# THE PRINCE'S SECRET BABY

## CHRISTINE RIMMER

**Harlequin**

SPECIAL EDITION

ISBN-13: 978-0-373-65662-2

THE PRINCE'S SECRET BABY

Copyright © 2012 by Christine Rimmer

THE ANNIVERSARY PARTY
Copyright © 2012 by Harlequin Books S.A.

Recycling programs
for this product may
not exist in your area.

The publisher acknowledges the following writers who contributed to
THE ANNIVERSARY PARTY: RaeAnne Thayne, Christine Rimmer,
Susan Crosby, Christyne Butler, Gina Wilkins and Cindy Kirk.

www.Harlequin.com

**Printed in U.S.A.**

## CONTENTS

**Books by Christine Rimmer**

# CHRISTINE RIMMER

came to her profession the long way around. Before settling down to write about the magic of romance, she'd been everything from an actress to a salesclerk to a waitress. Now that she's finally found work that suits her perfectly, she insists she never had a problem keeping a job—she was merely gaining "life experience" for her future as a novelist. Christine is grateful not only for the joy she finds in writing, but for what waits when the day's work is through: a man she loves who loves her right back and the privilege of watching their children grow and change day to day. She lives with her family in Oregon. Visit Christine at www.christinerimmer.com.

# THE PRINCE'S SECRET BABY

# Chapter One

"Stop here," Rule Bravo-Calabretti said to the driver.

The limousine rolled to a silent stop at the head of the row of parking spaces in the shadowed parking garage. The Mercedes-Benz sedan Rule had been following turned into the single empty space at the other end of the row, not far from the elevators and the stairs that led into the mall. From where he sat behind tinted windows, Rule could also see the breezeway outside the parking structure. It led directly into Macy's department store.

The brake lights of the Mercedes went dark. A woman emerged from the sedan, her head and shoulders appearing above the tops of the row of cars. She had thick brown hair that fell in well-behaved waves. Settling the strap of her bag on her shoulder, she shut the car door and emerged into the open aisle, where she turned back and aimed her key at the car. The Benz gave an obedient beep.

She put the key away in her bag. She looked, Rule decided, just as she'd looked in the pictures his investigators had taken of her—only more attractive, somehow. She wasn't a pretty woman. But there was something about her that he found much more interesting than mere prettiness. She was tall and slim and wore a blue silk jacket, which was perfectly and conservatively tailored. Her matching blue skirt kissed the tops of her slender knees. Her shoes were darker than her suit, with medium heels and closed toes.

He watched as she settled her bag in place again, straightened her jacket and turned for the door to the breezeway. He thought she looked very determined and somehow he found that determination utterly charming.

She hadn't glanced in the limousine's direction. He was almost certain she had no idea that he'd been following her.

And his mind was made up, just like that, in the sixty seconds it took to watch her emerge from her car, put her key in her purse and turn to go. He had to meet her.

Yes, he'd always told himself he never would. That as long as she was running her life successfully, taking good care of the child, it would be wrong of him to interfere. He'd relinquished all rights by law. And he had to live with the choices he had made.

But this wasn't about rights. This wasn't about challenging her for what was hers.

He had no intention of interfering. He simply had to… speak with her, had to know if his first reaction to seeing her in the flesh was just a fluke, a moment of starry-eyed idiocy brought on by the fact that she had what mattered most to him.

All right, it was playing with fire. And he shouldn't even be here. He should be finishing his business in Dallas and rushing back to Montedoro. He should be spending time with Lili, learning to accept that they could be a good match, have a good life.

And he *would* return to Montedoro. Soon.

But right now, today, he was going to do the thing he'd wanted to do for far too long now. He was going meet Sydney O'Shea face-to-face.

Sydney could not believe it.

The totally hunky—and oddly familiar—guy down the aisle from her in Macy's housewares department was actually making eyes at her. Men like that did not make eyes at Sydney. Men like that made eyes at women as gorgeous as they were.

And no, it wasn't that Sydney was ugly. She wasn't. But she wasn't beautiful, either. And there was something much too…practical and self-sufficient about her. Something a little too focused, as well. She also happened to be very smart. Men tended to find her intimidating, even at first glance.

So. Really. It was probably only her imagination that the drop-dead gorgeous guy by the waffle irons and electric griddles was looking at her. She pretended to read the tag on a stainless-steel sauté pan—and slid another glance in Mr. Eye Candy's direction.

He was pretending to read a price tag, too. She knew he was pretending because, at the exact moment she glanced his way, he sent a sideways look in her direction and one corner of that sinfully sexy mouth of his quirked up in a teasing smile.

Maybe he was flirting with someone behind her.

She turned her head enough that she could see over her shoulder.

Nope. Nobody there. Just more cookware racks brimming with All-Clad stainless-steel pots and pans, Le

Creuset enameled cast-iron casseroles and complete sets of Calphalon nonstick cookware—which, she firmly reminded herself, were what she *should* be looking at. She put all her attention on the business at hand and banished the implausibly flirty, impossibly smooth-looking man from her mind.

Yet another coworker was getting married, a paralegal, Calista Dwyer. Calista hadn't bothered to set up a bridal registry anywhere. The wedding was something of an impromptu affair. Tomorrow, Calista was running off with her boyfriend to some tropical island for a quickie wedding and a two-week honeymoon in paradise.

Sydney had left the office before lunch to choose a wedding gift. It was a task she had come to dislike. It happened so often and always reminded her that other people were getting married all the time. She really should do what a man in her situation would do, just have her assistant buy the wedding gifts—especially in a case like this, where she had no clue what Calista might be wanting or needing.

But no. She was still her grandmother's granddaughter at heart. Ellen O'Shea had always taken pride in personally selecting any gift she gave. Sydney continued the family tradition, even if she sometimes found the job annoying and a little bit depressing.

"Cookware. Necessary. But not especially interesting," a voice as warm and tempting as melted caramel teased in her ear. "Unless you love to cook?"

Good gravy. Mr. Hot and Hunky was right behind her. And there could be no doubt about it now. He was talking to her—and he *had* been giving her the eye.

Slowly, as if in a dream, Sydney turned to him.

Breathtaking. Seriously. There was no other word for this guy. Jet-black eyes, sculpted cheekbones, a perfect, square jaw, a nose like a blade. Broad, broad shoulders. And the way he was dressed…casual, but expensive. In light-colored trousers and a beautifully made navy jacket over a checked shirt.

He arched an ebony brow. "Do you?"

She forced herself to suck in a breath and then asked warily, "Excuse me?"

"Do you love to cook?" He gazed at her as though he couldn't tear his eyes away.

This could not be happening.

But wait. A gigolo? Maybe she looked like gigolo bait. Well-dressed and driven. Maybe it was the new black, to go trolling for a sugar mama in housewares.

And then again, well, he did look somehow familiar. She probably knew him from somewhere. "Have we met before?"

He gave her a slow once-over, followed by another speaking glance from those black-velvet eyes. That glance seemed to say that he wouldn't mind gobbling her up on the spot. And then he laughed, a low, sexy laugh as smooth and exciting as that wonderful voice of his. "I prefer to think that if we'd met in the past, you wouldn't have forgotten me so easily."

Excellent point. "I, um…" Good Lord. Speechless. She was totally speechless. And that wasn't like her at all. Enough with the stumbling all over herself. She stuck out her hand. "Sydney O'Shea."

"Rule Bravo-Calabretti." He wrapped his elegant, warm fingers around hers. She stifled a gasp as heat flowed up her arm.

The heat didn't stop at her shoulder. Arrows of what she could only categorize as burning excitement zipped downward into her midsection. She eased her hand from his grip and fell back a step, coming up short against the steel display shelves behind her. "Rule, you said?"

"Yes."

"Let me guess, Rule. You're not from Dallas."

He put those long, graceful fingers to his heart. "How did you know?"

"Well, the designer clothes, the two last names. You speak English fluently, but with a certain formality and no regional accent that I can detect. I'm thinking that not only are you not from Dallas, you're not from Texas. You're not even from the good old U.S. of A."

He laughed again. "You're an expert on accents?"

"No. I'm smart, that's all. And observant."

"Smart and observant. I like that."

She wished she could stand there by the cast-iron casserole display, just looking at him, listening to him talk and hearing his melted-caramel laugh for the next, oh, say, half century or so.

But there was still Calista's wedding gift to buy. And a quick lunch to grab before rushing back to the office for that strategy meeting on the Binnelab case at one.

Before she could start making gotta-go noises, he spoke again. "You didn't answer my question."

"Ahem. Your question?"

"Sydney, do you love to cook?"

The way he said her name, with such impossible passionate intent, well, she liked it. She liked it way, way too much. She fell back a step. "Cook? Me? Only when I have no other choice."

"Then why have I found you here in the cookware department?"

"*Found* me?" Her suspicions rose again. Really, what was this guy up to? "Were you *looking* for me?"

He gave an elegant shrug of those fine wide shoulders.

"I confess. I saw you enter the store from the parking garage at the south breezeway entrance. You were so... determined."

"You followed me because I looked determined?"

"I followed you because you intrigued me."

"You're intrigued by determination?"

He chuckled again. "Yes. I suppose I am. My mother is a very determined woman."

"And you love your mother." She put a definite edge in her tone. Was she calling him a mama's boy? Maybe. A little. She tended toward sarcasm when she was nervous or unsure—and he did make her nervous. There was just something about him. Something much too good to be true.

Mr. Bravo-Calabretti either didn't get her sarcasm— or ignored it. "I do love my mother, yes. Very much. And I admire her, as well." He studied Sydney for a moment, a direct, assessing kind of glance. "You're a prickly one, aren't you?" He seemed amused.

So he *had* picked up on her sarcasm. She felt petty and a little bit mean. And that made her speak frankly. "Yes, I am a prickly one. Some men don't find that terribly attractive."

"Some men are fools." He said it softly. And then he asked again, "Why are you shopping for pots and pans, Sydney?"

She confessed, "I need a wedding gift for someone at the office."

His dark eyes twinkled at her, stars in a midnight sky. "A wedding gift."

"That's right."

"Allow me to suggest..." He reached around her with his left hand. She turned to follow the movement and watched as he tapped a red Le Creuset casserole shaped like a heart. "This." She couldn't help noticing that he wore no wedding ring. And the casserole? Not bad, really.

"Very romantic," she said dryly. "Every bride needs a heart-shaped casserole dish."

"Buy it," he commanded. "And we can get out of here."

"Excuse me. We?"

He still had his arm out, almost touching her, his hand resting lightly on the red casserole. She caught a faint, tempting hint of his aftershave. It smelled fabulous—so subtle, so very expensive. He held her eyes, his dark gaze intent. "Yes. We. The two of us."

"But I'm not going anywhere with you. I don't even know you."

"That's true. And I find that very sad." He put on a teasingly mournful expression. "Because I want to know you, Sydney. Come to lunch with me. We can begin to remedy this problem." She opened her mouth to tell him that as far as she was concerned there was no problem and lunch was out of the question. But before she got the words out, he scooped up the heart-shaped dish. "This way." He gestured with his free hand in the direction of the nearest cashier stand.

She went where he directed her. Why not? The casserole was a good choice. And he was so charming. As soon as the clerk had rung her up, she could tell him goodbye and make him see that she meant it.

The clerk was young and blonde and very pretty. "Oh! Here. Let me help you!" She took the casserole from Rule and then kept sliding him blushing glances as she rung up the sale. Sydney sympathized with the dazzled girl. He was like something straight out of a fabulous romantic novel—the impossible, wonderful, hot and handsome, smooth and sophisticated lover who appears out of nowhere to sweep the good-hearted but otherwise perfectly ordinary heroine off her feet.

And did she actually think the word *lover?*

Really, she needed to get a grip on her suddenly too-vivid imagination.

"This casserole is the cutest thing. Is it a gift?" the clerk asked.

"Yes, it is," Sydney replied. "A wedding gift."

The girl slid another glance at Rule. "I'm sorry. We don't offer gift wrapping in the store anymore." She spoke in a breathy little voice. Rule said nothing. He gave the girl a quick, neutral nod and a barely detectable smile.

"It's fine," Sydney said. Like her grandmother, she not only bought gifts personally, she wrapped them, too. But she didn't have time to wrap this one if she wanted to give it to Calista before her wedding trip. So she would need to grab a gift bag and tissue somewhere. She swiped her card and signed in the little box and tried not to be overly conscious of the too-attractive man standing beside her.

The clerk gave Sydney the receipt—but she gave Rule the Macy's bag with the casserole in it. "Here you go now. Come back and shop with us. Anytime." Her tone said she would love to help Rule with a lot more than his shopping.

Sydney thanked her and turned to him. "I'll take that."

"No need. I'll carry it for you."

"I said I'll take it."

Reluctantly, he handed it over. But he showed no inclination to say goodbye and move on.

She told him, "Nice chatting with you. And I really have to—"

"It's only lunch, you know." He said it gently and quietly, for her ears alone. "Not a lifetime commitment."

She gazed up into those melting dark eyes and all at once she was hearing her best friend Lani's chiding voice in her head. *Seriously, Syd. If you really want a special guy in your life, you have to give one a chance now and then....*

"All right," she heard herself say. "Lunch." It wasn't a big deal. She would enjoy his exciting, flattering attention over a quick sandwich and then say goodbye. No harm done.

"A smile," he said, his warm gaze on her mouth. "At last."

She smiled wider. Because she did like him. He was not only killer-handsome and very smooth, he seemed like a great guy. Certainly there could be no harm in giving herself permission to spend a little more time with him. "So. First I need a store that sells gift bags."

He held her eyes for a moment. And it felt glorious. Just standing there in Macy's, lost in an endless glance with a gorgeous man. Finally, he said, "There's a mall directory, I think. This way." And then he shepherded her ahead of him, as he had when he ushered her to the cashier stand.

They found a stationery store. She chose a pretty bag and some sparkly tissue and a gift card. The clerk rang up the sale and they were on their way.

"Where to?" she asked, as they emerged into the mall again.

"This is Texas," he said, his elegant face suddenly open and almost boyish. "We should have steak."

He had a limo waiting for him outside, which didn't surprise her. The man was very much the limo type. He urged her to ride with him to the restaurant, but she said she would follow him. They went to the Stockyards District in nearby Fort Worth, to a casual place with lots of Texas atmosphere and an excellent reputation.

An antler chandelier hung from the pressed-tin ceiling

above their corner table. The walls were of pine planks and exposed brick, hung with oil paintings of cowboy boots, hats and bandannas. The floor was painted red.

They got a table in a corner and he ordered a beautiful bottle of Cabernet. She refused the wine when their waiter tried to fill her glass. But then, after he left them, she gave in and poured herself a small amount. The taste was amazing, smooth and delicately spicy on her tongue.

"You like it?" Rule asked hopefully.

"It's wonderful."

He offered a toast. "To smart, observant, determined women."

"Don't forget prickly," she reminded him.

"How could I? It's such a charming trait."

"Nice recovery." She gave him an approving nod.

He raised his glass higher. "To smart, observant, determined and decidedly prickly women."

She laughed as she touched her glass to his.

"Tell me about your high-powered job," he said, after the waiter delivered their salads of butter lettuce and applewood smoked bacon.

She sipped more of the wine she shouldn't really be drinking, given she had that big meeting ahead of her. "And you know I have a high-powered job, how?"

"You said the wedding gift was for 'someone at the office.'"

"I could be in data entry. Or maybe a top executive's very capable assistant."

"No," he said, with confidence. "Your clothing is both conservative and expensive." He eyed her white silk shell, her lightweight, fitted jacket, the single strand of pearls she wore. "And your attitude..."

She leaned toward him, feeling deliciously giddy. Feeling free and bold and ready for anything. "What about my attitude?"

"You are no one's assistant."

She sat back in her chair and rested her hands in her lap. "I'm an attorney. With a firm that represents a number of corporate clients."

"An attorney. Of course. *That,* I believe."

She picked up her fork, ate some of her salad. For a moment or two they shared a surprisingly easy silence. And then she asked, "And what about you? What do you do for a living?"

"I like variety in my work. At the moment, I'm in trade. International trade."

"At the moment? What? You change jobs a lot, is that what you're telling me?"

"I take on projects that interest me. And when I'm satisfied that any given project is complete, I move on."

"What do you trade?"

"At the moment, oranges. Montedoron oranges."

"Montedoran. That sounds exotic."

"It is. The Montedoran is a blood orange, very sweet, hinting of raspberry, with the characteristic red flesh of all blood oranges. The skin is smooth, not pitted like many other varieties."

"So soon I'll be buying Montedorans at my local Wal-Mart Supercenter?"

"Hardly. The Montedoran is never going to be for sale in supermarkets. We won't be trading in that kind of volume. But for certain gourmet and specialty stores, I think it could do very well."

"Montedoran…" She tested the word on her tongue. "There's a small country in Europe, right, on the Côte d'Azur? Montedoro?"

"Yes. Montedoro is my country." He poured her more

wine. And she didn't stop him. "It's one of the eight small-est states in Europe, a principality on the Mediterranean. My mother was born there. My father was American but moved to Montedoro and accepted Montedoran citizen-ship when they married. His name is Evan Bravo. He was a Texan by birth."

She really did love listening to him talk. He made every word into a poem. "So…you have relatives in Texas?"

"I have an aunt and uncle and a number of first cousins who live in and around San Antonio. And I have other, more distant cousins in a small town near Abilene. And in your Hill Country, I have a second cousin who married a veterinarian. And there are more Bravos, many more, in California and Wyoming and Nevada. All over the States, as a matter of fact."

"I take it that Calabretti is your mother's surname?"

"Yes."

"Is that what they do in your country, combine the hus-band's and wife's last name when they marry?"

He nodded. "In…certain families, anyway. It's similar to the way it's done in Spain. We are much like the Span-ish. We want to keep all our last names, on both sides of our families. So we string them together proudly."

"Bravo-Calabretti sounds familiar, somehow. I keep wondering where I've heard it before…"

He waited for her to finish. When she didn't, he shrugged. "Perhaps it will come to you later."

"Maybe so." She lowered her voice to a more confiden-tial level. "And I have to tell you, I keep thinking that *you* are familiar, that I've met you before."

He shrugged in a way that seemed to her so sophisti-cated, so very European. "They say everyone has a double. Maybe that's it. You've met my double."

It wasn't what she'd meant. But it didn't really matter.

"Maybe." She let it go and asked, "Do you have brothers and sisters?"

"I do." He gave her a regal nod. "Three brothers, five sisters. I'm second-born. I have an older brother, Maximilian. And after me, there are the twins, Alexander and Damien. And then my sisters—Bella, Rhiannon, Alice, Genevra and Rory."

"Big family." Feeling suddenly wistful, she set down her fork. "I envy you. I was an only child." Her hand rested on the tabletop.

He covered it with his. The touch warmed her to her toes—and thrilled her, as well. Her whole body seemed, all at once, completely, vividly alive. He leaned into her and studied her face, his gaze as warm as his lean hand over hers. "And you are sad, then? To have no siblings?"

"I am, yes." She wished he might hold her hand indefinitely. And yet she had to remember that this wasn't going anywhere and it wouldn't be right to let him think that it might. She eased her hand free. He took her cue without comment, retreating to his side of the table. She asked, "How old are you, Rule?"

He laughed his slow, smooth laugh. "Somehow, I begin to feel as though I'm being interviewed."

She turned her wineglass by the stem. "I only wondered. Is your age a sensitive subject for you?"

"In a sense, I suppose it is." His tone was more serious. "I'm thirty-two. That's a dangerous age for an unmarried man in my family."

"How so? Thirty-two isn't all that old." Especially not for a man. For a woman, things were a little different—at least, they were if she wanted to have children.

"It's time that I married." He said it so somberly, his eyes darker than ever as he regarded her steadily.

"I don't get it. In your family, they put you on a schedule for marriage?"

Now a smile haunted his handsome mouth. "It sounds absurd when you say it that way."

"It *is* absurd."

"You are a woman of definite opinions." He said it in an admiring way. Still, defiance rose within her and she tipped her chin high. He added, "And yes, in my family both the men and the women are expected to marry before they reach the age of thirty-three."

"And if you don't?"

He lowered his head and looked at her from under his dark brows. "Consequences will be dire." He said it in a low tone, an intimate tone, a tone that did a number on every one of her nerve endings and sent a fine, heated shiver dancing along the surface of her skin.

"You're teasing me."

"Yes, I am. I like you, Sydney. I knew that I would, the moment I first saw you."

"And when was that?"

"You've already forgotten?" He looked gorgeously forlorn. "I see I'm not so memorable, after all. Macy's? I saw you going in?" The waiter scooped up their empty salad plates and served them rib eye steaks with Serrano lime butter. When he left them, Rule slid her a knowing glance as he picked up his steak knife. "Sydney, I think you're testing me."

Why deny it? "I think you're right."

"I hope I'm passing this test of yours—and do your parents live here in Dallas?"

She trotted out the old, sad story. "They lived in San Francisco, where I was born. My mother was thrown off a runaway cable car. I was just three months old, in her arms when she fell. She suffered a blow to the head and died instantly, but I was unharmed. They called it a miracle at the time. My father was fatally injured when he jumped off to try and save us. He died the next day in the hospital."

His dark eyes were so soft. They spoke of real sympathy. Of understanding. "How terrible for you."

"I don't even remember it. My grandmother—my father's mother—came for me and took me back to Austin, where she lived. She raised me on her own. My grandfather had died several years before my parents. She was amazing, my grandmother. She taught me that I can do anything. She taught me that power brings responsibility. That the truth is sacred. That being faithful and trustworthy are rewards in themselves."

Now his eyes had a teasing light in them. "And yet, you're an attorney."

Sydney laughed. "So they have lawyer jokes even in Montedoro?"

"I'm afraid so—and a *corporate* attorney at that."

"I'm not responding to that comment on the grounds that it might tend to incriminate me." She said it lightly.

But he saw right through her. "Have I hit a nerve?"

She totally shocked herself by answering frankly. "My job is high-powered. And high-paying. And it's been... important to me, to know that I'm on top of a very tough game, that I'll never have to worry about where the next paycheck is coming from, that I can definitely take care of my own and do it well."

"And yet?"

She revealed even more. "And yet lately, I often find myself thinking how much more fulfilling it might be to spend my workdays helping people who really need me, rather than protecting the overflowing coffers of multibillion-dollar companies."

He started to speak. But then her BlackBerry, which she'd set on the table to the right of her water goblet the way she always did at restaurants, vibrated. She checked the display: Magda, her assistant. Probably wondering why she wasn't back at the office yet.

She glanced at Rule again. He had picked up his knife and fork and was concentrating on his meal, giving her the chance to deal with the call if she needed to.

Well, she didn't need to.

Sydney scooped up the phone and dropped it in her bag where she wouldn't even notice if it vibrated again.

With the smooth ease of a born diplomat, Rule continued their conversation as though it had never been interrupted. "You speak of your grandmother in the past tense...."

"She died five years ago. I miss her very much."

"So much loss." He shook his head. "Life can be cruel."

"Yes." She ate a bite of her steak, taking her time about it, savoring the taste and tenderness of the meat, unaccountably happy that he hadn't remarked on her vibrating BlackBerry, that he hadn't said he was "sorry," the way people always did when she told them she'd grown up without her parents, when she confessed how much she missed her grandmother.

He watched her some more, his dark head tipped to the side in way that had her thinking again how he reminded her of someone. "Have you ever been married?"

"No. I'm Catholic—somewhat lapsed, yes, but nonetheless, I do believe that marriage is forever. I've never found the man I want forever with. But I've had a couple of serious relationships. They...didn't work out." Understatement of the year. But he didn't need to hear it and she didn't need to say it. She'd done enough over-sharing for now, thank you very much. She added, "And I'm thirty-three. Does that seem…dire to you?"

"Absolutely." He put on a stern expression. On him, sternness was sexy. But then, on him, everything was sexy. "You should be married immediately. And then have nine children. At the very least. You should marry a wealthy man, Sydney. One who adores you."

"Hmm. A rich man who adores me. I wouldn't mind that. But the nine children? More than I planned on. Significantly more."

"You don't want children?" He looked honestly surprised.

She almost told him about Trevor right then. But no. This was a fantasy lunch with a fantasy man. Trevor was her real life. The most beautiful, perfect, meaningful, joyful part of her real life. "I didn't say I didn't want children. I do. But I'm not sure I'm ready for nine of them. Nine seems like a lot."

"Well. Perhaps we would have to settle for fewer than nine. I can be reasonable."

"We?"

"A man and a woman have to work together. Decisions should be jointly made."

"Rule." She put a hand to her breast, widened her eyes and asked him dramatically, "Could this be…oh, I can't believe it. Is it possible that you're proposing to me?"

He answered matter-of-factly, "As it happens, I'm wealthy. And it would be very easy for me to adore you." His dark eyes shone.

What was this feeling? Magical, this feeling. Magical and foolish. And that was the beauty of it. It was one of those things that happen when you least expect it. Something to remind her that life could still be surprising.

That it wasn't all about winning and staying on top—and coming home too late to tuck her own sweet boy into bed.

Sometimes even the most driven woman might just take a long lunch. A long lunch with a stranger who made her feel not only brilliant and clever, but beautiful and desired, as well.

She put on a tragic face. "I'm sorry. It could never work."

He played it stricken. "But why not?"

"You live in Montedoro." Grave. Melancholy. "My career—my whole life—is here."

"You might change careers. You might even decide to try a different kind of life."

Hah. Exactly what men always said. She wasn't letting him get away with it. "Or *you* might move to Texas."

"For you, Sydney, I might do anything."

"Perfect answer."

A moment ensued. Golden. Fine. A moment with only the two of them in it. A moment of complete accord.

Sydney let herself enjoy that moment. She refused to be guarded or dubious. It was only lunch, after all. Lunch with an attractive man. She was giving herself full permission to enjoy every minute of it.

## Chapter Two

The meeting on the Binnelab case was half over when Sydney slipped in at two-fifteen.

"Excuse me," she said as she eased through the conference room doors and they all turned to stare at her. "So sorry. I had...something of an emergency."

Her colleagues made sympathetic noises and went back to arguing strategy. No one was the least angry that she was late.

Because she was never late—which meant that of course there had to be a good reason for her tardiness. She was Sydney O'Shea, who graduated college at twenty, passed the bar at twenty-four and had been made partner at thirty—exactly one year before her son was born. Sydney O'Shea, who knew how to make demands and how to return a favor, who had a talent for forging strong professional relationships and who never slacked. She racked up the billable hours with the best of them.

If she'd told them all that she'd been sidetracked in Macy's housewares by a handsome orange salesman from Montedoro and allowed him to talk her into blowing off half of the Binnelab meeting, they'd have had zero doubt that she was joking.

She knew the case backward and forward. She only had to listen to the discussion for a few minutes to get up to speed on the direction her colleagues were taking.

By the end of the meeting, she'd nudged them in a slightly different direction and everyone seemed pleased with the result. She returned to her corner office to find her so-capable assistant, the usually unflappable Magda, standing in the middle of the room holding an orchid in a gorgeous purple pot. Magda stared in dismay at the credenza along the side wall where no less than twelve spectacular flower arrangements sprouted from a variety of crystal vases.

The credenza was not the only surface in the room overflowing with flowers. There were two vases on the coffee table and one each on the end tables in the sitting area.

Her desk had six of them. And the windowsill was likewise overrun with exotic blooms. Each arrangement had a small white card attached. The room smelled like a greenhouse.

*Rule.* She knew instantly. Who else could it be? And a quick glance at one of the cards confirmed it.

Please share dinner with me tonight. The Mansion at Turtle Creek. Eight o'clock. Yours, Rule

She'd never told him the name of her firm. But then again, it wouldn't have been that hard to find out. Just her name typed into a search engine would have done it.

"Smothered in flowers. Literally," she said to her nonplussed assistant. She felt that delicious glow again, that sense of wonder and limitless possibility. She was crushing on him, big-time. He made her feel innocent and free.

And beautiful. And desired…

Was there anything wrong with that? If there was, she was having trouble remembering what.

"They started arriving about half an hour ago," said Magda. "I think this orchid is the last of them. But I have nowhere left to put it."

"It would look great on your desk," Sydney suggested. "In fact, take the cards off and leave them with me. And then let's share the wealth."

Magda arched a brow. "Give them away, you mean?"

"Start with the data entry crew. Just leave me the two vases of yellow roses."

"You're sure?"

"Positive." She didn't think Rule would mind at all if she shared. And she wanted to share. This feeling of hope and wonder and beauty, well, it was too fabulous to keep to herself. "Tell everyone to enjoy them. And to take them home, if they want to—and hurry. We have Calista's party at four."

"I really like this orchid," said Magda, holding out the pot, admiring the deep purple lips suspended from the velvety pale pink petals. "It looks rare."

"Good. Enjoy. A nice start to the weekend, don't you think? Flowers for everyone. And then we send Calista happily off to her tropical honeymoon."

"Someone special must be wild for you," Magda said with a grin.

Sydney couldn't resist grinning right back at her. "Deliver the flowers and let's break out the champagne."

Calista loved the heart-shaped casserole. She laughed when she pulled it from the gift bag. "I guess now I'll just have to learn how to cook."

"Wait until after the honeymoon," Sydney suggested and then proposed a toast. "To you, Calista. And to a long and happy marriage."

After the two glasses of wine at lunch, Sydney allowed herself only a half glass of champagne during the shower. But the shortage of bubbly didn't matter in the least. It was still the most fun Sydney had ever had at a bridal shower. Funny how meeting a wonderful man can put a whole different light on the day.

After the party, she returned to her office just long enough to grab her briefcase, her bag and one of the vases full of yellow roses. Yes, as a rule she would have stayed to bill a couple more hours, at least.

But hey. It was Friday. She wanted to see her little boy before he went to bed. And she really needed to talk to Lani, who was not only her dearest friend, but also Trevor's live-in nanny. She needed Lani's excellent advice as to whether she should go for it and take Rule up on his invitation to dinner.

At home in Highland Park, she found Trevor in the kitchen, sitting up at the breakfast nook table in his booster chair, eating his dinner of spaghetti and meatballs. "Mama home! Hug, hug!" he crowed, and held out his chubby arms.

She dropped her briefcase and bag, set the flowers on the counter and went to him. He wrapped those strong little arms around her neck, smearing spaghetti sauce on her cheek when he gave her a big smacker of a kiss. "How's my boy?"

"I fine, thank you."

"Me, too." She hugged him harder. "Now that I'm home with you." He smelled of tomatoes and meatballs and baby shampoo—of everything that mattered.

At two, he was quite the talker. As he picked up his

spoon again, he launched into a description of his day. "We swim. We play trucks. I shout *loud* when we crash."

"Sounds like fun." She whipped a tissue from the box on the counter and wiped the red sauce off her cheek.

"Oh, yes! Fun, Mama. I happy." He shoved a meatball in his mouth with one hand and waved his spoon with the other.

"Use your spoon for eating," Lani said from over by the sink.

"Yes, Lani. I do!" He switched the spoon to the other hand and scooped up a mound of pasta. Most of it fell off before he got it to his mouth, but he only gamely scooped up some more.

"You're early," said Lani, turning to glance at her over the tops of her black-rimmed glasses. "And those roses are gorgeous."

"They are, aren't they? And as to being early, hey, it's almost the weekend."

"That never stopped you from working late before." Lani grabbed a towel and turned to lean against the sink as she dried her hands.

Her full name was Yolanda Ynez Vasquez and she was small and curvy with acres of thick almost-black hair. She'd been working for Sydney for five years, starting as Sydney's housekeeper. The plan was that Lani would cook and clean house and live in, thus saving money while she finished college. But then, even after she got her degree, she'd stayed on, and become Trevor's nanny, as well. Sydney had no idea how she would have managed without her. Not only for her grace and ease at keeping house and being a second mom to Trevor, but also for her friendship. After Ellen O'Shea, Yolanda Vasquez was the best friend Sydney had ever had.

Lani said, "You're glowing, Syd."

Sydney put her hands to her cheeks. "I do feel slightly warm. Maybe I have a fever...."

"Or maybe someone handsome sent you yellow roses."

Laughing, Sydney shook her head. "You are always one step ahead of me."

"What's his name?"

"Rule."

"Hmm. Very...commanding."

"And he is. But in such a smooth kind of way. I went to lunch with him. I really like him. He asked me to dinner."

"Tonight?" Lani asked.

She nodded. "He invited me to meet him at the Mansion at Turtle Creek. Eight o'clock."

"And you're going." It wasn't a question.

"If you'll hold down the fort?"

"No problem."

"What about Michael?" Michael Cort was a software architect. Lani had been seeing him on a steady basis for the past year.

Lani shrugged. "You know Michael. He likes to hang out. I'll invite him over. We'll get a pizza—tell me more about Rule."

"I just met him today. Am I crazy?"

"A date with a guy who makes you glow? Nothing crazy about that."

"Mama, sketti?" Trev held up a handful of crushed meatball and pasta.

"No, thank you, my darling." Sydney bent and kissed his plump, gooey cheek again. "You can have that big wad of sketti all for yourself."

"Yum!" He beamed up at her and her heart felt like it was overflowing. She had it all. A healthy, happy child, a terrific best friend, a very comfortable lifestyle, a job most high-powered types would kill for. And a date with the best-looking man on the planet.

Sydney spent the next hour being the mother she didn't get to be as often as she would have liked. She played trucks with Trev. And then she gave him his bath and tucked him into bed herself, smoothing his dark hair off his handsome forehead, thinking that he was the most beautiful child she had ever seen. He was already asleep when she tiptoed from the room.

Yolanda looked up when she entered the family room. "It's after seven. You better get a move on if you want to be on time for your dream man."

"I know—keep me company while I get ready?"

Lani followed her into the master suite, where Sydney grabbed a quick shower and redid her makeup. In the walk-in closet, she stared at the possible choices and didn't know which one to pick.

"This." Lani took a simple cap-sleeved red satin sheath from the row of mostly conservative party dresses. "You are killer in red."

"Red. Hmm," Sydney waffled. "You think?"

"I *know.* Put it on. You only need your diamond studs with it. And that garnet-and-diamond bracelet your grand-mother left you. And those red Jimmy Choos."

Sydney took the dress. "You're right."

Lani dimpled. "I'm always right."

Sydney put on the dress and the shoes and the diamond studs and garnet bracelet. Then she stood at the full-length mirror in her dressing area and scowled at herself. "I don't know..." She touched her brown hair, which she'd swept up into a twist. "Should I take my hair down?"

"No. It's great like that." Lani tugged a few curls loose at her temples and her nape. Then she eased the wide neckline of the dress off her shoulders. "There. Perfect. You look so hot."

"I am not the hot type."

"Yeah, you are. You just don't see yourself that way. You're tall and slim and striking."

"Striking. Right. Still, it would be nice if I had breasts, don't you think? I had breasts once, remember? When I was pregnant with Trevor?"

"Stop. You have breasts."

"Hah."

"And you have green eyes to die for."

"To die for. Who came up with that expression, anyway?"

Lani took her by the shoulders and turned her around so they faced each other. "You look gorgeous. Go. Have a fabulous time."

"Now I'm getting nervous."

"*Getting?* Syd. You look wonderful and you are going."

"What if he doesn't show up?"

"Stop it." Lani squeezed her shoulders. "Go."

Rosewood Mansion at Turtle Creek was a Dallas landmark. Once a spectacular private residence, the Mansion was now a five-star hotel and restaurant, a place of meticulous elegance, of marble floors and stained-glass windows and hand-carved fireplaces.

Her heart racing in mingled excitement and trepidation, Sydney entered the restaurant foyer, with its curving iron-railed staircases and black-and-white marble floor. She marched right up to the reservation desk and told the smiling host waiting there, "I'm meeting someone. Rule Bravo-Calabretti?"

The host nodded smartly. "Right this way."

And off she went to a curtained private corner on the

terrace. The curtains were pulled back and she saw that Rule was waiting, wearing a gorgeous dark suit, his black eyes lighting up when their gazes locked. He rose as she approached.

"Sydney." He said her name with honest pleasure, his expression as open and happy as her little boy's had been when she'd tucked him into bed that night. "You came." He sounded so pleased. And maybe a little relieved.

How surprising was that? He didn't look like a person who would ever worry that a woman might not show up for a date.

She liked him even more then—if that was possible. Because he had allowed her to see he was vulnerable.

"Wouldn't have missed it for the world," she said softly, her gaze locked with his.

Champagne was waiting in a silver bucket. The host served them.

Rule said, "I took the liberty of conferring with the chef ahead of time, choosing a menu I thought you might enjoy. But if you would prefer making your own choices…"

She loved that he'd planned ahead, that he'd taken that kind of care over the meal. *And* that he'd asked for her preference in the matter. "The food is always good here. Whatever you've planned will be perfect."

"No…dietary rules or foods you hate?" His midnight gaze scanned her face as though committing it to memory.

"None. I trust you."

Something flared in his eyes. "Fair enough, then." His voice wrapped around her, warm and deep and so sweet. He nodded at the host. "Thank you, Neil."

"Very good, then, your—" Neil paused almost imperceptibly, and then continued "—waiter will be with you shortly." With a slight bow, he turned to go.

"Neil seems a little nervous," she whispered, when the host had left them.

"I have no idea why," Rule said lightly. And then his tone acquired a certain huskiness. "You should wear red all the time."

"That might become boring."

"You could never be boring. And what is that old song, the one about the lady in red?"

"That's it. 'Lady in Red.'"

"You bring that song to mind. You make me want to dance with you."

How did he do it? He poured on the flattery—and yet, somehow, coming from him, the sweet talk sounded sincere. "Thank you for the flowers."

He waved a lean hand. "I know I went overboard."

"It was a beautiful gesture. And I hope you don't mind, but I shared them—with the data entry girls and the paralegals and the crew down in Human Resources."

"Why would I mind? They were yours, to do with as you wished. And sharing is good. You're not only the most compelling woman I've ever met, you are kind. And generous, too."

She shook her head. "You amaze me, Rule."

He arched a raven-black eyebrow. "In a good way, I hope?"

"Oh, yeah. In a good way. You make me want to believe all the beautiful things that you say to me."

He took her hand. Enchantment settled over her, at the warmth of his touch, at the lovely, lazy pulse of pleasure that seemed to move through her with every beat of her heart, just to be with him, to have her hand in his, flesh to flesh. "Would you prefer if I were cruel?"

The question shocked her a little. "No. Never. Why would you ask that?"

He turned her hand over, raised it to his lips, pressed a kiss in the heart of her palm. The pulse of pleasure within her went lower, grew hotter. "You fascinate me." His breath fanned her palm. And then, tenderly, he lowered their hands to the snowy tablecloth and wove his fingers with hers. "I want to know all about you. And truthfully, some women like a little more spice from a man. They want to be kept guessing. 'Does he care or not, will he call or not?' They might say they're looking for a good man who appreciates them. But they like…the dance of love, they revel in the uncertainty of it all."

She leaned closer to him, because she wanted to. Because she could. "I like you as you are. Don't pretend to be someone else. Please."

"I wouldn't. But I *can* be cruel." He said it so casually, so easily. And she realized she believed him. She saw the shining blade of his intention beneath the velvet sheath that was his considerable charm.

"Please don't. I've had enough of mean men. I…" She let the words trail off. The waiter was approaching their table. Perfect timing. The subject was one that desperately needed dropping.

But a flick of a glance from Rule and the waiter turned around and walked away. "Continue, please," Rule prompted softly. "What men have been cruel to you?"

*Way to ruin a beautiful evening, Syd.* "Seriously. You don't need to hear it."

"But I *want* to hear it. I meant what I said. I want to know about you, Sydney. I want to know everything." His eyes were so dark. She could get lost in them, lost forever, never to be found. And the really scary thing was that she almost felt okay with being lost forever—as long as he was lost right along with her.

"What can I say? There's just something about me…"

Lord. She did not want to go there. She tried to wrap it up with a generalized explanation. "I seem to attract men who say they like me because I'm strong and intelligent and capable. And then they get to work trying to tear me down."

Something flared in his eyes. Something…dangerous. "*Who* has tried to tear you down?"

"Do we have to get into this?"

"No. We don't. But sometimes it's better, I think, to go ahead and speak frankly of the past." Now his eyes were tender again. Tender and somehow completely accepting.

She let out a slow, surrendering sigh. "I lived with a guy when I was in law school. His name was Ryan. He was fun and a little bit wild. On the day we moved in together, he quit his job. He would lie on the sofa drinking those great big cans of malt liquor, watching ESPN. When I tried to talk to him about showing a little motivation, things got ugly fast. He said that I had enough ambition and drive for both of us and next to me he felt like a failure, that I had as good as emasculated him—and would I get out of the damn way, I was blocking his view of the TV?"

Rule gave one of those so-European shrugs of his. "So you got rid of him."

"Yes, I did. When I kicked him out, he told me he'd been screwing around on me. He'd had to, he said. In order to try and feel at least a little like a man again. So he was a cheater and a liar, too. After Ryan, I took a break from men. I stayed away from serious entanglements for the next five years. Then I met Peter. He was an attorney, like me. Worked for a different firm, a smaller one. We started going out. I thought he was nothing like Ryan, not a user or runaround or a slacker in any way. He never formally moved in with me. But he was…with me, at my house, most nights. And then he started pressuring me to get him in at Teale, Gayle and Prosser." She said the name of her firm with another long sigh.

"You weren't comfortable with that?"

"No, I wasn't. And I told him so. I believe in networking, in helping the other guy out. But I didn't want my boyfriend working at the same firm with me, especially not if he was hired on my say-so. There are just too many ways that could spell trouble. He said he understood."

Rule still had his fingers laced with hers. He gave her a reassuring squeeze. "But he didn't understand."

"Not in the least. He was angry that I wouldn't give him 'a hand up,' as he put it. Things kind of devolved from there. He said a lot of brutal things to me. I was still an associate at the firm then. At a party, Peter got drunk and complained about me to one of the partners. By the time he and I were over, I…" She sought the right way to say it.

He said it for her. "You decided you were through with men." She glanced away. He caught her chin, lightly, gently, and guided it back around so that she met his eyes again. "Are you all right?" He sounded honestly concerned. She realized that her answer really mattered to him.

She swallowed, nodded. "I'm okay. It's just…when I talk about all that, I feel like such a loser, you know?"

"Those men. Ryan and Peter. *They* are the losers." He held her gaze. "I notice you haven't told me their last names."

"And I'm not going to. As I said, it's long over for me, with both of them."

He gave her his beautiful smile. "There. That's what I was waiting to hear." He let go of her hand—but only to touch her in another way. With his index finger, he traced the line of her jaw, stirring shivers as he went. He caught one of the loose curls of hair that Lani had pulled free of her French twist, and rubbed it between his fingers. "Soft," he whispered. "Like your skin. Like your tender heart…"

"Don't be too sure about that. I'm not only prickly, I can be a raving bitch," she whispered back. "Just ask Ryan and Peter."

"Give me their last names. Ryan and Peter and I will have a long talk."

"Hah. I don't think so."

He touched her cheek then, a brushing caress of such clear erotic intent that her toes curled inside her Jimmy Choos. "As long as you're willing to give men another chance."

"I could be. If the *right* man ever came along."

He took her untouched champagne flute and handed it to her. Then he picked up his own. "To the right man."

She touched her glass to his, echoed, "The right man." It was excellent champagne, each tiny bubble like a burst of magic on her tongue. And when she set the glass down again, she said, "I always wanted to have children."

He answered teasingly, "However, not nine of them."

Suddenly, it came to her. She realized where she'd been going with her grim little tale of disappointed love. It hadn't really been a case of total over-sharing, after all.

"Actually," she said. "This is serious."

"All right."

"There's something I really do need to tell you."

His expression changed, became…so still. Waiting. Listening. He tipped his head to the side in that strangely familiar way he had. "Tell me."

She wanted—needed—for him to know about Trevor. If learning about Trev turned him off, well, she absolutely *had* to know that now, tonight. Before she got in any deeper with him. Before she let herself drown in those beautiful black eyes. "I…" Her mouth had gone desert-dry. She swallowed, hard.

This shouldn't be so difficult, shouldn't matter so very much. She hardly knew this man. Holding his interest and his high regard shouldn't be this important to her.

Yet it *was* important. Already. She cared. A lot. Way, way too much.

He seemed too perfect. He *was* too perfect. He was her dream man come to vivid, vibrant, tempting life. The first minute she saw him, she'd felt as though she already knew him.

Yes, she should be more wary. It wasn't like her to be so easily drawn in.

And yet she was. She couldn't stop herself.

She thought of her grandmother, who had been a true believer in love at first sight. Grandma Ellen claimed she had fallen for Sydney's grandfather the first time she met him. She'd also insisted that Sydney's father had fallen in love with her mother at first sight.

Could falling in love at first sight be a genetic trait? Sydney almost smiled at the thought. She'd believed herself to be in love before—and been wrong, wrong, wrong.

But with Ryan, it hadn't been like this. Or with Peter. Nothing like this, with either of them.

Both of those relationships had developed in the logical, sensible way. She'd come to believe that she loved those men over a reasonable period of time, after getting to know them well—or so she had thought.

And look what had happened. She learned in the end that she hadn't really known either Ryan or Peter. Not well enough, she hadn't. With both men, it had ended in heartbreak. Those failures should have made her more wary. Those failures *had* made her more wary.

Until today. Until she met Rule.

With Rule, her heart seemed to have a will of its own. With him, she wanted to just go for it. To take the leap, take a chance. She didn't want to be wary with him. With him, she could almost become a believer in love at first sight.

If only he wasn't put off by learning that she already had a child....

"It's all right," he said so gently. "Go on."

And she did. "I was almost thirty, when it ended with Peter. I wanted to make partner in my firm and I wanted a family. I knew I could do both."

He gave a slow nod. "But the men were not cooperating."

"Exactly. So I decided...to have a family anyway. A family without a man. I went to a top cryobank—a sperm bank, at a fertility clinic?"

"Yes," he said in a way that could only be called cautious. "I know what a cryobank is."

"Well, all right." Her hands were shaking. She lowered them to her lap so he wouldn't see. "I went to a sperm bank. I had artificial insemination. The procedure was successful. I got pregnant. And now I have a beautiful, healthy two-year-old son."

"You have a child," he repeated, carefully. "A boy."

She folded her hands good and tight in her lap to still the shaking. And her heart seemed to have stopped dead in her chest—and then commenced beating way too hard and too fast. It hurt, her own heart, the way it pounded away in there. Because she *knew,* absolutely, that it was over, between her and Rule, over before it had even really begun. And it didn't matter *how* perfect he was for her. It didn't matter if he just happened to be her dream-come-true. It didn't matter that he made her want to believe in love at first sight. She was absolutely certain at that moment that he wouldn't accept Trevor. And if he didn't accept her son, she wanted nothing to do with him.

In a moment, she would be rising, saying good-night. Walking away from him and refusing to look back.

She drew her shoulders tall. Her hands weren't shaking anymore. "Yes, Rule. I have a son, a son who's everything to me."

## Chapter Three

And then, just as she was dead certain that it was finished between them, Rule smiled.

A *real* smile. He laid his warm, lean hand along the side of her face. "How wonderful. I love children, Sydney— but I already said that, didn't I? When can I meet him? Tomorrow, I hope."

She blinked, swallowed. Almost sick with emotion, she put her hand against her churning stomach. "I... You what?"

He laughed, a beautiful, low, sexy sound. "You thought I wouldn't want to meet your son?" And then he frowned. "You don't know me very well."

"I... You're right. I don't know you." She took slow, deep breaths, ordering her stomach to settle down, stunned at how much it mattered, that he wasn't rejecting Trevor. That it wasn't over after all, that she didn't have to rise and walk away and not look back. She could stay right here, in this beautiful restaurant, at this private table, with this incredible man. She chided, "I have to keep reminding myself that I don't know you well, that we only met this afternoon."

"Unbelievable." His frown had faded. "I had forgotten. Somehow, it seems that I've known you forever."

She confessed, "I have that feeling, too." And then she laughed, a laugh that felt as light and bubbly as the excellent champagne. "I had it the first moment I saw you."

"You did?" He wore that boyish look, the one that made her think of Trev.

"Yes. I thought how you couldn't be looking at me. And then I thought how familiar you looked, that I must have met you before…."

"Of course I was looking at you," he said it with a definite note of reproach. "But you were very busy reminding yourself that you were through with men."

"I was. I admit it. How dumb was that?"

"It's all right. Now that you've told me why you gave up men, I thoroughly understand. And I'm not complaining. If you hadn't decided to stay away from the male sex, you might have found someone else by now and I wouldn't have a chance with you."

"And that would have been a tragedy," she teased.

"Yes, it would. A true catastrophe. But you did give up men. Now all I have to do is convince you to give one more man a chance." He raised his glass again. She clinked hers against it. "Are you ready for the first course?"

Suddenly, she was starving. "I am, yes."

He cast a glance beyond the open curtain. That was all. Just a glance. The waiter appeared again and made straight for their table.

Two hours later, Rule walked her out to the valet stand and had her car brought around. He tipped the valet generously and then took her hand and led her away from her waiting Mercedes. "Just for a moment…"

She went with him, down the sloping front entrance, to a shadowed area next to a large brick planter thick with greenery, beneath a beautiful old oak. The spring night felt warm and close around them.

He turned to face her. His eyes gleamed like polished stones through the darkness and his fingers trailed up her bare arm, a long, slow, dancing caress that left her strangely weak and slightly breathless. "Sydney…" He clasped her shoulders, and then framed her face between both wonderful hands. "Sydney O'Shea. I was becoming frightened."

His words confused her. She scanned his shadowed features. "But why?"

"That I would never find you. Never meet you…"

"Oh. That." She felt a glad smile curve her lips.

"Yes. That." His sweet breath stirred the loose curls at her temples as he bent his head closer to her.

A kiss. *His* kiss. Their first kiss. She tipped her face up to him, offering her mouth.

He held her eyes as he lowered his lips to hers.

Warm. Soft. Easy…

Her eyes drifted shut as his mouth touched hers, lightly, cherishingly. And she trembled, the moment was so exactly as she'd imagined it might be during their lunch that afternoon, during the long, glorious meal just past.

"Sydney…" He whispered her name against her mouth and she opened for him.

Instantly, she wanted more, wanted to be closer. *Had* to be closer.

Surging up, she wrapped her arms around him. A tiny, hungry cry escaped her at the sheer glory of such a perfect moment.

He took her cue and deepened the kiss, gathering her into him, cradling her against his body, so that she felt his warmth and solidness all along the length of her. He tasted of coffee and the heavenly pistachio mascarpone cake they'd shared for dessert. And the way he kissed her, the way his warm, rough-tender tongue caressed her…oh, there was nothing, ever, in her experience, to compare to it.

Nothing to compare.

To his kiss…

She wished it would never end.

But of course, it had to end. He took her shoulders again and reluctantly lifted his mouth from hers.

"Tomorrow," he said, gazing down at her, his eyes heavy-lidded, holding her a willing captive with his light touch at her shoulders, with his tender glance.

"Yes," she vowed, though she didn't even know yet what he planned for tomorrow.

He brushed the backs of his fingers against her cheek, and then up to her temple, causing those lovely shivers to course across her skin. "In the morning? I could come and collect you and your little boy. We could…visit a park, maybe. A park with swings and slides, so he'll have a chance to play. My little niece and nephew love nothing so much as a few hours in the sunshine, with a sandbox and a slide."

"You didn't tell me you had a niece and a nephew."

He nodded. "My older brother, Max, has two children— say yes to tomorrow."

"But I already did, didn't I?"

"Say it again."

"Yes—and why don't you come for breakfast first? You can meet my best friend, Lani, who has a degree in English literature, is a fabulous cook and takes care of Trevor while I'm at work."

"I would love breakfast. And to meet your friend, Lani."

"I have to warn you. Breakfast comes early at my house."

"Early it is."

"Seven-thirty, then." She took his hand, automatically threading her fingers with his, feeling the thrill of touching him—and also a certain rightness. Her hand fit perfectly in his. "Come on." She pulled him back toward her car. "I'll give you my address and phone number."

"Where's Michael?" Sydney asked, when she let herself in the house at quarter of eleven and found Lani sitting on the sofa alone, wearing Tweety Bird flannel pajama bottoms and a yellow cami top.

"How was the big date?" Lani asked, with a too-bright smile.

Sydney slipped off her red shoes and dropped to the sofa beside her friend. "It was better than…anything. Wonderful. I'm crazy about him. He's coming for breakfast at seven-thirty."

"Good. I can check him out. See if he's good enough for you."

"He's good enough. You'll see. I thought maybe one of your fabulous frittatas…"

"You got it." Lani took off her glasses and set them on the side table.

"Hey." Sydney waited until her friend looked at her again. Then she guided a thick swatch of Lani's dark, curly hair behind her ear. "You didn't answer my question about Michael."

Lani's big eyes were a little sad, and her full mouth curved slightly down. "Tonight, when I watched you getting ready to meet this new guy, putting on your makeup, fixing your hair, waffling over that perfect red dress…"

"Yeah? Tonight, what?"

"I thought, '*That*. What Syd's feeling. I want *that*.'"

"Oh, sweetheart…"

Lani's shoulders drooped. "And then you left and Michael came over and I thought what a nice guy he is…but I couldn't go on with him. Because he's not *the* guy." She laughed a little, shaking her head. "Do you know what I mean?"

Sydney reached out. Lani sagged against her and they held each other. "Yeah," Sydney whispered into her friend's thick, fragrant hair. "Yeah, I know exactly what you mean."

The next morning, the doorbell rang at seven-thirty on the nose.

"I get it!" Trevor fisted his plump hand and tapped the table twice. "Knock, knock!" he shouted. "Who's there?"

Sydney kissed his milk-smeared cheek. "Eat your cereal, Bosco."

"Banana!" Trev giggled. "Banana who?"

Lani said, "The coffee's ready and the frittata's in the oven. Answer the door, Syd."

"Orange. Banana." Trevor was totally entranced with his never-quite-right knock-knock joke. He banged his spoon gleefully against the tabletop. "Orange your… banana…"

Lani took his spoon from him. "Well, I guess I'll have to feed you, since you're not doing it."

"Lani, no! I eat. I do it myself."

"You sure?"

"Yes!"

She handed him back the spoon. "Go," she said to

Sydney, canting her head in the general direction of the front door.

Her heart doing somersaults inside her chest, Sydney went to let Rule in.

"Hi." She said it in the most ridiculous, breathy little voice.

"Sydney," he replied in wonderful melted-caramel tones. Could a man get more handsome every time a woman saw him? Rule did. The bright April sunshine made his hair gleam black as a crow's wing, and his smile had her heart performing a forward roll. He had a big yellow Tonka dump truck in one hand and a red ball in the other.

"I see you've come armed for battle," she said.

He shrugged. "In my experience, little boys like trucks. And balls."

"They do. Both. A lot." She stared at him. And he stared back at her. Time stopped. The walls of her foyer seemed to disappear. There was only the man on the other side of the open door. He filled up the world.

Then, from back in the kitchen, she heard her son calling out gleefully, "Orange. Banana. Banana. Orange..."

Lani said something. Probably, "Eat your cereal."

"It's the never-ending knock-knock joke," she said, and then wondered if they even had knock-knock jokes in his country. "Come in, come in..."

He did. She shut the door behind him. "This way..."

He caught her elbow. Somehow he had managed to shift the toy truck to the arm with the ball in it. "Wait." He said it softly.

She turned back to him and he looked down at her and...

Was there anything like this feeling she had with him?

So fine and shining and full of possibility. He pulled her to him.

She went willingly, eagerly. Close to him was where she wanted to be. She moved right up, snug and cozy against his broad chest, sharing his strong arms with the red ball and the yellow truck. "What?"

"This." And he kissed her. A brushing kiss, tender and teasing. Just right for early on a sunny Saturday morning. She felt his smile against her own.

When he lifted his mouth from hers, his eyes were soft as black velvet and full of promise. "May I meet your son now?"

"Right this way."

Trevor was shy with Rule at first.

Her little boy stared with big, solemn dark eyes as Sydney introduced Rule to Lani.

"And this is Trevor," Sydney said.

"Hello, Trevor. My name is Rule."

Trevor only stared some more and stuck a big spoonful of cereal in his mouth.

"Say hello," Sydney instructed him.

But Trevor turned his head away.

Rule sent her an oblique glance and a slight smile that said he knew about kids, and also knew how to be patient. He put the ball and the truck under the side table against the wall and accepted coffee, taking the empty chair between Lani and Sydney.

Lani served the frittata and they ate. Rule praised the food and said how much he liked the coffee, which Lani prepared to her own exacting tastes, grinding the beans with a top-quality grinder and brewing only with a French press.

He asked Lani about her degree in literature. The two

of them seemed to hit it off, Sydney thought. Lani was easy with him, and friendly, from the first. She told him her favorite Shakespeare play was *The Tempest.* He confessed to a fondness for *King Lear,* which had Lani groaning that she might love *Lear,* too. But she had no patience for thickheaded, foolish kings. Sydney didn't know a lot about Shakespeare, but it did kind of please her, that Rule seemed well-read, that he could carry on a conversation about something other than the Mavericks and the Cowboys.

He turned to her. "And what about you, Sydney? Do you have a favorite Shakespeare play?"

She shrugged. "I saw *A Midsummer Night's Dream* once. And I enjoyed it. Everybody falling in love with the wrong person, but then it all worked out in the end."

"You prefer a happy ending?"

"Absolutely," she told him. "I like it when it all works out. That doesn't happen often enough in real life."

"I like trucks!" Suddenly, Trev was over his shyness and back in the game.

Rule turned to him. "And do you like balls?"

"Red balls! Yes!"

"Good. Because that truck and that ball over there beneath the table? They're for you."

Trevor looked away again—too much attention, apparently, from this intriguing stranger.

Sydney said, "Tell Rule 'thank you.'"

"Thank you, Roo," Trev parroted obediently, still looking away, the soft curve of his round cheek turned down.

But Rule wasn't looking away. He seemed honestly taken with her little boy. Her heart did more wild and lovely acrobatics, just to look at the two of them, Rule watching Trev, Trev not quite able to meet this new guy's eyes.

Then Rule said, "Knock, knock."

Trev didn't look, but he did say, "Who's there?"

"Wanda."

Trev peeked, looked away, peeked again. "Wanda who?"

"Wanda cookie?"

Slowly, Trev turned and looked straight at Rule. "Cookie! Yes! Please!"

Rule actually produced an animal cracker from the pocket of his beautifully made lightweight jacket. He slid a questioning glance at Sydney. At her nod, he handed the cookie over.

"Grrr. Lion!" announced Trev and popped the lion-shaped cookie in his mouth. "Yum." He chewed and swallowed. "Thank you very much—Orange! Banana! Knock, knock."

Rule gamely went through the whole joke with him twice. Trev never got the punch line right, but that didn't have any effect on his delight in the process.

"It never ends," Lani said with a sigh. But then she grinned. "And you know we wouldn't have it any other way."

"All done," Trev told them. "Get down, Mama. Play trucks!"

So Sydney wiped his hands and face with a damp cloth and swung him down from his booster seat. He went straight for Rule. "Roo. Come. We play trucks!"

"It appears you have been summoned," Sydney said.

"Nothing could please me more—or *almost* nothing." The teasing heat in his glance hinted that whatever it was that pleased him more had something to do with her. Very likely with kissing her, an activity that pleased her a bunch, too.

He tossed his jacket across the family room sofa and went over and got down on the floor with Trev, who gathered all his trucks together so they could roll them around making *vrooming* noises and crash them into each other. Sydney and Lani cleared the table and loaded the dishwasher. And soon enough, it was time to head for the neighborhood park. Lani begged off, so it was just the three of them. Since the small park was only a couple of blocks away, they walked, Trev between Sydney and Rule, holding both their hands.

Trev was an outgoing child, although he was usually pretty reserved around new people. It took him a while to get comfortable with someone. But apparently, with Rule, he was over his shyness after those first few moments at the breakfast table.

Trev chattered away at him as they strolled past the pretty, gracious homes and the wide, inviting lawns. "I walk fast, Roo. I strong! I happy!"

Rule agreed that he was very fast, and so strong—and wasn't it great that he was happy? "I'm happy, too," Rule said, and shared a speaking glance with Sydney.

Trev looked up at them, at Rule, then at Sydney, then back at Rule again. "Mama's happy, too!" he crowed. "Knock, knock!"

"Who's there?" asked Rule. And then he went through the endless loop of the joke two more times.

They stayed at the park for three hours. Sydney watched for a sign that Rule might be getting tired of pushing Trev on the swings, of sitting with him on the spinner, of playing seesaw—Trev and Sydney on one end, Rule on the other.

But Rule seemed to love every minute of it. He got down and crawled through the concrete tunnels with Trev, heedless of his designer trousers, laughing as Trev scuttled ahead of him calling out, "You can't catch me, I too fast!" Trev popped out of the tunnel.

Rule was right behind him. Rule growled, playing it scary. Trev let out a shriek of fear and delight.

Finally, at a little after eleven, Trev announced, "Okay. All done." And he was. All the fun had worn him out.

The walk back to the house took a little longer than the stroll over there. When Trevor was tired, he dragged his feet and kept trying to sit down instead of moving forward.

But they got him there, eventually. Lani took over, hustling him to the bathroom to change him out of the diaper she'd put on him for the park and back into the lighter-weight training pants he wore most of the time now.

Alone with Rule for the first time since their kiss at the front door, Sydney said, "You were wonderful with him."

His gaze held hers. She did love the way he looked at her—as though he couldn't get enough of just staring into her eyes. He said, "It wasn't difficult, not in the least. I enjoyed every minute of it." And then he added in that charming, formal way of his, "Thank you for inviting me, Sydney."

"It was my pleasure—and clearly, Trev's, too. Had enough?"

He frowned. "Are you saying you would like for me to go now?"

She laughed. "No way. I'm just giving you an out, in case you've had enough of crashing trucks and knock-knock jokes for one day."

"I want to stay, if you don't mind."

"Of course I don't mind." Now her heart was doing cartwheels. "Not in the least."

Yes, all right. Maybe she should be more cautious. Put the brakes on a little. But she didn't *want* to put the brakes on. She was having a great time and if he didn't want to go, well, why should she feel she should send him away?

He could stay for lunch if he wanted, stay for dinner.

Stay…indefinitely. That would be just fine with her. Every moment she was with him only convinced her that she wanted the *next* moment with him. And the one after that. Something about him had her throwing all her usual caution to the winds.

Was she in for a rude awakening? She just didn't think so. Every moment she was with Rule only made her more certain that he was the real deal: a great guy who liked her—a lot. A great guy who liked children, too, a guy who actually enjoyed spending the morning playing in the park with her and her little boy.

As long as he gave her no reason to doubt her confidence in him, well, she *wouldn't* doubt him. It was as simple as that.

He said, "Perhaps we could take Trevor and Lani to lunch?"

"I wish. But no. Trev's going to need to eat right away, and since he's been on the go since early this morning, he's probably going to be fussy. So we'll get some food down him and then put him to bed. His nap will last at least a couple of hours. You sure you won't mind just hanging around here for the afternoon?"

"There's nothing I would rather do than hang around here with you and your son." He said it so matter-of-factly, and she knew he was sincere.

"I'm glad." They shared a nod of perfect understanding.

As Sydney had predicted, Trev was cranky during lunch, but he did pack away a big bowl of chicken and rice. He went right to sleep when Sydney put him in bed.

Then she and Rule raided the refrigerator and carried their lunch of cheese, crackers and grapes out to the backyard. They sat under an oak not far from the pool and he told her more about his family, about how his older brother

Max's wife had tragically drowned in a water-skiing accident two years before, leaving Max with a broken heart and two little children to raise on his own.

"They were so happy together, Max and Sophia," Rule said, his eyes full of shadows right then. "They found each other very young, and knew they would marry when they were both hardly more than children. It's been terrible for him, learning to live without her."

"I can't even imagine how that must be for him. I've always envied people who find true love early and only want a chance to have a family, to grow old side by side. It's just completely wrong that your brother and his wife didn't get a whole lifetime of happiness together."

They were sitting in a pair of cushioned chaises, the platter of cheese and fruit on the low teak table between them. He held out his hand to her. She took it without hesitation and let him pull her over to his chaise.

He wrapped an arm around her, using his other hand to tip her chin up. They shared a slow, sweet kiss. And then he spoke against her softly parted lips. "I love the taste of your lips, the feel of your body pressed close to mine…."

She reached up, touched the silky black hair at his temple. A miracle, to be here with him, like this. To be free to touch him at will, to be the one *he* wanted to touch. "Oh, Rule. What's happening with us?"

He kissed her again, a possessive kiss, hard and quick. "You don't know?"

"I…think I do. But I've waited so long to meet someone like you. It almost seems too good to be true."

"You're trembling." He held her closer.

She laughed, a torn little sound. "Not so prickly now, huh?"

"Come here, relax…" He stretched out in the chaise and pulled her with him, so she lay facing him, tucked against his side, his big arms around her, his cheek touching her hair. A lovely breeze came up, stirring the warm afternoon air, making it feel cool and comfortable beneath the oak tree. "Don't be afraid. I would never hurt you. I'm only grateful that I've found you, at last."

"So, then," she teased, "you lied yesterday when you said you weren't looking for me."

"Can you forgive me?"

She took a moment, pretended to think it over and finally whispered, "I'll try."

"Good. Because I've been looking for you all my life. And now that I have you in my arms, I never want to let you go."

"I want to be with you, too." She laid her hand against his chest, felt the steady, strong beating of his heart. "And I'm not afraid," she added. And then she sighed. "Well, okay. That's not so. I *am* afraid—at least a little."

"Because of those fools Ryan and Peter?"

She nodded. "I haven't had good luck with men."

He kissed her hair. "Maybe not."

"Definitely not."

"Until now," he corrected her.

She tipped her head back and met those shining dark eyes and…well, she believed him. She honestly did. "Until now," she repeated, softly, but firmly, too.

"Come out with me tonight. Let me come for you. We'll have dinner, go dancing."

It was Lani's night out. But Sydney had more than one sitter she could call. "I would love to."

Trev woke at a little before three, completely refreshed and ready to play some more.

Rule was only too happy to oblige him. Together, they built a wobbly Duplo castle—which Trev took great delight in toppling to the floor the moment it was finished.

Then the three of them took the red ball outside to Trev's fenced play area and rolled the ball around. Finally, inside again, Rule and Trev played more trucks until Lani announced it was time for Trev's dinner.

The man amazed Sydney. He seemed completely content to spend hours entertaining her toddler. He honestly did seem to love children and Sydney couldn't help thinking that he would make a wonderful father.

Rule called his driver at five-twenty-five.

"Bye, Roo. Come back. See me soon!" Trev called, pausing to wave as Lani herded him toward the stairs for his bath.

"Goodbye Trevor."

"We play trucks!" Trev started up the stairs in his usual way, using both hands and feet.

"Yes." Rule nodded, watching his progress upward. "Trucks. Absolutely."

Trev turned to Lani and started his knock-knock joke as he and Lani disappeared on the upper landing. The moment they were out of sight, Sydney moved into Rule's open arms.

They shared a kiss and then he took her hand and brushed his lips across the back of it. "Your son is amazing. So smart. Just like his mom."

She answered playfully, "And don't forget strong. Trev is very strong. Just ask him."

"Yes, I remember. Very strong and very loud when he wants to be—and I'm honored that you shared the story of his birth so honestly with me. And that you've trusted me enough to tell me about those idiots Ryan and Peter."

"I think it's better," she said, "to be honest and forthright."

"So do I." Something happened in his eyes—a shadow of something. Uneasiness? Concern?

Her pulse beat faster. "Rule. What is it? What's the matter?"

"I'm afraid I have a confession to make."

Now her pulse was racing dizzyingly fast. And she felt sick, her stomach churning. So, then. He really *was* too good to be true. "Tell me," she said softly, but not gently. She couldn't hide the thread of steel that connected the two simple words.

"Remember how I told you I admired my mother?"

She wasn't getting it. "This confession is about your mother?"

He touched her cheek, a light touch that made her heart ache. She really liked him. So very much. And now she just knew it was all going wrong. He said, "No, it's not about my mother. Not essentially."

"What do you mean? It is, or it isn't."

"Sydney, I admire my mother for any number of reasons. And I revere her as the ruler of my country."

She was sure she must have misunderstood him. "Excuse me? Your mother rules your country?"

"My mother is Adrienne II, Sovereign Princess of Montedoro. And my father is His Serene Highness Evan, Prince Consort of Montedoro."

"Okay. You'll have to say that again. I'm sure I misunderstood. Sovereign Princess, you said?"

"Yes. My mother holds the throne. My father is Prince Consort and my brother Maximilian is the heir apparent. Before Max had his son and daughter, I was second in line to the throne."

## *Chapter Four*

Sydney gaped up at him. "A prince. You're telling me that you're a prince? And not just as in, 'a prince of a guy,' but a *real* prince? A…royal prince?"

He chuckled. "My darling, yes. That is, more or less, what I'm telling you."

"Um. More or less?"

"The truth is that Montedoro is ruled by a prince, not a king. And, in terms of his or her title, a ruling prince is said to have a throne, but not a crown. And only those who are the children or grandchildren of ruling kings or queens, or are the spouses of royalty, are given the honorific of royal. However, in the sense that 'royal' means 'ruling,' yes. I am of the royal family of Montedoro, or more correctly, the princely family. And even though we are not addressed as royal, both our family coat of arms and our individual monograms contain the image of a crown."

She was still gaping. "I don't think I understood a word you just said."

He frowned. "I see your point. Perhaps that was more information than you require at the moment."

A prince. A prince of Montedoro. Should she have known this? "Wait. Evan Bravo. I remember now. Your dad was in the movies, right?"

He nodded. "It was a big story in all the newspapers and tabloids of the day. My mother married a film actor and he returned with her to Montedoro, where they had many children and lived happily ever after." He gave a wry smile. "Sydney, you look pale. Would you like to sit down?"

"No. No, really. I'm fine. Just fine."

"Perhaps you would like to see my diplomatic passport…."

"Ohmigod. No. Really. I believe you. I do." Still, she couldn't help looking around nervously, half expecting Ashton Kutcher and the *Punk'd* camera crew to be making their appearance any second now. She turned her gaze up to him again and tried to look stern. "You should have told me."

"I know." He did seem honestly contrite. "But the moment never seemed right. I wanted you to know me, at least a little, before we got into all of that."

"Last night. At the Mansion. The nervous host…"

"Yes. I'm staying there. He knows who I am." He took her chin, tipped it up to him. "But none of that matters."

"Rule. Of course it matters."

"Only if you let it. To me, what matters most of all, more than anything, is this…" And he lowered his dark head and claimed her lips.

And by the time that kiss was through, she was inclined

to agree with him. "Oh, Rule…" She clung to him, feeling light-headed and slightly weak in the knees.

"I'll leave you now," he said ruefully, stroking her hair, his eyes full of tenderness and understanding. She thought how crazy she was for him—and how she would look him up on Google the minute he was out the door. One side of his mouth curled up in the gorgeous half smile that totally enchanted her. He said, "You'll have time to look me up on the internet before I come to collect you for the evening."

She shook her head. "You know me too well. How is that possible? We only met yesterday."

"Forgive me. For taking so long to tell you…"

"I'll consider forgiving you as soon as my head stops spinning."

"One last kiss…"

She gave it. She simply could not resist him—and beyond that, she didn't *want* to resist him.

When he lifted his head that time, he released her. She opened the door and watched him jog down the front walk to his waiting limousine.

As soon as the long, black car disappeared from sight, she shut the front door and went upstairs to get with Lani about her plans for the evening.

She found her friend on her knees filling the tub. Trev sat on the bathroom floor in his training pants, putting a new face on his Mr. Potato Head.

"Lani…"

"Hmm?" Lani tested the water, turned the hot water tap up a little.

"Just wondering if you were going out tonight?"

"Nope, I'm staying in. And yes, I'd be happy to watch Trev."

"Wonderful." So that was settled.

"Mama, see?" Trev held up Mr. Potato Head, whose

big, red lips were now above his moustache and who had only one eye in the middle of his forehead. She bent down and kissed him. He asked, "Mama read a story?"

"After your bath, I promise."

"O-*kay!*" He removed Mr. Potato Head's red hat and reached for a blue plastic ear.

Sydney kissed him again and then ran back downstairs to her office off the foyer. She kept a PC in there and she figured she had maybe twenty minutes before Trev finished his bath and would come looking for her.

Sydney was good at research, and she knew how to get a lot of information quickly. By the time Trev came bouncing down the stairs and demanded her attention again, she intended to know a whole lot more about Rule.

She found pages and pages of references to the courtship and marriage of Rule's father and mother.

Evan Bravo was born in San Antonio, second of seven sons, to James and Elizabeth Bravo. Several sources cited early estrangement from his overbearing father. Determined to make his mark in Hollywood, Evan Bravo moved West at the age of eighteen. Talent and luck were on his side. He was never a big star, but at twenty-five, he won a Golden Globe and a Best Supporting Actor Oscar for his portrayal of a charming but crooked L.A. detective in a big-budget box office hit called *L.A. Undercover.* Then he met Princess Adrienne of Montedoro. There ensued a whirlwind courtship, a fabulous palace wedding—and celebrating in the streets of the whole of Montedoro when their first child, Maximilian, was born. Princess Adrienne, as the last of her line, was expected to provide her country with an heir and a spare and then some. She did exactly that, bearing eight more children in the succeeding eleven years.

Sydney read the story of the tragic death of Maximilian's wife, Sophia—drowning while water-skiing, just as Rule had already told her. Also, she learned that third-born Alexander had been captured by terrorists in Afghanistan and held prisoner for four years, until somehow engineering a miraculous and daring escape only a few months ago.

Prince Rule, she learned, had obtained his degree in America, from Princeton. He was the businessman of the family, the glamorous bachelor, big in international trade, and was known to champion and generously contribute to several worthy causes. Over the years, his name had been linked with any number of gorgeous models and actresses, but those relationships had never seemed to last very long. Some sources claimed that he was "expected" to marry his longtime friend from childhood, HRH Liliana, aka Princess Lili, heir presumptive to the throne of the island state of Alagonia. However, no actual announcement of an engagement had so far been made.

Sydney went looking for images of the princess in question and found several. Liliana of Alagonia was blonde, blue-eyed and as beautiful as a princess in a fairy tale.

Sudden apprehension had Sydney catching her lower lip between her teeth and shifting in her swivel chair. Princess Lili, huh? Rule had never mentioned this supposed "childhood friend." Tonight, she would definitely have a few questions for him.

"Mama, read me books!"

Sydney looked up from the computer to find her little boy and Lani standing in the open doorway to the front hall.

Lani said, "Sorry to interrupt, but he hasn't forgotten that you said you would read to him."

"And I will, absolutely."

Trev, all pink and sweet from his bath, wearing his Captain America pajamas, marched over and tugged on her arm. "Come *on,* Mama."

Further research on Princess Liliana would have to wait. Sydney swung him into her arms and carried him upstairs where he'd already picked out the books he wanted her to read to him.

Later, after he was in bed, as she hurried to get ready for the evening, she told Lani that Rule was a Montedoran prince.

"Whoa. And I didn't even curtsy when you introduced me to him."

"It's a little late to worry about protocol." Sydney leaned close to the mirror as she put on her makeup. "Which is fine with me."

"What would it be like to marry a prince?" Lani wondered out loud.

"Did I mention marriage? We've only just met."

"But it's already serious between you two, I can tell. Isn't it?"

Sydney set down her powder brush and turned to her friend. "Yeah. I think it is—and I may be late coming home tonight." Unless Rule confessed that he intended to marry the lovely Princess Lili. In that case, she would be coming home early, crying on Lani's shoulder and swearing off men for the next decade, at least.

"Oh, Syd…" Lani grabbed her and gave her a hug. And then she took Sydney by the shoulders and held her away. "You look wonderful. I love that dress. It brings out the color of your eyes." Lani sighed. "Enjoy every moment."

"I will." Sydney smoothed her hair and tried to banish any thought of pretty Princess Lili from her mind.

Rule arrived in his limousine at eight.

Once on the inside of the tinted-glass windows, Sidney

saw there were two men in the front seat: the driver in his dark livery and chauffeur's cap and also a thick-necked military-looking guy with a crew cut, who had a Bluetooth device in his ear and wore sunglasses even though it was nearly dark.

Sydney leaned close to Rule, drawn to his strength and his warmth and the fine, subtle scent of the aftershave he wore. She whispered, "Don't tell me. You keep the Secret Service on retainer."

He gave a shrug. "Effective security is something of a necessity. It's a sad fact of life in this modern age."

They went to another really wonderful restaurant, where they were once again ushered into a private room.

She waited until they were served the main course before she brought up the subject that had been bothering her. "So tell me about Princess Liliana of Alagonia."

He sent her a wry sort of smile. "I see you've been checking up on me."

"Did you think I wouldn't?"

"I absolutely knew that you would."

She told him exactly what she'd learned. "Rumor has it that you and the princess are 'expected' to marry."

He held her gaze. "You should know better than to put your faith in rumors."

"You're hedging, Rule." She sat back in her chair and took a drink from her water goblet.

"Lili's eight years younger than I am. She's like one of my little sisters."

"But she's *not* your sister—little or otherwise."

"All right, enough." He said it flatly. "I am not going to marry Liliana, Sydney. We are not affianced. I have never proposed marriage to her."

She took a wild guess. "But *she* wants to marry *you.* It's *assumed* that you will marry her."

He didn't look away. But his eyes were definitely guarded now. "She...looks up to me."

Did he imagine she would wimp out and leave it at that? Hah. "Just say it. She *does* want to marry you."

He sat back in his chair, too. And he looked at her so strangely, so distantly. When he spoke, his voice was cold. "I would not presume to speak for Liliana. She's a sweet and lovely person. And yes, if I married Lili, it would be considered a brilliant match, one that would strengthen the bonds between our two countries."

She said sharply, "So, then you *should* marry her."

"Not only that." His eyes were so dark right then, dark and full of secrets, it seemed to her. Suddenly, she was thinking that she didn't know him at all, that this brief, magical time she'd shared with him had truly been just that: magic, not reality. Nothing more than a beautiful, impossible fantasy. That the truth was coming out now and the fantasy was over.

So soon. Way too soon...

He spoke again. "Do you recall how I told you I had to marry by my thirty-third birthday?"

"Yes."

"Did you think I was only teasing you?"

"Well, I thought you meant that there was pressure in your family, as there is in a lot of families, for you to settle down, start providing your parents with grandchildren, all that."

"It's considerably more than just pressure. It's the law."

She looked at him sideways. "Now you really are kidding."

"On the contrary, I'm completely serious. My country was once a French protectorate. And France...casts a long shadow, as they say. We have signed any number of treaties with France, treaties wherein the French promise to guarantee Montedoro's sovereignty."

As a lawyer, she knew what he was getting at. "And the simple fact that another country is in a position to guarantee your sovereignty is…problematic?"

"Precisely. Although my family is officially in charge of succession, the French government must approve the next ruling prince or princess. There is even a stipulation that, should the throne go vacant, Montedoro will revert to a French protectorate. That is why we have a law designed to ensure that no prince will shirk his—or her—obligation to produce potential heirs to the throne. Montedoran princes and princesses are required to marry before their thirty-third birthday or be stripped of all titles and income. I will be thirty-three on June twenty-fourth."

"Two and a half months from now."

"Yes," he said softly.

Sydney was certain of it then. No matter what he'd said a few moments ago, he did intend to marry the lovely Lili. This thing between the two of them was only…what? A last fling before his ingrained sense of duty finally kicked in, before he went back to Montedoro and tied the knot with the pretty blonde princess he'd known since childhood—and then got to work having a bunch of little princes with her.

And why, oh, why, if he just *had* to have a final fling, couldn't he have chosen someone else? Sydney was a hard-driving, overworked single mom and the last thing she needed was a whirlwind romance with a man who was planning to marry someone else. Plus, she'd already suffered through more than her share of disappointments when it came to the male gender, thank you very much.

Bottom line? She really did not have time for this crap.

And she wanted desperately to be furious with him.

But she wasn't. The whole situation only made her miserable. She longed to put her face in her hands and burst into tears.

But no—in fact, *hell* no. She was an O'Shea and an O'Shea was tougher than that. No way was she letting him see her break down and cry. Instead, coolly, she advised, "Don't you think you're cutting it a little close?"

"More than a little. And the truth is I *have* considered asking Liliana to be my wife."

Surprise, surprise. "So what's stopped you?"

"No man wants to marry a woman he thinks of as a sister. Not even if she is a fine person, not even to keep his inheritance, not even for the good of his country. And so I've hesitated. I've put off making my move."

"Rule. I have to say it. You need to stop dithering and get with the program."

That slow smile curved his beautiful mouth. "A prince does not *dither.*"

"Call it what you want. Looks like dithering to me."

"If I *was* dithering, Sydney—and I'm not admitting that I was—I'm not dithering anymore."

She cast a pained glance toward the ceiling. "Okay. You lost me there."

"I'm absolutely certain now that Liliana will never be my bride. In one split second, everything changed for me."

She didn't get where this was going. She really didn't. And she told herself firmly that she didn't care. What mattered was that it was over between them. It had to be, she saw that now. Over and done before it even really got started. "In one split second," she parroted with a heavy dose of sarcasm. "So...the realization that you're definitely not marrying dear Princess Lili hit you like a lightning bolt, huh?"

"No."

"I'm not following you."

"It's quite simple. While everything changed for me in an instant, it took a little longer than that for me to accept that marriage to Lili had become impossible."

"I have no idea what you're telling me."

"*That* happened after lunch yesterday."

"*What* happened?"

"You said goodbye and got into your car and drove away. I stood and watched you leave and tried to consider the concept of never seeing you again. And I couldn't do that. Right then, marrying Lili became impossible."

"So there was no lightning bolt, after all."

"Of course there was a lightning bolt. It struck the moment I saw you, striding into Macy's, indomitable. Unyielding. Ready to take on the world. At that moment, Liliana was the last thing on my mind. Right then, all I could think of was you."

Sydney reached for her untouched glass of wine and took an extra-large gulp of it. She set the glass down with care. "Well, I…" Her voice had a definite wobble to it. She drew in a slow, steadying breath. "You're not marrying the princess. You're sure about that?"

"Yes. Absolutely certain."

"You mean that? You really mean that?"

"I do, Sydney. With all my heart."

"Don't mess with me, Rule."

"I promise you, I'm not."

Her throat felt tight, so tight it ached. She gulped to relax it a little. "Okay," she said softly, at last. "You're not marrying the princess, after all."

"I'm so glad we're finally clear on that." His voice was gentle, indulgent. "You've hardly touched your food. Is it unsatisfactory?"

"Oh, no. It's fine. Really. Delicious." She picked up her fork again.

They ate in silence for a while.

Finally, he spoke. "I like you in that emerald-green satin. Almost as much as I like you in red."

"Thank you."

"I still want to take you dancing."

She sipped her wine again, suddenly as certain as he seemed to be. About the two of them. About…everything. Whatever happened in the end, she wanted this night with him. She wanted it so much. She wanted *him*. "I have a suggestion."

"And I am always open to suggestion. Especially if the suggestion is coming from you."

"Take me back to the Mansion, Rule. Take me to your room. We can dance there."

## Chapter Five

His room was one of the two Terrace Suites on the Mansion's top floor. It was over thirteen hundred square feet of pure luxury.

There was champagne waiting for them in the sitting room—champagne and a crystal bowl full of Montedoran oranges. He took off his jacket and tie and they sat on the sofa, sipping the champagne. She slipped off her shoes as he peeled an orange for her.

"Oh, this so good," she said, savoring the ruby-red sections, one by one. They tasted like no orange she'd ever had before.

He bent close and kissed her then, a slow kiss that started out light and so tender and deepened until she was slightly breathless—scratch that. More than slightly. A lot more than slightly. "Very sweet," he said when he lifted his mouth from hers. He wasn't talking about the orange.

She only gazed at him, her heart beating in a slow, deep,

exciting way, her body warm and lazy, her eyelids suddenly heavy.

The sofa was nice and fat and comfortable. She considered stretching out on the cushions, reaching for him as she went down, pulling him with her, so they were stretched out together.

But he set his half-full flute aside and picked up the remote on the coffee table. The large flat screen above a bow-fronted cabinet flared to life. Before she could ask him why he suddenly wanted to watch *Lockup,* he changed the channel to a music station. A slow romantic song was playing.

"Come." He offered his hand and they rose together. They went out to the terrace, where the lights of downtown Dallas glittered in the balmy darkness of the April night.

They danced. It was like a dream, a dream come to life, just the two of them, holding each other, swaying to the music, not saying anything.

Not needing to speak.

Then he put a finger under her chin and she looked up into his eyes, into the light shining within that velvet darkness. She tried to remind herself that she still wasn't sure about the whole love at first sight thing, didn't really believe that you could meet someone and know instantly that here was the person you wanted to spend the rest of your life with. It took time to know another person, time to learn his ways, time to discover if there really was any chance for the relationship in the long-term.

But when Rule looked at her, well, she believed that *he* believed. And his belief was powerful. His belief made her want to believe, too.

"I see you," he whispered, and she couldn't help smiling. He reminded her of Trev again, Trev playing peekaboo: *I see you, Mama. I see you, I do.* "I know," he said. "It sounds silly when I say it. It sounds self-evident. And not important in the least."

"I didn't say that. It was only, for a moment, you reminded me of Trev."

"Ah." He searched her eyes some more. "Well, good, then. I'm pleased if I make you think of him. And it *is* important that I see you. I see in you all that I've been looking for, though I didn't even realize I *was* looking until yesterday. I see in you the best things, Sydney. The things that matter. I see that with you I can be a better man, and a happier man. I see that you will always interest me. That you will challenge me. I want to…give you everything. I want to spend my life making sure you have it all, whatever makes you happy, whatever your heart desires."

She searched his astonishingly gorgeous face. "You are tempting me, you know that?"

"I hope so." He brushed one soft, warm kiss against her lips, a kiss that lingered like a tender brand on her skin even after he had lifted his head to gaze down at her once more. "I want to tempt you, Sydney. Because I've never met anyone like you. You amaze me. I want to be with you. I never want to let you go." He kissed her again, an endless kiss, as they danced. His mouth was so soft, not like the rest of him at all. His mouth was hot and supple and his tongue eased past the trembling barrier of her lips, sliding hot and knowing, over the edges of her teeth, across the top of her tongue, and then beneath it.

She felt…lost. Lost in a lovely, delicious kind of way. She didn't know where she was going. And Sydney Gabrielle O'Shea *always* knew where she was going. She'd always kept her focus, because she had to. Who would keep her on track if she didn't? Her parents were gone without her even knowing them. And then, too soon, so was her strong, steady grandmother. The men to whom she gave her trust were not dependable.

There was only Lani, her true, forever friend. And then there was Trevor to light up her days.

And now this. Now Rule.

At last. Long after she'd been sure there would never be a man for her. Her doubts, her hesitations were falling away. *He* was peeling them away. With his tenderness and his understanding, with his honesty and his frank desire for her.

Who had she been kidding? She *could* believe in love at first sight. Like her beloved grandmother before her, she *did* believe in love at first sight.

As long as it was love at first sight with a certain man. With the *right* man. The one she could trust. The one she could count on to be there when she needed someone to lean on. The one who honestly seemed to like everything about her, even her prickly nature and her sometimes sharp tongue.

Maybe that wasn't so surprising, that he had no issues with her strength and determination, with her ambition and her drive. After all, she had no issues with him— or whenever she did have issues, he would patiently and calmly put them to rest.

And she certainly liked the feelings he roused in her. The excitement, the desire. And the unaccustomed trust. Every time she felt her doubts rising—about him, about the impossibility of this thing between them—he stepped right up and banished them. He kept proving to her that he was exactly the man he seemed to be, exactly the man she'd never dared to dream she might someday find.

They danced some more, still kissing. She wrapped her arms around his neck, threaded her fingers up into the warm silk of his dark, dark hair. He lifted his head, but only to slant his mouth the other way and continue to kiss her, endlessly, perfectly. She sighed and lifted closer to him, loving the feel of her breasts against his hard chest, of her body and his body, touching so lightly, striking off sparks.

Sparks of promise, sparks of building desire.

He broke the kiss. She sighed at the loss. But then he only lowered his mouth again and kissed her cheek and then her temple. He caught her earlobe between his teeth, worried it so gently.

She made a soft, pleasured sound and pressed her body even closer to him, wanting to melt right into him, wanting to become a part of him, somehow—his body, her body, one and the same. He went on kissing her—his wonderful lips gliding over the curve of her jaw, down the side of her neck.

Her green dress had spaghetti straps. With a lazy finger, he pushed the left strap out of his way and kissed her shoulder, a long, lingering kiss. She felt his tongue, licking her, sending hot shards of pleasure radiating out along her skin. And then his teeth…oh, those teeth. He nipped her, but carefully, tenderly.

They had stopped dancing. They stood in the shadow of a potted palm, in a corner of the terrace. He eased the side of her dress down. She felt the sultry night air touch her breast.

And then he kissed her there. He took her nipple into his mouth and sucked it, rhythmically. He whispered her name against her skin.

She cradled his head, close—closer, her fingers buried in his hair. The heat of him was all around her, and down low, she was already liquid, weak, yearning. A silver thread of pure delight drew down through the core of her, into the womanly heart of her, from her breast, where he kissed her endlessly. He drew on her eager flesh in a slow, tempting rhythm, making her bare toes curl on the terrace flagstones. She moaned, held him closer, murmured his name on a slow, surrendering sigh.

And then he lifted his head. She blinked, dazed, and gazed up at him, feeling like a sleepwalker, wakened from the sweetest dream.

"Inside." He bent close again, caught her lower lip between his teeth, licked it, let it go. "Let's go in…"

She trembled, yearning. Her nipple was drawn so tight and hard, it ached. It ached in such a lovely, thrilling way. "Yes. Oh, yes…" And she tried to pull her strap back up, to cover herself.

"Don't." He caught her hand, stilled it, then brought her fingers to his lips and kissed them. "Leave it." His voice was rough and infinitely tender, both at once. "Leave it bare…" He bent, kissed her breast again, but only briefly that time. "So beautiful…"

And then he swept her up as though she weighed nothing and carried her through the open door into the sitting room, pausing only to turn and slide the door shut. A new song began.

He stopped in midstride. Their gazes locked. "'Lady in Red,'" he whispered.

"Not tonight," she whispered.

"It doesn't matter, whether you happen to be wearing red or not. To me, this song is you. This song is *yours*. You're my lady in red…"

"Oh, Rule." She touched his cheek with the back of her hand. His fine tanned skin was slightly rough with the beginnings of his dark beard, slightly rough and so very warm.

He took her mouth again, in a hard, hot kiss. She surrendered to that kiss. She let him sweep her away with the heat of it. She was seduced by the carnal need in it.

And he was moving again, carrying her through the door that led to his bedroom. The bed was turned back. He bent to put her down on the soft white sheets, so carefully, as though she might break, as though she was infinitely precious to him.

He laid her down and he rose to his height again. Swiftly, without ceremony, he took off his shirt, undid his belt, took down his trousers and his briefs. He sat and removed his shoes and socks. And then he rose once more to toss everything carelessly onto the bedside chair. The view of his magnificent body from behind stole every last wisp of breath from her body.

And then he turned to face her again. His eyes were molten.

Naked. He was naked and he was as beautiful—*more* so—than she had even imagined, the muscles of his chest and arms and belly so sharply defined. His legs were strong and straight and powerful, dusted with black hair, black hair that grew dense and curly where his big thighs joined.

The proof that he wanted her jutted out hard and proud. She dragged in a ragged breath and let it out with care.

And then he came down to her.

More kisses. Long, deep kisses, until she was pliant and more eager than ever. Until she whimpered with need. He took down the other strap of her dress and he kissed her right breast so slowly and deliciously, with the same erotic care he had lavished on the left.

By the time he eased her to her side facing away from him and took the zipper of her dress down, she was ready.

For him. For the two of them. For whatever he might

do to her, do *with* her. Ready for tonight. And tomorrow night. And all the nights to come.

With him. Beside him. Always.

Was this a dream? If it was, she prayed she might never wake up.

Tucked close behind her, his front to her back, he eased the dress down, gently, carefully, making the simple act of peeling the fabric away from her body into a caress. A long, perfect thrilling caress.

She lifted enough that he could take the dress down over her thighs and off. She wore no bra. She didn't need one.

He cupped her breasts, one and then the other, his hand engulfing them. He whispered that they were beautiful. "Delicate," he said. "Perfect."

She believed him. Seduced by the magic of his knowing touch, she had relinquished everything, even the wisdom of a little healthy skepticism. She believed all the things he whispered to her. She believed every last rough-tender, arousing word. Every knowing, skilled caress. He touched her face and she smelled the tart sweetness of blood oranges on his fingers. And it seemed to her that the scent was his scent—sweet, tempting, ruby-red.

His hand moved downward, over her breasts again and lower, along her belly. She gasped as his fingers eased under the elastic of her panties.

He found the feminine heart of her. He whispered that she felt like heaven there, so wet and hot and slick for him. He stroked her, a touch that quickly set every last nerve she possessed ablaze. Her whole body seemed to be humming with excitement, with electricity, with heat. She was liquid and burning and close to the brink.

She wanted it to last, wanted the climb to the top to go on forever, wanted to hold off on completion until she had him within her. But in no time, she was shuddering, going over the edge, moaning his name, working her hips against his fingers—oh, those fingers of his: magic, just…magic. She cried out.

He whispered, "Yes, like that. Just like that."

And then she was sailing out from the peak, into the wide open, drifting slowly, slowly down into her body again, her body that had his body wrapped around it.

"You feel…so good," she murmured, lazy. And she took his hand and tucked it tenderly close to her heart.

But he wasn't through yet.

Which was totally fine with her. She could go on like this, touching him, *being* touched by him, forever.

He was moving, shifting her onto her back, resettling himself close against her side. She sighed and let him do as he wished with her. She was drifting, satisfied, deeply content, on the borderline of sleep.

"Sydney…"

Reluctantly, still lost in the echoes of so many beautiful sensations, she opened her eyes. He was up an elbow, gazing down at her, his eyes liquid, black as the middle of a very dark night.

She reached up, touched his mouth. "So soft. You're such a good kisser…"

He bent near again, kissed her with that mouth of his, her fingers still on his lips, so he kissed them, too. "Sydney…" He kissed her name against her mouth, against her fingers.

"Mmm." She eased her hand away, parted her lips, took his tongue inside. "Mmm…" Maybe she wasn't so sleepy after all. She clasped his hard shoulder, loving the rock-like contour of it, and then she let her hand glide around to his strong nape. She caressed the amazing musculature of his broad back. "I just want to touch you…"

He didn't object. He went on kissing her, as she indulged herself. She wanted to touch every inch of him—his back, his powerful arms, his fine, strong chest. He had a perfect little happy trail and she did what a woman tends to do—she followed it downward.

And when her fingers closed around him, she took great satisfaction in the low groan he let out. She drank in that groan like wine.

Was there ever a guy like this? She doubted it. Every part of him was beautiful, her fairy-tale prince made flesh.

She closed her eyes again and reveled in the feel of him. She wanted…everything from him. All of him. Now.

She whispered in a shattered sort of wonder, against his beautiful lips. "Oh, Rule. Now. Please, now…" And she urged him to come even closer, all the way closer, opening her thighs for him, pulling him onto her, so eager, so hungry.

More than ready.

"Wait…" He breathed the word against her parted lips.

"What?" She moaned in frustration. "No. I don't want to wait."

"Sydney…" He took his mouth from hers.

And again, she lifted her heavy eyelids and gazed up at him, impatient. Questioning. "What?"

He gave her one of those beautiful, wry, perfect smiles of his. And he tipped his dark head toward his raised hand. She tore her gaze away from all that manly beauty to see what he held.

A condom.

"Oops." She felt her cheeks flush even redder than they already were. She let out a ragged sigh. "I can't believe it. I didn't even think about that. How could I not think of that? I'm never that foolish, that irresponsible."

His shining midnight gaze adored her—and indulged

her. "It's all right. There are two of us, after all. Only one of us had to remember. And I haven't minded at all seeing you so carried away that you didn't even think about using protection."

"I *should* have thought of it."

He shook his head, slowly, lazily, that tempting smile of his a seduction in itself. "You are so beautiful when you're carried away." His smile, his tender words, the hot-candy sound of his voice. She was seduced by every aspect of him.

Seduced and loving it.

Still, she tried to hold out against him. "I'm not beautiful, Rule. We both know that."

"You *are* beautiful. And please give me your hand and stop arguing with me."

Really, the guy was irresistible. She held out her hand.

He put the little pouch in the center of her palm. "Do the honors?"

She laughed, a soft, husky laugh, a laugh that spoke so clearly of her desire. "Now you're talkin'."

He lay back on the pillows and watched her, his eyes so hot now, molten, as she removed the wrapper and set it aside.

She bent over him, kissed him, in the center of his chest, on that silky trail of hair, not far from his heart. His skin was hot. He smelled so good. She rained a flood of kisses on him, to each side of his big chest, over his rib cage, on his ridged, amazing belly, all the way to her goal.

When she got there, she kissed him once more, a light, feathery breath of a kiss. He moaned. The sound pleased her. She stuck out her tongue and she licked him, concentrating first on the flare, then centering on the sensitive tip. And then, at last, taking him inside—then slowly, by agonizing degrees, lifting once more to release him.

A strangled sound escaped him. And he touched her hair, threading his fingers through it, lifting himself toward her, begging wordlessly, on another groan, for more.

She gave him what he asked for. She took him in again slowly, all the way, relaxing her throat to accommodate him, and then, just as slowly, let him out. She used her tongue on him, licking, stroking, swirling, teasing.

His moans and his rough, ragged breathing told her that he couldn't take much more. Good. She wanted to lead him all the way to the brink. She wanted to make him go over, into a perfect satisfaction, as he'd done to her.

But then he caught her face between his hands and he guided her up his body again, until she was looking right into those beautiful eyes.

"Put it on," he commanded in a rough, hungry growl. "Put it on now."

And she realized she was fine with that. More than fine. She rolled on the condom carefully. Once it was on, she rose onto her knees, intending to take the top position.

But then he reached for her, and he lifted up from the pillows and she happily surrendered as he guided her so gently down onto her back again. He eased her thighs wide and settled between them, his arms against the mattress to either side of her head, his fingers in her hair.

"Sydney…" His mouth swooped down to claim another kiss. Deep and hot and perfect, that kiss.

And she felt him, nudging against her, so slick and hard and wonderfully insistent. He pressed in slowly, filling her. She opened for him eagerly, her mouth fused to his as he came into her.

Oh, it was glorious, thrilling, nothing like it.

Not ever.

Not ever in her life before.

He began to move, rocking into her, his hips meeting hers, retreating—and returning. Always, returning.

She lifted herself up to him, wrapped her legs around his waist, her arms around his shoulders, clasping his strong neck, her fingers clutching his hair.

She was lost, flying, burning, free. There was nothing, just this. This beauty. This magic. The two of them: her body, his body—together. One.

Retreating. Returning. Over and over. Wet and hot and exactly as she'd never realized she'd always wished it might be.

Nothing like it.

Not ever.

Not ever in her life before.


"Sydney…" His voice in her ear. His breath against her skin. "Sydney…"

She sighed, turned her head away, so luxuriously comfortable, only wanting to sleep a little more.

"Sydney…" He nuzzled her temple, caught the curling strands of hair there between his lips, gave them a light, teasing tug.

She kept her eyes stubbornly shut, grumbled, "I was sleeping…"

His mouth on her cheek. Warm. Tempting. His words against her skin. "But you have to wake up now."

Wake up. Of course. She knew he was right. She turned her head to him, opened her eyes, asked him groggily, "What time is it?"

"After three." He was on his side, braced up on an elbow, the sheet down around his lean waist, clinging like an adoring lover to the hard curve of his left hip.

With a low groan, she sat up, raked her hair back off her forehead, stretched and yawned. Then she let her arms drop to the sheets. "Ugh. You're right. I do have to get home." She started to push back the covers.

He caught her hand. "Wait."

She smiled at him, searched his wonderful face. "What?"

"Sydney…" His mouth was softer than ever and his eyes gleamed and he looked so young right then. Young and hopeful and…nervous.

He did. He actually looked nervous. Prince Rule of Montedoro. Nervous. How could that be? He really wasn't the nervous type.

"Rule?" She laid her palm against his beard-roughened cheek. "Are you okay?"

He took her wrist, turned his head until her hand covered those soft lips of his. And he kissed her, the most tender, sweetest kiss, right in the heart of her palm, the way he had done the night before when he asked her if she would prefer him to be cruel.

A shiver went through her, a premonition of…

What? She had no idea. And already the strange, anxious feeling had passed.

There was only his mouth, so soft against her palm. Only the beauty of the night they had shared, only the wonder that he was here with her and he was looking at her like she hung the moon, as though she ruled the stars.

He lowered her hand so it no longer covered his lips. And then, raising his other hand, he put something in her palm, after which he closed her fingers tenderly over it.

And then he said the impossible, incredible, this-must-be-a-dream-and-can't-really-be-happening words, "Marry me, Sydney. Be my bride."

## *Chapter Six*

Still trying to believe what she thought he'd just said, Sydney uncurled her fingers and stared down in what could only be called shock and awe at the ring waiting there.

The brilliant emerald-cut diamond was huge. And so icily, perfectly beautiful. Flanking it to either side on the platinum band were two large, equally perfect baguettes.

She looked up from the amazing ring and into his dark eyes. "Just tell me…"

"Anything."

"Is this really happening?"

He laughed, low, and he brushed the hair at her temple with a tender hand. "Yes, my darling. It's really happening. I know it's crazy. I know it's fast. But I don't care about any of that. In my heart, I knew the moment I saw you. And every moment since then has only made me more certain. Until there is nothing left. Nothing but absolute certainty that you are the woman for me."

"But you... I... We can't just—"

"Yes. We can. Today. We can fly to Las Vegas and be married today. I don't want to wait. I want you for my wife now. I have to return to Montedoro on Tuesday. I want you and Trevor with me."

"I don't... I can't... Oh, Rule. Wait."

He shook his head. "My darling, I don't want to wait. Don't make me wait."

"But, I mean, I have a c-career," she sputtered. "I have a house. I live in Texas. Can you even marry someone from Texas?"

"Of course I can. As long as that someone will have me."

"But you can't possibly... I mean, now that I think about it, well, don't you have to marry someone with at least a title? A duchess. A countess. A Lady Someone-or-Other?"

"My mother married an American actor and it's worked out quite well, I think. Times change. And I'm glad. I can marry whomever I choose, Sydney. I choose you—and I hope with all my heart that you choose *me*."

"I can't... I don't..."

"My love, slow down."

"Slow down? You're telling *me* to slow down? You just asked me to marry you and you meant today!"

He laughed then. "You're right. I'm no position to talk about slowing down. But I do think it wouldn't hurt if you took a breath. A nice, deep one." It was pretty good advice, actually. She drew in a slow breath and let it out with care. "Better?" he asked so tenderly.

She looked down at the ring again. "I think I might faint."

"No." He chuckled. "You are not a woman who faints."
Still, he pulled her against him. She went, leaning her head
on the hard bulge of his shoulder, loving the warmth and
solidity of him, the scent of him that was so fine, yet
at the same time so undeniably male. Loving everything
about him.

*Love.* Was it possible? She knew that *he* thought it was.

And yet, still. Even given the possibility that it really
was love at first sight between the two of them, well, she'd
thought she would have a little more time than this before
he asked her to commit to forever…

She pulled away, enough that she could meet his eyes.
"It's so fast, Rule. I mean, so soon to jump into marriage.
It's just…really, really fast."

"I know. I don't care." His gaze was steady on hers. He
spoke with absolute certainty. "I know what I want now.
At last. I told you, I've waited my whole life for this, for
*you.*"

"Yes. I know. We've…spoken of that. But still. Marriage. That's a lot more than talk as far as I'm concerned.
For me, marriage would be a lifetime thing."

"Yes. I know. We agree on that, on what it is to be married, that it's forever."

She searched his face. "It's the marriage law, right? You
have to choose a wife and you have to do it soon."

"I do, yes."

"But not until June. You have until then. We could…
have more time together, a few weeks, anyway. We could
get to know each other better."

"I don't need more time, Sydney. You're the one. I know
it. More time isn't going to change that—except to make
me even more certain that you are the woman for me. I
don't need to be more certain. I need…you. With me. I
need at last to begin the life I've always wanted. The life

my parents have. The life Max had with Sophia before he lost her. I want you to be mine. I want to be yours. I want every moment that God will grant us, together. Because fate can be cruel. Look what happened to Max. He thought he had a whole life ahead of him with Sophia. And now he's alone. Every day they did have is precious to him. I don't want to waste a day, an hour, a moment now, Sydney. I want us to begin our lives together today."

"Oh, Rule…"

"Say yes. Just say yes."

She wanted to. So much. But her inner skeptic just had to ask, "But…for a lifetime? I mean, come on. I looked you up on Google. You're the sexy bachelor prince. I'm pretty certain you've never dated a woman like me before. A really smart, really capable, average-looking, success-driven career woman."

His eyes flashed fire. "You are not average-looking."

"Oh, fine. I'm not average. I'm attractive enough. But I'm no international beauty."

"You are to me. And that's all that matters. Plus, you're brilliant. You're charming. People notice you, they want to…follow you. I don't think you realize your own power. I don't think you truly see yourself as you appear to others. I don't think you understand that strength and determination and focus in a woman—in the right woman—can be everything to a man. You're not the only one who knows how to use a search engine, Sydney. I looked you up. I read of how you graduated college at twenty. I read about the cases you've won for your law firm. And with all that ambition and drive, you have a good heart. And a deep, honest, ingrained sensuality. And last but in no way least, you're a wonderful mother—and you *chose* motherhood. Even with all your accomplishments, you also wanted a family. And when the men around you refused to be worthy of you, you found a way to be a mother, to make your own family. Of course I want you for my wife. You're everything I've been looking for." He brushed a hand, so lightly, along the curve of her cheek and he whispered, "Marry me, Sydney."

"I…" Her throat felt tight. She had to gulp to relax it. "You make me sound so amazing."

"Because you *are* amazing." He pulled her into his arms again.

She went without resisting. "Oh, Rule…"

"Say yes."

She tried to order her thoughts. "Can you move here, to Texas?"

His lips touched her hair. "That, I can't do. I have obligations to my country, obligations I couldn't bring myself to set aside."

She puffed out her cheeks with another big breath. "Just like a man. I knew you were going to say that."

"We can return often. My business dealings bring me to the States several times a year. Would it be so terrible, to live in Montedoro?"

"No. Not terrible. Just…huge. I would have to leave Teale, Gayle and Prosser…"

He rubbed her arm, a soothing, gentle caress. "I seem to recall that you said you were ready for a change in your work, that you would like a chance to help people who really needed your help."

"Yes. I said that. And I meant it."

"As my wife, there would be any number of important causes you might tackle. You would have many opportunities to make a difference."

"But what causes? What opportunities?"

He tipped up her chin, kissed the tip of her nose. "My darling, I think that would be for you to discover." She knew he was right on that score. And she was strong and smart and she learned fast. There wasn't a lot she couldn't do, once she set her mind and heart to doing it.

What about Trevor? He was young enough that the move probably wouldn't be as big a deal for him as it might have been—if he were already in school, if he had to leave close friends behind.

She thought of Lani then. "My God. Lani…"

"What about your friend?"

"I would lose Lani."

"You wouldn't *lose* her. A friend is a friend, no matter the miles between you—and who knows? If you asked her to come with us, she might say yes."

"So, Lani could come, too? If that worked for her. You wouldn't mind?"

"Of course not. What I know of her, I like very much. And I want you to be happy. I want you to have your dear friend with you."

"She might find it interesting. She writes, did I tell you?"

"No, I don't believe you did."

"She does. Right now she's working on a novel. She might find lots to write about in Montedoro. She might enjoy the experience of living somewhere she's never been before. Maybe she *will* want to come…."

"So, then. You will ask her." He kissed her again, on the cheek.

And she wanted more than that. So she turned her head enough that their lips met.

Heaven. Just heaven, kissing Rule. He guided her back onto the pillows and kissed her some more. She could have gone on like that indefinitely. But it was after three in the morning—on what she was actually starting to let herself think of as her wedding day.

She had a thousand things to do before they left for Las Vegas. She pushed at his chest.

He leaned back then, enough to capture her gaze. "What is it?"

"You really want to fly to Vegas today?"

"Yes. That's exactly what I want. Be my wife, Sydney. Make me the happiest man in the world. Bring your beautiful child and your excellent friend and we'll be married today. And after that, come live with me in Montedoro."

She reached up, touched that soft mouth of his. Oh, she did love touching him. Lightly, she smoothed the dark hair at his temples. She loved everything about him. And she was ready, to make a change.

To take a chance on love.

He spoke again, those black eyes shining. "I think Trevor would thrive if we married. I know you already have so much to offer him, that you're giving him an excellent start in life. But if we're together, he can have even more. For one thing, you would be able to spend more time with him. You could plan the work you choose to do specifically around him, during these years when he needs his mother most of all. And I would hope that, in time, we can speak of my adopting him."

Was there a more fabulous man in the whole world? She doubted it. "You would want to adopt him?"

"I would. So much. And I would hope that we also might have more children—I know, I know. I promise not to expect *eight* more. But maybe one or two...?"

"Oh, Rule..."

"Say yes."

She still had her hand on his chest, where she could feel the sure, steady beat of his heart. "I would need more time, here, in Dallas, before I could move to Montedoro. I have to give my partners reasonable notice. I can't leave them scrambling when I go. *I* may be ready to move on, but it would be wrong to leave *them* high and dry."

"Is it possible that you could be ready to go in two weeks?"

She gasped. "No way. Cases have to be shuffled, clients reassigned. I was thinking three months, if I really pushed it."

"What if you brought them more clients, big clients, as a…compensation for making a quick exit?" He named a couple of big oil companies, a major health food and vitamin distributor and a European bank that had branches in the U.S.

Sydney realized her mouth was hanging open. She shut it—and then she asked, "You're serious? You can deliver those?"

"Yes. I have a number of excellent connections worldwide. And if it doesn't work out with one or two of those particular companies, I'm sure I can offer others just as good."

"Well, I could possibly get away in a month or so, if my partners were grateful enough for what I brought them before I left."

"I'll get to work on that potential client list in the next few days. And I'll arrange the introductions, of course. I think you might be surprised at how quickly you can wrap things up with Teale, Gayle and Prosser, once they know exactly how much business you'll be bringing in before you go."

He was right. It would make all the difference, if she brought in some big clients. "I can't do it in two weeks. But if you bring the right clients, I'll give it my best shot. I could manage it in a month. Maybe."

His whole fabulous face seemed to light up from within. "I believe that you just said yes."

"Yes." She said the beautiful word out loud. "I did. Yes, Rule. Yes." And she threw her arms around his neck and let her kisses say the rest.

"Wow, Syd. When you finally go for it with a guy, you *really* go for it." Lani, in her pj's, still groggy from sleep, was shaking her head as she reached for her glasses. But at least she was smiling.

It was ten of five on Sunday morning. Sydney had headed for Lani's room the moment she walked in the front door and they were sitting on Lani's bed. Rule had said he would return at eight and Sydney had promised to be ready to go. He'd told her that he would have a private jet waiting at the airport. It helped to be a rich prince when you wanted to elope to Vegas at a moment's notice.

"So...you don't think I'm crazy?" Sydney asked, apprehensions rising.

"No way. I knew he was the one for you the moment I saw him."

"Uh, you did?"

"Oh, yeah. I mean seriously, Syd. The guy is your type."

"Well, yeah. In my wildest fantasies."

"Which have now become reality. He's intelligent, smooth and sophisticated. He's tall, dark, killer handsome—and I really think he's a good man. It's quite the major bonus that he happens to be a prince. And seeing him with Trevor, well, he's terrific with Trev. And have you noticed they look enough alike to be father and son?"

Sydney chuckled. "I have, actually."

"I go a lot on instinct," Lani said. "You know that. And my instinct with Rule is you've made the right choice."

Sydney beamed. "You are the best friend any woman ever had."

"Likewise."

"Say you'll come to Vegas with us." Sydney put on her most pitiful, pleading expression.

"Are you kidding? Like I would miss that? No way. I'm going."

"Oh, I'm so glad!" Sydney grabbed her friend and hugged her hard.

"How long am I packing for?" Lani asked when Sydney released her.

"Just overnight. I'll take tomorrow off. But Tuesday, I've got to get back to the office and start wrapping things up for the move to Montedoro."

"Oh. My. God. You're marrying a prince and moving to Europe. I don't believe it—or, I *do* believe it. But still. It's beyond wild."

"Yep. I think I need to pinch myself." Sydney let out a joyous laugh. "Is this really real?"

"Oh, yes, it is!" Lani replied. "Let me see the ring again." She grabbed Sydney's hand. "Just gorgeous. Absolutely gorgeous." And then she stuck out her lower lip and made out a small, sad puppy-dog sound. "But you know I will be sulking. I'll miss you way too much. And Trev, oh, how will I get along without him?" She put her hand on her chest and pantomimed a heartbeat.

Sydney had the answer to that one ready. "You don't have to miss us, not if you come with us."

"Come with you? You mean, permanently?"

"Oh, yeah. I would love that."

Lani blinked. "You're serious."

"You bet I am. I've already discussed it with Rule. He's good with it. More than good. And I would love it if you were there—I mean, if that could work for you."

"Me. Living in Montedoro with my best friend, the prince's bride. Interesting."

"I was hoping you might think that. But don't decide now. Take your time. No pressure. I mean that."

Lani bumped her shoulder affectionately. "I'll give it serious consideration—and thank you."

"Hey. Don't thank me. I'll miss you like crazy if you decide you don't want to do it. If you come, *I'll* be the grateful one."

"I'll think about it," Lani promised. "And we'd better get cracking if we're going to be ready to head for Vegas at eight."

As it turned out, Rule had Bravo relatives in Las Vegas. Aaron and Fletcher Bravo ran a pair of Las Vegas casino/hotels. Rule was a second cousin to both men. His grandfather James and their grandfather Jonas had been brothers.

"Fletcher and Aaron are half brothers," Rule told Sydney during the flight to Nevada. "They have different mothers, but both are sons of Blake Bravo."

"I have to ask. You don't mean *the* Blake Bravo?"

"Ah. You've heard of the infamous Blake?"

She nodded. "He died in Oklahoma about a decade ago, and at the time, the story made the front page of every paper in Texas. He *was* pretty notorious."

Rule nodded. "Yes, he was. Kidnapping his own brother's son for a fortune in diamonds, marrying all those women…" Beyond the whole kidnapping thing, Blake Bravo had been a world-class polygamist. He'd married any number of women all over the country and he'd never divorced a single one of them. Each woman had believed she was the only one.

Sydney said, "A very busy man, that Blake."

"*Busy* is not the word I would have chosen," Rule said dryly. "But yes, both Aaron and Fletcher are his sons."

The flight took a little under three hours, but they

gained two hours because of changing time zones, so they touched down at McCarran International Airport at ten after ten in the morning.

There was a limo waiting. The driver loaded the trunk with their luggage, the security guy who had flown from Dallas with them got in front on the passenger side and off they went to High Sierra Resort and Casino.

Aaron Bravo was CEO of High Sierra. The resort was directly across Las Vegas Boulevard from Impresario Resort and Casino, which Fletcher ran. The two giant complexes were joined by a glass breezeway five stories up, above the Strip.

Aaron greeted them at the entrance to his resort. Tall and lean with brown hair, Aaron wasn't classically handsome. But he was attractive, very much so, with a strong nose, sharp cheekbones and a square jaw. He said how pleased he was to meet Sydney and Lani—and Trevor, too. Then he introduced them to his wife, Celia, who was cute and friendly, a redhead with big hazel eyes.

Celia led the way to their suite, which had its own kitchen, a large living area and four bedrooms branching off of it. The security guy, whose name was Joseph, had the room next door.

The first order of business was to get the marriage license. Lani stayed behind with Trevor. Sydney, Rule and Joseph headed for the Las Vegas Marriage Bureau. An hour later, they were back in the suite, where Trev was playing with his trucks and Lani was stretched out on the sofa with her laptop.

"Ready for pampering?" she asked. "Celia says the spa is called Touch of Gold and it's full service…."

"Go," said Rule. "Both of you. The wedding's not until four." The short ceremony would be held in the wedding chapel right there at High Sierra. "I'll watch Trevor."

Sydney hesitated to let him do that. How strange. Here she was about to marry this wonderful man, and she felt reluctant to leave him alone with her son.

But no. Her reaction was only natural. It was one thing to trust her own heart. Another to leave her child alone with someone for the first time—even someone like Rule, who was so good with Trevor.

Lani spoke up. "Uh-uh. I'm onto something with this chapter and I'm not giving it up now. You go, Syd. I'm staying."

"Roo!" called Trev from under the table. "Come. We play trucks!"

So Rule and Lani both stayed in the suite with Trevor. Sydney went by herself to the spa. On the way, she stopped in at the resort's florist and ordered a bouquet of yellow roses, which she told them she would pick up personally in a few hours. She also asked to have a yellow rose boutonniere sent up to the suite for Rule.

At Touch of Gold, she decided to start with a hot rock massage. After the massage, she had it all, mani-pedi, haircut and blow dry and the expert attention of the spa's cosmetician, too.

And then, when she was perfectly manicured, with her hair smooth and shiny and softly curling to her shoulders and her makeup just right, Celia appeared with a tall, stunning brunette, Cleo, who was Fletcher's wife. The two women took Sydney to the bridal boutique not far from the spa.

Sydney chose a simple sleeveless fitted sheath dress of white silk and a short veil. Her shoes were ivory satin platform high heels, with side bows and peep toes. Celia had Sydney's street clothes sent back to the suite and Sidney left the boutique dressed for her wedding. After that, they stopped off at the florist to pick up her bouquet.

And then the two women led her straight to the High Sierra wedding chapel. Sydney waited in the chapel's vestibule for the "Wedding March" to begin. Staying to the side, out of sight, she peeked around the open door.

The rest of the small wedding party was already there: Lani, holding Trev, and Aaron and another dark-haired man who was obviously Cleo's husband, Fletcher Bravo. She saw him in profile and noted the family resemblance between him and Aaron—and Rule, too, she realized.

Her groom was waiting for her, standing down in front with the justice of the peace, looking fabulous as always in a black silk suit with a lustrous cobalt-blue tie and a shirt the color of a summer sky. In his lapel, he wore the yellow rose she'd sent him.

Sydney's pulse beat faster, just at the sight of him. And she smiled to herself, thinking of all the years she'd been so sure she would never find him—the right man, a good man, solid, smart and funny and true. The fact that he'd turned out to be a real-life prince who was total eye candy and had a voice that turned her insides to jelly, well, that was just the icing on the cake.

He was exactly the man for her. He made her feel beautiful and bold and exciting—or maybe he simply saw her beauty and made her see it, too. It didn't matter. With him, she could have it all. She could not wait to start their life together.

The only thing that could have made this day more perfect was if her Grandma Ellen could have been here, too.

Cleo helped Sydney pin the short veil in place.

And then the "Wedding March" began.

With a smile of pure happiness curving her lips and the glow of new love in her heart, Sydney walked down the aisle toward her waiting groom. She was absolutely certain she was making the right choice, marrying a man who saw beyond the walls she had erected to protect her injured heart. A man who had loved her the first moment he saw her, a man who wanted to be a real father to her son. A man who had been charmingly reluctant to reveal his princely heritage. A man of honor, who spoke the truth.

A man who did not have a deceptive bone in his body.

## Chapter Seven

The justice of the peace said, "I now pronounce you husband and wife. You may kiss the bride."

His eyes only for her, Rule raised the short veil and guided it back over her head.

And then he drew her closer to him and he kissed her, a tender, perfect kiss. A kiss that promised everything: his love and his devotion, the bright future they would share. Sydney closed her eyes and wished the special moment might last forever.

After the ceremony, they all went to dinner in a private dining room in High Sierra's nicest restaurant. More children joined them there, six of them. Celia and Aaron had three, as did Fletcher and Cleo. The food was great and the company even better.

Aaron and Fletcher proposed a series of excellent toasts and when the kids were done eating, they were all allowed to get down and play together. There was much childish laughter. Trev loved every minute of it. He seemed quite taken with Fletcher and Cleo's oldest child, Ashlyn. He followed her around the private dining room, offering her dazzling smiles whenever she glanced his way. Ashlyn didn't seem to mind. And she knew several knock-knock jokes. She patiently tried to teach them to Trev, who inevitably got carried away and started playing both parts.

"Knock, knock," Ashlyn would say gamely.

And Trev would crow, "Who's there? Bill! Orange! Wanda!"

There was a cake, three tiers tall, a yellow cake with white fondant icing and edible pearls, crowned with a circle of yellow rosebuds. Celia took pictures as Sydney and Rule fed each other too-big bites of the sweet confection.

Trev tore himself away from his adoration of Ashlyn to join them at the cake table. "Roo, Mama, cake! Now!" He reached up his chubby arms.

So Rule swept him up against his chest and Trev laughed in delight. "Roo!" he cried. "Kiss," and puckered up his little mouth.

Rule puckered up as well and kissed him with a loud, smacking sound, which made Trev laugh even harder. A second later, he demanded, "Cake, Mama!"

"Cake, *please?*" she suggested.

And he shouted, "Cake! Please!"

So Sydney fed him a few bites of cake while Celia snapped more pictures. Then they served everyone else. The kids were silent—for a few minutes anyway—as they devoured their dessert.

After that, everyone lingered, reluctant to call an end to an enjoyable event. The adults chatted, the children went back to running in and out under the table, laughing, playing tag.

Eventually though, the little ones started getting fussy. Lani said she would take Trev up to the suite. Sydney offered to go, but Lani said she wanted to get back to her writing anyway. She could handle Trevor and work on her book at the same time, and often did. She would keep her laptop handy and sneak in a sentence or two whenever Trevor gave her a moment to herself.

So Lani took him up. Soon after, Celia and Cleo gathered their respective broods and left for the onsite apartments each family kept in the resort complex.

That left Fletcher and Aaron playing dual hosts to the newlyweds. The men talked a little business. The Bravo CEOs agreed that Montedoran oranges would be a perfect addition to the complimentary fruit baskets they offered in their luxury suites.

Rule invited his two second cousins and their families to Montedoro. Both said they would love to come. They would stay at the Prince's Palace and visit the fabulous casino in Montedoro's resort ward of Colline d'Ambre.

Finally, after more good wishes for a long and happy life together, the half brothers went to join their families. Rule and Sydney were left alone in the private dining room.

He drew her close to him, tipped up her chin and kissed her slowly and so sweetly. "My wife…" he whispered against her lips. "My own princess."

She chuckled. "Just like that? I only have to marry you and I get to be a princess?"

He took her hand, laid it against his chest. "And you will always rule my heart."

She laughed then. "Oh, you are so smooth." And then she frowned.

He kissed her furrowed brow. "What?"

"Your mother, the princess. Your family. This will be quite a surprise to them."

"A happy surprise," he said.

"So...you haven't told them anything about me yet?"

"Only my father. He knows...everything. And by now he will have told my mother that I've married the only woman for me."

She searched his face. "The way you say that. *Everything.* It sounds mysterious somehow."

He touched her cheek, smoothed a few strands of hair behind her ear. "Not mysterious at all. I spoke with my father this morning, before I came to take you to the airport. He wished us much happiness and he looks forward to meeting his new daughter-in-law and grandson."

"So he's not overly disappointed that you're not marrying Princess Lili?"

He traced the neckline of her wedding dress, striking sparks of excitement. "My father is a great believer in marrying for love. So he wants me to be happy. And he understands that I *will* be happy—with you."

"And your mother?"

"I know that she will be happy for me, as well." He kissed her again, slowly. A kiss that deepened, went from tender to scorching-hot. Her mind went hazy and her body went loose.

When he lifted his mouth from hers that time and the small dining room swam into focus again, a busman stood at the door. "Excuse me. I'll come back...."

Rule shook his head. "No. We're just leaving." He stood and pulled back her chair for her. "Shall we try our luck in the casino?"

"I'm terrible at games of chance."

"Never admit that. Lady Luck will hear you."

Her bouquet and her short veil, which she'd removed a while ago, lay on the table. Rule signaled the busman over, tipped him hugely and asked him to have both items delivered to their suite.

The busman promised it would be done.

Sydney took the rose from Rule's lapel, feeling wonderfully wifely and possessive of him as she did it. "This, too," she told the busman. "And the cake. I want the rest of the cake."

The busman promised he'd have the cake boxed and sent to their suite with the veil, the bouquet and the boutonniere.

They took the wide glass breezeway across the Strip to Impresario, which was all in blacks and reds and golds, a Moulin Rouge theme. They played roulette for over two hours. Sydney surprised herself by winning steadily. When they left the roulette table she was up more than a thousand dollars.

She caught sight of Joseph a few feet away and leaned close to her new husband to whisper, "Joseph is following us."

He brushed a kiss against her hair. "Joseph is always following us. That's his job."

"You're kidding. You mean every time I've been out with you…?"

"That's right. Joseph has been somewhere nearby."

"I swear I never noticed before."

"You're not supposed to notice. He's paid to be invisible until he's needed."

"Well, he's very good at it."

"He'll be pleased to hear that. Joseph takes great pride in his work—and what would you like to play next?"

"I was kind of thinking it would be fun to try my luck at blackjack."

"Blackjack it is, then." They found a table and played for another hour. Sydney won some more.

When they left the blackjack table it was after ten.

He leaned close. "I think you're lucky, after all."

"I think it's you," she whispered back. "You bring me luck."

He had his arm around her and pulled her closer, right there in the aisle, on their way toward the elevators that led up to the fifth floor and the breezeway back to High Sierra. Their lips met.

And a flash went off.

She laughed. "I think I'm seeing stars."

But he wasn't smiling. "The jackals are onto us."

"Ahem. Excuse me….?"

"Paparazzi. We have to go." He already had her hand and was moving fast toward the elevators. She hurried to keep up. More flashes went off.

A balding guy in tight pants and a black shirt with a big gold chain around his neck stepped in front of them. He stuck a microphone in Rule's face and started firing questions at him, racing backward to keep up with them. "Enjoying your visit to America, Your Highness? Who is the woman in white? Is that a wedding ring I see on the lady's finger?"

Rule only said, "Excuse me, no comment," and kept walking fast.

That was when Joseph appeared. He must have grabbed the guy with the microphone, because the man stumbled and fell back, out of their path.

Rule forged on. They reached the elevators and one rolled open as if on cue. He pulled her in there, pushed the button for the fifth floor and the doors slid shut.

"Whew," she said, laughing a little. "Looks like we're safe."

He just looked grim. "I should have known they would spot us." A moment later, the doors slid open wide. They got off and a group of men in business suits got on. Rule had her hand again. They were headed for the breezeway. Halfway across it, Joseph caught up with them. "Is it handled?" Rule asked low.

"Too many cameras." Joseph spoke softly, but his face looked carved in stone. "And they refused to deal, anyway. They got away with the shots they took."

Rule swore under his breath and pulled her onward.

On the High Sierra side, they took an elevator up to their floor. When the elevator stopped and the door opened, Joseph stuck his head out first. "We're clear," he said and signaled them out.

They walked at a brisk clip down the hallway to their suite. Rule had the key ready. He swiped it through the slot and they were in as Joseph entered the room next door.

The suite was silent. Trev had been put to bed hours ago and Lani must have retreated to her room. She'd left the light in the suite's granite-tiled foyer on for them.

Sydney sagged against the door. "Wow. That was exciting."

Rule braced a hand by her head and bent to kiss her—a hard, passionate kiss that slowly turned tender. When he pulled away, he whispered, "I'm sorry…"

"Whatever for? I had a great time."

"I knew it was unwise, to take you out on the casino floor and then stay there for hours. We were bound to be spotted."

She touched the side of his face, brushed the backs of her fingers along the silky, beautifully trimmed hair at his temples. "It's not the end of the world, is it, if our pictures end up in some tabloid somewhere?"

"In my family, we prefer to control the message."

"Meaning?"

"I was hoping we could keep our marriage private for the next few weeks, until I had you with me in Montedoro. From there, a discreet and carefully worded announcement could be made. And pictures could be taken by the palace photographer to send to the press, pictures of our choosing."

"What? A candid shot of you and me racing down a hallway with our mouths hanging open in surprise isn't discreet enough for you?"

He laughed then. But his eyes were troubled. "No, it's not."

She smoothed his lapel, straightened his collar. "Well, no matter how bad it is, just remember how much fun we had. As far as I'm concerned, I had so much fun, it's worth a few ugly pictures in some scandal sheet. Plus, I won almost two thousand dollars, about which I am beyond thrilled. I never win anything. But all I have to do is marry you, and suddenly it's like I've got a four-leaf clover tattooed on my forehead."

He was looking at her in *that* way again. The lovely, sexy way. The way that set small fluttery creatures loose in her stomach and had her feeling distinctly sultry lower down. "There is no four-leaf clover on your forehead." He kissed the spot where it might have been.

"Oh, it's there," she said softly, breathlessly. "You just can't see it. I was clever that way. I insisted on an invisible tattoo."

"Wait. I think I see it, after all." He breathed the words against her skin. And then he kissed his way down between her brows, trailing that wonderful mouth along the top of her nose. He nipped her lips once and then kissed her chin. "And I'm glad you enjoyed yourself."

"Oh, I did." Her voice was now more breath than sound. "I really did...."

He covered her mouth with his again. Luckily, she had the door at her back to lean against. She stayed upright even though her knees had gone deliciously wobbly. And as it turned out, she didn't need to hold herself upright much longer anyway. Still kissing her, he scooped her up in his arms carried her through the open archway to the central room of the suite.

The busman had kept his promise. On the dining table, she saw the large cake box, her veil and bouquet and also Rule's boutonniere. She smiled against his lips as he turned and carried her through the open door to their room, where the lamp by the bed had been left on low. Also, on a long table against the wall, a pair of crystal flutes flanked an ice bucket holding a bottle of champagne. The covers on the king-size bed were turned invitingly down.

She stretched out an arm to push the door shut behind them. Rule carried her to the side of the wide bed and set her down on her feet. They shared another kiss, one that went on for a lovely, endless space of time.

When he lifted his head, he guided her around so her back was to him. She read his intention and smoothed her hair to the side. He lowered the zipper at the back of her dress.

She took it from there, easing her arms free, pushing the dress down. Stepping out of it, she bent and picked it up and carried it to the bedside chair, where she took time to lay it down gently, to smooth the white folds.

"Come back here," he said, his voice rough with wanting.

"In a moment..." She sent him a teasing glance over her shoulder as she returned to the door long enough to engage the privacy lock. From there, she went to the dressing table on the far side of the room. She took off her shoes, her bra, her white lace panties and pearl earrings. And after that, she removed the single strand of pearls her grandmother had given her and the blue lace garter provided by the bridal boutique. Finally, wearing nothing but a tender smile, she faced him again. "Your turn."

He made a low sound in his throat, his gaze moving over her, hot and possessive. "Don't move. I'll be right back."

The room had a walk-in closet. He entered it and came back out a moment later. Returning to the side of the bed, he laid two wrapped condoms on the nightstand.

She told him softly, "We won't need those."

Something flared in his eyes—triumph? Joy? But then he stood very still. "Are you sure?"

She nodded. "We both want more children. I'm thinking there's no time like the present to get going on that."

"Sydney O'Shea Bravo-Calabretti," he said. "You amaze me."

She did like the sound of her name, her new name, on his lips. And she had no doubts. None whatsoever. She told him so. "I know what I want now, Rule. I want you. I want a family, with you and Trev. And I'm greedy. I want more babies. I honestly do."

He took a step toward her.

She put up a hand. "Your clothes. All of them. Please."

He didn't argue. He undressed. He did it swiftly, with no wasted motion, tossing the beautifully tailored articles of clothing carelessly aside as he removed them. His body was so fine and strong. Just looking at him stole her breath.

When he had everything off, she went to him. She lifted her arms to him and he drew her close. Nothing so fine as that, to be held in his powerful arms, to feel the heat and hardness of him all around her.

He smoothed her hair, caressed her back with a long stroke of his tender hand. "I think I'm the happiest man in the world tonight."

She tipped her head up to him. "I'm glad. So glad…"

He kissed her and she thought how she would never, ever get enough of his kisses. That with him, she'd finally found everything she'd almost let herself forget that she'd been looking for.

She pulled him down onto the bed with her and gave herself up to his touch, to the magic of his lips on her skin.

He kissed her everywhere, each secret hollow, each curve, even the backs of her knees and the crooks of her elbows. He kissed her breasts, slowly and thoroughly, and then he moved lower. He kissed all her secret places, until she cried out and went over the edge, clutching his dark head, moaning his name.

She was still sighing in sweet satisfaction when he slid up her body again. All at once, he was there, right where she wanted him most. She wrapped her arms around him, so tightly. And he came into her, gliding smoothly home. Her body was as open to him as her mind and her heart. She accepted him eagerly, the aftershocks of her climax still pulsing through her. And when he filled her, she let out a soft cry of joyous abandon.

Did it get any better than this?

She didn't see how it could. Somehow, she'd finally found the man she wanted for a lifetime—or rather, *he* had found *her*.

There was nothing, ever, that could tear them apart.

Rule wasn't sure what woke him.

A general sense of unease, he supposed. He turned to

look at the woman sleeping beside him. The lamp was off and the room in darkness. Still, he could hear her shallow, even breathing. So peaceful. Content. He could make out her shadowed features, just barely. A soft smile curved her mouth.

She pleased him. Greatly. In so many ways.

No, she wasn't going to be happy with him when she found out the truth. But she was a very intelligent woman. And there was real chemistry between them. Surely, when the time came, she would forgive him for his deception. He would rationally explain why he'd done what he had done. She would see that, even if he hadn't been strictly honest with her, it had all worked out perfectly anyway. She wanted to be with him and he wanted her *and* the boy. They could work through it and move on.

He wanted to touch her. To kiss her. To make love to her again. When he was touching her, he could forget that he'd married her without telling her everything.

But no. He wouldn't disturb her. Let her have a few hours of uninterrupted sleep.

Settling onto his back, he stared into the darkness, not happy with himself, wondering why he had become so obsessive over this problem. His obsession served no one. It was going to be a long time before he told her the truth, anyway. Maybe he never would.

In the past twenty-four hours or so, he'd found himself thinking that there was no real reason she ever had to know....

Except that he'd always considered himself an honest man. And it gnawed at his idea of his own character and his firm belief in fair play, to have this lie between them.

Which was thoroughly ironic, the more he considered it. He'd chosen the lie when he realized he wanted her for his wife. He'd seen it as the only sure way to his goal. So he supposed that meant his idea of himself as an honest man was only another lie.

And damned if he wasn't giving himself a headache, going around and around about this in his mind, when he was set on his course and there was no going back now.

He heard a faint buzzing sound: the cell phone in his trouser pocket, flung across that nearby chair.

Slowly, carefully, so as not to wake her, he eased back the covers and brought his feet to the floor. By then, the phone had stopped buzzing. He collected it from the trousers and tiptoed to the room's bath, where he checked to see who had called.

His father.

The voice mail signal beeped. He called to pick up the message.

His father's voice said "Rule. Call me on this line as soon as you get this. We need to touch base on the subject of Liliana."

Lili. What now?

With the nine-hour time difference, it would be around noon in Montedoro, which made it as good a time to call as any.

But not from the bathroom, where Sydney might wake up and walk in on him.

So he returned to the dark bedroom, where his bride was still sleeping the untroubled slumber of the blameless. He found his briefs and his trousers and put them back on. He tiptoed to the door and pulled it slowly open. The hinges played along and didn't squeak. He slipped through and closed it soundlessly behind him.

The suite had a balcony. He went out there, into the warm desert night, and closed the slider behind him.

His father answered on the first ring. "I understand congratulations are in order?"

The balcony had a café table and a couple of chairs. He dropped into one of them. "Thank you. I'm a very happy man."

"How is the boy?"

"Trevor is…a revelation to me. More than I ever might have wished for. Wait till you see him."

"I'm looking forward to that. When will you bring them home to us?"

"Sydney needs a month, she says. I'll come home ahead for a week or so and take care of my commitments there, and then return to help her through the transition."

"I heard that you had a little run-in with the press."

Rule didn't ask how his father knew. Joseph could have turned in a report—or the information could have come from any number of other sources. "Yes. They got away with pictures. And they put it together—Sydney's white dress, her engagement diamond and wedding band."

"So I understand. It won't take the story long to end up in the tabloids."

"I know." Rule felt infinitely weary thinking of that.

"Liliana is still here, still our guest at the palace. She has no idea that you've already married someone else."

"I know," Rule said again. He got up, stood at the iron railing, stared down at the resort pool, at the eerie glow the pool lights made, shining up through the water, at the rows of empty lounge chairs.

"Your mother is waiting to hear from you. She's always thought of you as the most considerate and dependable of her children."

"I've disappointed her."

"She'll get over it." His father's voice was gentler now.

"I'm trusting you to keep my secret," he reminded his father.

"I haven't told anyone, not even your mother." His father sighed.

"I should have spoken to Lili first, I know, for the sake of our long friendship—and in consideration of Montedoro's sometimes strained relationship with Leo." King Leo was Lili's hot-tempered, doting father. "But it was awkward, since I had made no proposal to her. How exactly was I to go about telling her that I *wouldn't* be proposing? Also there was the timing of it. As soon as I finally met Sydney and made my decision, I felt it was imperative to move forward, to attain my goal before leaving the States."

"You are so certain about this woman you have married, this woman you have only just met?"

"Yes," Rule said firmly. "I am."

"You *wanted* to marry her, for herself? Not simply for the child. You feel she is…right for you?"

"Yes. I did. I do."

"Yet you don't feel confident enough of her trust in you to tell her the basic truth of the situation?"

Rule winced. His father had cut a little too close to the bone with that one. He said, "I made a choice. I'm willing to live with the consequences."

His father was silent. Rule braced himself for criticism, for a very much deserved lecture on the price a man pays for tempting fate, for doing foolish, thoughtless, irresponsible things and telling himself he's breaking free, that he's trying to help others.

More than three years ago, Rule had let his hunger for something he didn't even understand win out over his good sense. And now, when he'd finally found what he was looking for, he'd lied to secure the prize he sought. And he was continuing to lie….

But then his father only said, "Fair enough, then. I see

your dilemma. And I sympathize. But still, it's only right that you explain yourself to Liliana, face-to-face, as soon as possible. She should hear it from you first. She's an innocent in all this."

"I agree. I was planning to return on Tuesday, but I'll try to get away Monday...I mean, today."

"Do your best."

Rule promised he would and they said goodbye.

He turned to go inside and saw Sydney, her hair tangled from sleep, her green eyes shadowed, full of questions. Wearing one of the white terrycloth robes provided by the resort, she stood watching him through the sliding glass door.

## Chapter Eight

He'd been facing away from the suite, he reminded himself. And speaking in low tones. She couldn't have heard the conversation through the thick glass of the door.

Tamping down his anxiety that she might have overheard something incriminating after all, he pulled the door open and murmured regretfully, "I woke you...."

"No. The *absence* of you. That's what woke me." She took his hand, pulled him into the suite and slid the door shut. After that, she stood gazing up at him, and he had that feeling he so often had with her, the feeling he'd just described to his father. The feeling of rightness, that he was with her, that he had finally dared to approach her, to claim her. Too bad the sense of rightness was liberally mixed with dread at the way-too-possible negative outcome of the dangerous game he played. "Is there something wrong?" She searched his face.

He still had her hand in his, so he pulled her back to

their room. Once he had her inside, he shut and locked the door.

"Rule, what?"

He framed her sweet, proud face between his hands. He loved her wide mouth, her nose that was perhaps a little too large for her face. A nose that made her look interesting and commanding, a nose that demanded a man take her seriously. One lie, he had already told her. A huge lie of omission. All else must be the absolute truth. "You're going to be angry with me...."

"You're scaring me. Just tell me what's going on. Please."

He caught her hand again, took her to the bed, sat her down and then sat beside her. "That was my father, on the phone. He asked me to come back to Montedoro today. He thinks I should talk to Liliana, that I owe her an explanation, that I should be the one to tell her that any proposal she might have been expecting is not forthcoming, that I'm already married."

She pulled her hand from his and drove right to the point. "And what do *you* think, Rule?"

"I think my father is right."

She speared her fingers through her night-mussed hair, scraping it back off her forehead. He wanted to reach for her, but he didn't dare. "Princess Lili is still waiting, I take it, for you to ask her to marry you?"

"That's the general assumption. She's a guest at the palace. It would be pretty unforgivable of me to let her find out in the tabloids that I'm already married."

"*Pretty* unforgivable?"

"All right. Simply unforgivable. As I said before, she's like a sister to me. While a man doesn't want to marry his sister—he doesn't want to see her hurt, either."

"I understand that."

"Sydney…" He tried to wrap his arm around her.

She dodged away from his touch. "Why, exactly, is she expecting you to marry her?" She looked at him then. Those green eyes that could be so soft and full of desire for him, were cool now, emerald-bright.

"I told you, she's always believed herself to be in love with me, ever since we were children. She's looked up to me, she's…waited for me. And as the years have gone by and I never married, it has been spoken of, between our two families, that I would need to marry soon due to the laws that control my inheritance. That Lili would be a fine choice in any number of ways."

"What ways?"

He suppressed an impatient sigh. "Ways of state, you might say. Over the years, there has been conflict, off and on, between Montedoro and Alagonia."

"Wars, you mean?"

"No. Small states such as ours rarely engage in wars. In Montedoro, we don't even have a standing army. But there has been discord—bad feelings, you could say—between our two countries. The most recent rift occurred because King Leo, Lili's father, wanted to marry my mother. My mother didn't want to marry him. She wanted to rule Montedoro and she wanted, as much as possible, to protect our sovereignty. If she'd married a king, he could so easily have encroached on her control of the throne. Plus, while she's always been fond of King Leo, she didn't feel she could love him as a husband. And she wanted that, wanted love in her marriage. She managed to avoid a situation where Leo might have had a chance to propose to her. And then she met my father."

"Don't tell me." At least there was some humor in her voice now. "It was love at first sight."

"So my mother claims. And my father, as well. They

married. King Leo is known for his hot temper. He was angry and even went so far as to put in place certain trade sanctions as something of a revenge against my mother and Montedoro for the injury to his pride. But then he met and married Lili's mother, an Englishwoman, Lady Evelyn DunLyle. The king loved his new wife and found happiness with her. He gave up his vendetta against my mother and Montedoro. Leo's queen and my mother became fast friends. Though Queen Evelyn died a few years ago, relations between our countries have been cordial for nearly three decades and we all think of Lili as one of our family."

"You're saying that if you'd married the princess, it would have bolstered relations between your countries. But now that you've essentially dumped her, if she goes crying to her father, your country and her country could end up on the outs again."

"I have not dumped her." He felt his temper rising, and quickly restrained it. "A man cannot dump a woman he's never been with in any way. I swear to you, Sydney, I have never so much as kissed Liliana, except as a brother would, chastely, on the cheek."

"But she thinks you're *going* to kiss her for real. She thinks you're going to *be* with her. She thinks that she'll be married to you before the twenty-fourth of June."

"Yes." He said it resignedly. "I believe she does."

"You realize that's kind of pitiful, don't you? I mean, if you've never given her any sort of encouragement, why would she think that you'll end up proposing marriage—unless she's a total idiot?"

"Lili is not an idiot. She's a romantic. She's more than a little…fanciful."

"You're saying she's weak-minded?"

"Of course not. She's a good person. She's…kind at heart."

Sydney shook her head. "You strung her along, didn't you?"

"No. I did no such thing. I simply…failed to disabuse her."

"Come on, Rule. She was your ace in the hole." Those green eyes were on him. He had the rather startling intuition that she could see inside his head, see the cogs turning as he tried to make excuses for what he had to admit was less than admirable behavior. "You never encouraged her. But you didn't *need* to encourage her. Because she'd decided you were her true love and she's a romantic person. You figured if you never met anyone who…worked for you, as a partner in life, you could always marry Lili when your thirty-third birthday got too close for comfort."

"All right." He threw up both hands. "Yes. That's what I did. That is exactly what I did."

She gave him a look that seared him where he sat. "And it was crappy what you did, Rule. It was really crappy."

"Yes, Sydney. It was…crappy. And I feel accountable and I want to apologize to her in person."

"I should hope so." She huffed out a disgusted breath.

And then there was silence. He stared straight ahead and hated that she was angry with him.

And by God, if she was angry over Lili, what was he in for when she found out about Trevor?

He couldn't stop himself from pondering his own dishonesty. About Trevor. About Lili. He was beginning to see that he wasn't the man he'd believed himself to be. That he was only an honest man when it suited him.

Such thoughts did not make him proud.

Plus, he found himself almost wishing he'd told her another lie just now, given her some other excuse as to why he had to go back right away to Montedoro. He hated this—the two of them, so late on their wedding night it was already the next morning, sitting side by side on the edge of their marriage bed, not looking at each other.

"We'll leave right after breakfast," she said. "You can go straight to Montedoro. I'll get a commercial flight for Lani and Trevor and me."

"I will take you to Dallas," he said.

"Really. It's fine. I'll—"

"No." He cut her off in a voice that brooked no argument. "I will take you to Texas. And then I'll go straight on from there."

A half an hour later, they lay in bed in the darkness together, but not touching, facing away from each other. Sydney knew it was the right thing, for him to go, to make his peace with the woman he'd kept on a string.

She knew it was the right thing…

But she didn't like it one bit. She was disappointed in Rule. And more than a little angry that because of him, their wedding night had ended in such a rotten, awful way.

Here she'd married her prince, literally. She'd been so sure he was the perfect man for her—and the day after their wedding, he had to leave her to fly back to his country and apologize to the woman everyone had *thought* he would marry. A woman Rule said was like a sister to him, a woman who was pretty and delicate and romantic at heart. Sydney was none of those things. Not pretty. Not the least delicate.

Okay, maybe she *was* a bit of a romantic. But she'd never had the luxury of indulging her romantic streak— not until her own personal prince came along.

Maybe her prince wasn't such a fine man, after all. Maybe she should have slowed things down between them, at least a little, given herself more time to make sure that marrying him was really right for her. She'd been hurt before, and badly. She should have kept those past heartaches more firmly in mind. Ryan and Peter had proved that she didn't have the best judgment when it came to giving her heart. And yet, after knowing Rule for—*oh, dear God,* under forty-eight hours—she'd run off to Vegas and married him.

Sydney closed her eyes tightly. Was she a total fool, after all? She'd followed her heart yet again. And look at her now, hugging the edge of the bed on her wedding night, curled into a tight ball of pure misery.

And then the truth came to her, cool and sweet as clean water poured on a wound. Rule wasn't Ryan or Peter. He hadn't lied to her or manipulated her.

He'd told her the truth about Princess Lili on Saturday night *before* he'd asked her to marry him. And when his father had called him home to make peace with Lili, Rule hadn't lied to her about what was going on. Even though he so easily could have, he hadn't taken the easy way, hadn't made up some story for why he needed to get back. After all, she knew he had responsibilities in Montedoro and she would have most likely accepted any credible story he'd told her about the sudden necessity for him to go.

But he *hadn't* lied. He'd taken the hard way, the way that proved his basic integrity. He'd told her what was really going on, and told her honestly. Told the truth, even when the truth didn't show him in the greatest light.

All at once, her stomach didn't feel quite so tight anymore. And her heart didn't ache quite so much.

Carefully, slowly, she relaxed from the tight little ball she'd curled herself into. She stretched out her legs and then, with a sigh, she eased over onto her back.

She could feel him beside her, feel his stillness. A concentrated sort of stillness. She couldn't hear his breathing. He must be awake, too. Lying there in misery, hating this situation as much as she did.

No, she didn't forgive him, exactly. Not yet, anyway. She couldn't just melt into his arms, just send him off to Princess Lili with a big, brave smile and a tender kiss goodbye.

But she could...understand the position he was in. She could sympathize.

The sheet between them was cool. She flattened her hand on it, and then moved her fingers, ever so slowly, toward his unmoving form.

He moved, too. Only his hand. His fingers touched hers and she didn't pull back.

She lay very still. No way was she going to let him wrap those big, warm arms around her.

But when his fingers eased between hers, she let them. And when he clasped her hand, she held on.

She didn't let go and neither did he. In time, sleep claimed her.


Rule had a car waiting for them in Dallas. He exited the jet to say goodbye to them as their bags were loaded into the trunk and airport personnel bustled about, preparing the jet for the flight to Montedoro.

Trev went eagerly into his arms. "Bye, Roo! Kiss!" And he kissed Rule's cheek, making a loud, happy smacking sound.

Rule kissed him back. "I will see you very soon."

"Soon. Good. Come see me soon."

"You be good for your Mama and Lani."

"I good, yes!"

Rule handed Trev over to Lani and turned to Sydney. "A moment?" he asked carefully. Lani left them, carrying Trev to the open backseat door where the driver had already hooked in his car seat. Rule brushed a hand down Sydney's arm—and then instantly withdrew it. She felt his touch like a bittersweet echo on her skin, even through the fabric of her sleeve. He said, "You haven't forgiven me." It wasn't a question.

"Have a safe trip." She met his eyes, made her lips turn up in a fair approximation of a smile.

He muttered, low, "Damn it, Sydney." And then he reached for her.

She stiffened, put her hands to his chest, started to push him away. But then he was kissing her. And he tasted so good and he smelled like heaven and…

Well, somehow, she was letting her hands slide up to link around his neck. She melted into him and kissed him back. A little moan of frustrated confusion escaped her, a moan distinctly flavored with unwilling desire.

And when he finally lifted his head, she couldn't make up her mind whether to slap him or grab him around the neck, pull him down and kiss him again.

"Kisses don't solve anything," she told him tightly, her hands against his chest again, keeping him at a safer distance. She should have jerked free of his hold completely. But he would be gone in a minute or two. And she'd already kissed him. She might as well go all the way, remain in the warm circle of his arms until he left her.

"I know they don't. But damned if I can leave you without a goodbye kiss."

Okay, he was right. She was glad he had kissed her. Sometimes a kiss said more than words could. She lifted a hand and laid it cherishingly against his lean cheek. "Tell the princess I…look forward to meeting her."

He turned his lips into her palm, kissed her there, the way he had that first night, in their private alcove at the

Mansion restaurant, his breath so warm and lovely across her skin. "I'll return for you. Within the week."

A week wasn't going to cut it. He should know that. She reminded him, "I told you I would need a month, at least, to tie up loose ends at the firm—and that's with you giving my partners a few rich clients as a going-away present."

"I will do what I said I would. And I'm still hoping you can be finished faster."

"Well, that's not going to happen. Get used to it."

"I'll try. And when I return, you're going to have to make room for me at your house." He added, so tenderly, "Because I can't live without you."

His words softened her heart and she wasn't sure she wanted that. She was all turned around inside, wanting him so very much, *not* wanting to be vulnerable to him. She rolled her eyes. "Can't live without me. Oh, right. Kissing up much?"

He took her by the arms. "Correction. I don't *want* to live without you. I'm wild for you. And you know that I am."

Well, yeah. She did, actually. She relented a little. "Of course you'll be staying at my house. I don't want to live without you, either, no matter how angry I happen to be with you."

"Good."

"After all, we're only just married—we only just *met,* if you want to get right down to it."

"Don't." He said it softly. But his eyes weren't soft. His eyes were as black and stormy as a turbulent sea. "Please." He took her hand and kissed the back of it and the simple touch of his mouth on her skin worked its way down inside her, into the deepest part of her. It warmed her and thrilled her—and reassured her, too. "One week," he said fervently. "At the most. I will miss you every day

I'm away from you. I will call you, constantly. You'll be sick and tired of hearing the phone ring."

"I won't mind running to answer the phone. I'll answer and answer gladly," she confessed in a near-whisper. "As long as it's you on the other end of the line."

"Sydney…" He kissed her again, a quick, hard press of his lips against hers. "A week."

And he let her go. She watched him mount the steps to the plane. And she waited to wave to him, when he paused to glance back at her one more time before going in.

Finally, too soon, he was gone.

Rule arrived at Nice Airport at five in the morning. From there, it was only a short drive to Montedoro. He was in his private apartments at the Prince's Palace before six.

At eight, Caroline deStahl, his private secretary, brought him the five newspapers he read daily—*and* the three tabloids that contained stories about him and Sydney. All three tabloids ran the same pictures, one of the two of them kissing, and another of them fleeing down an Impresario hallway. And all three had similar headlines: The Prince Takes a Bride and Wedding Bells for Calabretti Royal and Prince Rule Elopes with Dallas Legal Eagle.

It was a little after 1:00 a.m. in Dallas. Sydney would be in bed. He hated to wake her.

But he did it anyway.

She answered his call on the second ring. "It's after one in the morning, in case you didn't notice," she grumbled sleepily.

"I miss you. I wish I was there with you."

"Is this an obscene phone call?"

He laughed. "It could become one so easily."

"Are you there yet?"

"In my palace apartment, yes. My secretary just delivered the tabloids. We are the main story."

"Which tabloids?"

He named them. "I'm sure we're all over the internet, as well. You are referred to by name. And also as my bride, the 'Dallas Legal Eagle.'"

"Ugh. I was hoping to explain things to my partners at the firm before the word got out. Have you spoken with Princess Liliana yet?"

"No. But I will right away, this morning."

"What can I say? Good luck—and call me the minute it's over."

He pictured her, eyes puffy, hair wild from sleep. It made an ache within him, a sensation that some large part of himself was missing. He said ruefully, "I'll only wake you again if I call…."

"Yeah, well. It's not like I'll be able to go back to sleep now. At least, not without knowing how it went."

He felt thoroughly reprehensible. On any number of levels. "I shouldn't have called."

"Oh, yeah. You should have. And call me right away when it's over. I mean it."

"Fair enough. Sydney, I…" He sought the words. He didn't find them.

She whispered, "Call me."

"I will," he vowed. And then he heard the faint click on the line, leaving him alone, half a world away from her, with just his guilty conscience to keep him company.

Two hours later, he sat in the small drawing room of the suite Liliana always took whenever she visited the palace. He'd been waiting for half an hour for her to appear and he didn't know yet whether she had heard about his marriage or not. Her attendant, one of Lili's Alagonian cousins,

Lady Solange Moltano, had seemed welcoming enough, so he had hopes that he'd arrived in time to be the first to tell her what she didn't want to know.

The door to the private area of the suite opened. He stood.

Lili emerged wearing all white, a pair of wide-legged trousers and a tunic-length jacket, her long blond hair loose, her Delft-blue eyes shining, her cheeks pink with excitement. She was absolutely beautiful, as always. And he really was so fond of her. He didn't want to see her hurt.

He'd never wanted to see Lili hurt.

"Rule." She came toward him, arms outstretched.

They shared an embrace. He looked down at the golden crown of her head and wished he were anywhere but there, in her sitting room, about to tell her that a brilliant, opinionated and fascinating brunette from Texas had laid claim to his heart.

She caught his hands in her slender ones, stepped back and beamed up at him. "You're here. At last…"

So. She didn't know.

"Lili, I came to see you right away, as soon as I got in. I have something important to tell you."

She became even more radiant than a moment before— if that was possible. "Oh." She sounded breathless. "Do you? Really? At last…"

What if she fainted? She'd always been so delicate. "Let's…sit down, shall we?"

"Oh, absolutely. Let's." She pulled him over to a blue velvet sofa. They sat. "Now. What is it you'd like to say to me?"

He had no idea where to begin. His tongue felt like a useless slab of leather in his mouth. "I… Lili. I'm so sorry about this."

Her radiance dimmed, marginally. "Ahem. You're… sorry?"

"I know you've always had an expectation that you and I would eventually marry. I realize I've been wrong, very wrong, to have let things go on like this, to have—"

She cut him off. "Rule."

He coughed into his hand. "Yes?"

Her perfect face was now scarily composed. "All right. So, then. You're not here to propose marriage to me."

"No, Lili. I'm not. I'm here to tell you that I'm already married."

Lili gasped. Her face went dead-white.

He got ready to catch her as she collapsed.

## Chapter Nine

But Lili remained upright on the sofa. She asked in a voice barely louder than a whisper, "Would you mind telling me her name, please?"

"Sydney. Sydney O'Shea."

"Not Montedoran?"

"No. I met her in America. In Texas."

Lili swallowed, her smooth white throat working convulsively. "Sydney O'Shea. From Texas."

"Yes. Lili, I—"

She waved a hand at him. "No. Please. I… Fair enough, then. You've told me. And I hope you'll be very happy together, you and this Sydney O'Shea." Her huge blue eyes regarded him, stricken. Yet she remained so calm-seeming. She even forced a tight smile. "I hope you will have a lovely, perfect life." She shot to her feet. "And now, if you don't mind, I think I would like you to go."

"Lili…" He rose. He wanted to reach out to her. But that

would be wrong. He would only be adding insult to injury. What good could he do for her now? None. There was no way he could help her through this, nothing he could do to make things better.

He *was* the problem. And he really needed to leave, now, before she broke down in front of him and despised him even more for bearing witness to her misery.

"Go," she said again. "Please just go."

So he did go. With a quick dip of his head, he turned on his heel and he left her alone.


He called Sydney again the moment he reached his own rooms.

"How did it go?" she asked.

"Not well. She sent me away as soon as I told her."

"Is there someone with her? Someone she can talk to?"

"She has a cousin with her. But I don't think that they're close."

"Who *is* she close to?"

"My God, Sydney. What does it matter? What business is it of mine or yours?"

"Men are so thickheaded. She needs someone to talk to, someone to comfort her, someone who understands what she's going through."

*He* needed a stiff drink. But then again, it was barely eleven in the morning. "You don't know her, Sydney. How can you possibly know what she needs?"

"Rule. She's a woman. I *know* what she needs. She needs a true friend with a shoulder she can cry on. She needs that friend now."

"Sydney. I adore you," he said in his coolest, most dangerous tones. "You know that. And I'm very sorry to have made such a balls-up of all this. But you don't know Liliana and you have no idea what she needs. And I'll thank you to stop imagining that you do."

"I'm getting seriously pissed off at you. You know that, right?"

"Yes. I realize that. And we're even. Because I am becoming pretty damn brassed off at *you.*"

Dead silence on the line. And then, very flatly, "I think I should hang up before I say something I'm bound to regret."

"Yes. I agree. Go back to sleep, Sydney."

"Hah. Fat chance of that." *Click.* And silence.

"Goodbye," he said furiously, though it wasn't in any way necessary, as she had already hung up.

He put down the phone and then he just stood there, staring blindly at an oil painting of a pastoral scene that hung over the sofa, wanting to strangle someone. Preferably his bride.

A tap on the outer door interrupted his fuming. "Enter."

His secretary, Caroline, appeared to inform him that Her Sovereign Highness and Prince Evan wished to speak with him in the Blue Sitting Room of their private apartment.

In his parents' private rooms, they didn't stand on ceremony.

His mother embraced him and told him she forgave him for running off and marrying his Texas bride without a word to the family beforehand. His father congratulated him as well and said he was looking forward to meeting Sydney and her son. Prince Evan said nothing about the secret Rule had finally shared with him a few weeks before. Rule was grateful to see that his father, at least at this point, was keeping his word and telling Her Sovereign Highness nothing about how Rule had come to meet his bride in the first place.

And when his mother asked him about that, about how he and Sydney had met, he told her the truth, as far as it went. "I saw her going into a shopping mall. One look, and I knew I wanted to know her. So I followed her. I convinced her that she should have lunch with me and after that, I pursued her relentlessly until she gave in and married me. I knew from that first sight of her, getting out of her car, settling her bag on her shoulder so resolutely, that she was one of a kind."

His mother approved. She'd more or less chosen his father that way, after seeing him across a room at a Hollywood party during a visit to the States. "You did have us worried," she chided. "We feared you would fail to make your choice before your birthday. Or that you would marry our darling Lili and the marriage would not suit in the end."

Rule had to keep from gaping. "If you thought that Liliana and I were a bad match, you might have mentioned that to me."

His mother gave a supremely elegant shrug. "And what possible good would that have done? Until you met the *right* woman, you were hardly likely to listen to your mother telling you that the perfectly lovely Lili, of whom you've always been so fond, was all wrong for you."

Rule had no idea how to reply to that. He wanted to say something angry and provoking. Because he felt angry and provoked. But that had more to do with his recent conversation with Sydney than anything else. So he settled for saying nothing.

And then his mother and father shared a look. And his mother nodded. And his father said, "I hope you'll be having a private word with Liliana soon."

At which point he went ahead and confessed, "As it happens, I've already spoken with her."

His mother rose abruptly. Rule and his father followed suit. She demanded, "Why ever didn't you say so?"

Yes. No doubt about it. To strangle someone or put his fist through a wall about now would be extremely satisfying. "I *did* tell you. I told you just now."

"When did you speak with her?" his mother asked.

He glanced at his wristwatch. "Forty-five minutes ago."

"You told her of your marriage?"

"Yes." His parents shared a speaking glance. "What? I *shouldn't* have told her?"

"Well, of course you needed to tell her."

"Then I don't understand what—"

"Is she alone now?"

"I have no idea. Solange Moltano answered the door to me. I'm assuming she's still there, in Lili's apartment."

"The Moltano woman will never do. Lili will need someone to *talk* with, someone to comfort her."

It was exactly what Sydney had said. And that made him angrier than ever. He gritted his teeth and apologized, though he was sick to death of saying how sorry he was. "It's all my fault. I can see now I've handled everything wrong."

His mother put her cool hand against his cheek. "No, darling. You did what you had to do—except for not telling me the moment you left her. Lili will need me now. I'll go to her right away." And with that, she swept from the room.

Into the echoing silence after her departure, Rule said, "I think I would like to hit someone."

His father nodded. "I know the feeling."

"I've broken Lili's heart. And my wife is furious at me."

"Lili will get over this, Rule. Leave it to your mother.

She loves Lili like one of our own and she will know just what to say to comfort her—and why is your bride angry with you?" His father frowned. "You've *told* her already, about the boy?"

Rule swore. "No. Not yet. And I won't. Not…for a while, in any case. Sydney's upset about Lili. She sympathizes with Lili. She says I used Lili as my 'ace in the hole,' as a way to hedge my bet in case I didn't find someone I really wanted to marry before Montedoran law took my title and my fortune."

"She sounds like a rare person, your new wife. Not many brides have sympathy for the 'other' woman."

"Sydney is like no one I've ever known," he said miserably.

"That's good, don't you think?"

"I don't know what to think. She has me spinning in circles. I don't know which end is up."

"A good woman will do that, turn your world upside down."

"I've mucked everything up." Rule sank to the sofa again, shaking his head. "Sydney believes absolutely in honesty and truth and integrity. She's disappointed in me because I wasn't honest with Lili, because I didn't make my true feelings—or lack of them—clear to Lili long ago. I keep thinking, if Sydney can hardly forgive me for not being totally honest with Lili, how can I ever tell her the truth about Trevor?"

His father sat down beside him. He said gently, "You have a real problem."

"I used to see myself as a good man, a man who did what was right.…"

"Do you want my advice?"

"You'll only tell me to tell her, and to tell her now."

His father's lips curved in a wry smile. "So that would be a no, then. You don't want my advice?"

"I can't tell her. Honesty is everything for her. If I was going to tell her, I should have done it at the beginning, that first day I met her, before I pushed for marriage…"

"Why didn't you?"

"She confided in me concerning her past romantic relationships. I knew she had very good reasons not to put her trust in men. If I'd told her before I married her, she might never have allowed me to get close to her. Certainly she wouldn't have let me near her in the time allotted before the twenty-fourth of June. It's as I said to you on the phone. There was no good choice. I made the choice that gave me a fighting chance. Or at least, so I thought at the time."

"What do you have on your calendar?"

Rule arched a brow. "And what has my schedule got to do with my complete failure to behave as a decent human being?"

"I think you should clear it."

"My calendar?"

"Yes. Fulfill whatever obligations you can't put off here and do it as quickly as possible. Reschedule everything else. And then return to Texas. Make it up with Sydney, get through this rough patch, spend time with Trevor, strengthen your bonds with both of them. And return to Montedoro when your wife is ready to come with you."

That morning, Sydney actually had two reporters lurking on her front lawn. When she backed out of her garage on the way to the office, she stopped in the driveway, rolled her window down and let them snap away with their cameras for a good sixty seconds.

They fired questions at her while they took the pictures.

She told them that yes, she had married her prince and she was very happy, thank you. No, she wasn't willing to share any of their plans with the press.

One asked snidely if she'd met the Alagonian princess yet. She said no, but she was looking forward to making Princess Liliana's acquaintance—and in case they hadn't noticed, hers was a gated community. She would be calling neighborhood security the next time she found them on her property. That said, she drove away.

At the firm, she met with three of her partners. They already knew about her marriage.

And they weren't surprised when she told them she would be leaving Teale, Gayle and Prosser. They weren't happy with her, either. She was a valued and very much counted-on member of the team, after all. And they were going to be scrambling to fill the void that would be created by her absence.

When she told them she hoped to leave for her new home within the month, an icy silence descended. After which there was talk of her obligations, of the contract she had with the firm.

Then she told them about the potential clients she would be bringing in before she left. She named the ones Rule had mentioned the night before their wedding. And she explained that His Highness, her husband, had excellent business connections worldwide—connections he was willing to share with Teale, Gayle and Prosser.

By the time the meeting was over, her partners were smiling again. Of course, they would be waiting to see if she delivered on her promises. But at least she had a chance of getting out quickly with her reputation intact and zero bridges burned.

She went to work with a vengeance, getting her office and workload in order.

Rule hadn't called since the second time she'd talked to him the night before, when she'd gotten all up in his face. Had she been too hard on him?

Oh, maybe. A little.

But she couldn't believe he'd just dropped the bomb of his elopement on the poor, lovesick princess and then left her all on her own because she'd *asked* him to. Sydney hoped her harsh words had put a serious bug up his butt— as her Grandma Ellen might have said—and that he'd found a way to make sure Liliana had the confidant she needed at a time like this.

At five that afternoon, Sydney was called into the main conference room, which was packed with her partners, the associates, the paralegals, the secretarial staff and even the HR people. There was champagne and a pile of wedding gifts and a cake.

Sydney couldn't believe it. It was really happening. She was getting the office wedding shower she'd been so certain she'd never have.

She thanked them and made a little speech about how much they all meant to her and how she would miss them. And then she ate two pieces of cake, sipped one glass of champagne and did the rounds of the room, her spirits lifted that her colleagues had made a party just for her.

It was nine at night when she left the office. She was seriously dragging by then. Sleep had been in short supply for five days now—since last Friday, when her whole life had changed in an instant, because she'd gone into Macy's to buy a wedding gift for Calista Dwyer.

At home, Lani helped her carry in the gifts from the party. "You look exhausted," Lani said. "Just leave everything on the table. I'll deal with it tomorrow."

Sydney dropped the last box on the stack and sank into a chair. "How was your day?"

"Fabulous. Trevor took a three-hour nap and I got ten pages done. And then later, we went to the park. He seems to have slacked off on the endless knock-knock jokes."

"That's a relief."

"I so agree—he asked twice about 'Roo.' He wanted to know when Rule was coming to see him again so they could play trucks."

Sydney was happy that her son was so taken with his stepfather. She only wished she didn't feel edgy and unsure about everything. But it had all happened so fast between them, and now he was gone. A sense of unreality had set in.

She told Lani, "He said he'd be back in a week."

"Well, all right. Good to know—and is everything okay with you two?"

Sydney let her shoulders slump. "There are some issues."

Lani knew her so well. "And you're too wiped out to talk about them now." At Sydney's weary nod, she asked, "Hungry?"

"Naw. I had takeout at the office—and two pieces of cake at the party. I think I'll go upstairs and kiss my sleeping son and then take a long, hot bath."

Forty-five minutes later, Sydney climbed into bed. She set the alarm for six-thirty, turned off the light and was sound asleep almost as soon as her head hit the pillow.

Rule didn't call that night. Or the next morning.

Apparently, he really was "brassed off" at her. She thought it was rather childish of him, to cut off communication because she'd pissed him off. Then again, nothing was stopping her from picking up the phone and calling *him*.

She felt reluctant to do that, which probably proved that she was being every bit as childish as he was. And she did wonder how things had worked out with Liliana, if he'd done what she'd asked him to do and found someone for the poor woman to talk to.

And okay, she hadn't *asked*. She'd more like *commanded*. And he hadn't appreciated her ordering him around.

Maybe she shouldn't have been so hard on him. Maybe she should have...

Who knew what she should have done? She was totally out of her depth with him. She'd only known him since Friday and now they were married and already he was halfway around the world from her. No wonder they were having "issues."

She hardly knew him. And how would she *get* to know him, with him there and her here?

All she knew for certain was that she ached with missing him. The lack of him was like a hole in her heart, a vacancy. She needed him with her, to fill that lack. She wanted him there, with her, touching her. She wanted it so bad. She wanted to grab him in her arms and curl herself into him, to hold on so tight, to press herself so close. She wanted to...somehow be inside his skin.

She wanted the scent of him, the sound of his voice, the sweet, slow laugh, the feel of his hands on her, the touch of his mouth...

She was totally gone on him. And he'd better return to her in a week, as he'd promised, or she would do something totally unconstructive. Track him down and shoot him, maybe. Not fatally, of course. Just wing him.

At the office the next day, she got calls from a couple of oil company executives, representatives of two of the companies Rule had said he could deliver to her firm. The calls eased her mind a little.

Okay, he hadn't been in touch the way he'd promised

that he would. But he was moving ahead with his plans to help her get away from Texas gracefully. That was something. A good sign.

Before the end of the day, she'd set up the first getting-to-know-you meetings between her partners and the reps from the oil companies.

Thursday morning at six-thirty, at the exact moment that her alarm went off, the phone rang. Jarred awake, she groped for the alarm first and hit the switch to shut it off.

Then she grabbed the phone. "Hello, what?" she grumbled.

"I woke you."

Even half-asleep, gladness filled her. "Hello."

"Are you still angry with me?"

She rolled over onto her back, and raked her sleep-scrambled hair back off her face. "I could ask you the same question."

"I know I said I'd call every day..." God. His voice. How could it be better, smoother, deeper, just plain sexier than she remembered?

She corrected him. "You said you would call *constantly*. That's *more* than every day."

"Will you ever forgive me?"

She chuckled, a low, husky sound. She just couldn't help it. All he had to do was call and her world was rosy again. "I would say forgiveness is a distinct possibility."

"I'm so glad to hear that." He said it tenderly. And as if he really, really meant it.

"I miss you, Rule. I miss you so much."

"I miss you, too."

"How can I feel this way? I've only known you for, what, five days?"

"Four days, nineteen hours and...three minutes—and

you'd better miss me. You're my wife. It's your job to miss me when we're apart."

"Well, I'm doing my job, then."

"Good."

"And I'm sorry," she said, "that we argued."

"I am, too."

"Those two oil men called yesterday. I set them up with my partners."

"Excellent."

She hesitated to ruin the conciliatory mood by bringing up a certain princess. But she really did want to know what had happened. "Did everything work out then, with Liliana?"

"You were right," he said quietly. "I should have sent someone to be with her."

"Oh, no. What *happened?*"

"When I told my mother that Lili hadn't seemed to take the news of our marriage well, she rushed off to comfort her. Lili wasn't in her rooms. Lili's attendant said that she'd fled in tears."

"Omigod. She's missing, then?"

"No. They found her shortly thereafter. She simply turned up, looking somewhat disheveled, or so I was told, and insisting she was perfectly fine."

"Turned up?"

"One of the servants found her in the hallway between Maximilian's apartments and Alexander's. She claimed she'd simply gone for a stroll."

"A *stroll?*"

"That's what she said."

"Is she friends with your brothers? Did she talk it out with one of them?"

"Not possible."

"Why not?"

"Max is with his children, at his villa. And Alex and Lili have never gotten on, not since childhood."

"That doesn't mean he might not have been kind to her, if he saw that she was upset."

"Sydney, he's hardly come out of his rooms since he returned from Afghanistan. But you're right, of course. Anything is possible. Perhaps she talked to him, though no one told me that she did."

"But…she's all right, then?"

"Yes. She did end up confiding in my mother. And in the end, Lili promised my mother that she is perfectly all right and that no one is to worry that her father's famous temper will be roused. Lili said she had finally realized that she and I were not right for each other, after all. She told my mother to wish me and my bride a lifetime of happiness. My mother believes that Lili was sincere in what she said."

"Okay. Well. Good news, huh?"

"I believe so, yes. Lili departed yesterday morning for Alagonia. King Leo has not appeared brandishing a sword or insisting on pistols at dawn, so I'm going to venture a guess that renewed animosity between our two countries has been safely averted."

"I'm so glad. I have to admit, I was worrying—that Liliana might have done something crazy, that her father might have taken offense. And then, when you never called, I only worried more."

"I'm a complete ass."

"Do you hear me arguing? Just tell me you're coming back here to me by Tuesday or Wednesday, as promised."

"Sorry. I can't do that." He said it teasingly.

Still, her heart sank. She tried to think of what to say, how to frame her disappointment in words that wouldn't get them started fighting all over again.

And then he said, "I'll be there tomorrow."

She felt deliciously breathless. "Oh, Rule. Say that again."

"You *do* miss me." The way he said that made her heart beat faster.

"Oh, yes, I do," she fervently agreed. "I want to have *time* with you. I want you near me. Here we are, married. We're going to spend our lives together, yet in many ways we hardly know each other."

"Tomorrow," he said. "It'll be late, around ten at night, by the time I reach your house."

"Tomorrow. Oh, I can't believe it—and late is fine. I'm lucky to get home by nine-thirty, anyway. I'll be here. Waiting."

"I have work to do there, too, you know. I have to introduce your partners to any number of excellent potential clients, so they'll realize they owe it to you to let you go right away."

She beamed, even though he wasn't there to see it. "I can't tell you how glad I am that you're coming back now. It will be so good, to be with you every day—even if I do spend way too much of every day at work. But I'm going to change that. When I'm through at the firm, I'm going to make sure I never again take a job where I hardly see my son, where I'm rarely with my husband."

"I do like the sound of that."

"Good— Oh, and I forgot to tell you. Trevor will be so pleased to see you. He's been asking for you."

"Tell him I'm on my way."

## Chapter Ten

Sydney was waiting at the picture window in the living room Friday night when the long, black limo pulled in at the curb. The sight of his car had her heart racing and her pulse pounding so hard, it made a roaring sound in her ears.

With a glad cry, she spun on her heel and took off for the door. Flinging it wide, she ran down the front steps and along the walk. He emerged from the car and she threw herself into his arms.

He kissed her, right there beneath the streetlight. A hard, hot kiss, one that started out desperate and ended so sweet and lazy and slow.

When he lifted his head, he said, "I thought I'd never get here."

She laughed, held so close and safe in his arms. "But you *are* here. And I may never let you go away from me again." She took his hand. "Come inside…"

The driver was already unloading Rule's bags. He followed them up the front walk. Joseph followed, too.

In the house, the driver carried the bags up to the master suite and then, with a tip of his cap, took his leave.

Joseph remained. For once, he wasn't wearing those dark glasses. But he still had the Bluetooth device in his ear. And he carried a black duffel bag.

Rule looked slightly embarrassed. "I'm afraid Joseph goes where I go."

Sydney spoke to the bodyguard. "I hope you don't mind sleeping in a separate room from His Highness."

The severe-looking Joseph almost cracked a smile. "Ma'am, if you have a spare room, that would be appreciated. If not, the sofa will do well enough."

"I have a guest room." She indicated the doorway at the end of the hall. "The kitchen is through there. While you're here, make yourself at home. You're welcome to anything you find in the pantry or the fridge."

"Thank you, ma'am."

She turned to Rule. "Are you hungry?"

His dark eyes said, *Not for food,* and she felt the loveliest warmth low in her belly, and a definite wobbliness in her knees. He told her, "I ate on the plane."

So she led the way up the stairs and showed Joseph to his room, indicating Trevor's bathroom across the hall. "I'm afraid you'll have to share the bathroom with my son."

"Thank you. This will suit me very well."

Before joining Rule in her room, she tapped on Lani's door and told her friend that Rule's bodyguard was staying in the guest room.

Lani, reading in bed, looked up from her eReader, over the top rims of her glasses. "Thanks for the warning—and don't stay up all night."

"Yes, Mother."

"Say hi to Rule."

"Will do."

She went to her own room and found Rule standing in the bow window, staring out at the quiet street. "Lani says hi."

He turned to her. "I like your house. It's comfortable, and the rooms are large. Lots of windows..."

She hovered in the open doorway, her stomach suddenly all fluttery. "We've been happy here. It will be strange, to live in a palace."

"I have other properties. Villas. Town houses. You might prefer one of them."

All at once, the life that lay before her seemed alien, not her own. "We'll see." The two words came out on a breath.

He held out his hand to her. "Are you shy of me now, Sydney?"

Her throat clutched. She spoke through the tightness. "A little, I guess." A nervous laugh escaped her. "That's silly, isn't it?"

He shook his dark head. "Come here. Let me ease your fears."

Pausing only to shut the door and engage the lock, she went to him and took the hand he offered. His touch burned her and soothed her at once.

He reached out with the hand not holding hers and shut the blinds. "I put my suitcases in your closet...."

She moved in closer. He framed her face. She said, "It seems like forever, since you left...."

"I'm here now."

"I'm so glad about that."

He kissed her. And the throat-tight nervousness faded. There was only his mouth on her mouth, his hands against her cheeks, brushing down the sides of her throat, tracing the collar of her cotton shirt, and then going to work on the buttons down the front of it.

She was breathless and sighing, pulling him closer. He took away her shirt and her bra. He pushed down the leggings she had pulled on after work. She kicked away her little black flats and wiggled the rest of the way out of the leggings.

And then he went to work on his own clothes, kissing her senseless as he ripped off his jacket, his shirt, his trousers...everything. She had only her panties on and he was completely naked when he started walking her backward toward the bed.

"Wait," she breathed against his lips.

He only went on kissing her—until she gave a gentle shove against his chest. With an impatient growl, he lifted his mouth from hers. "You know you're killing me...."

She put her finger to those amazing lips of his. "Only a moment..."

"A moment is too long." But he did let her go.

She turned around and pulled the covers down, smoothing them. "There."

"Sydney..." He clasped her by the hips and drew her back against him.

"I'm here. Right here..." She lifted her arms and reached for him, clasping his neck, turning her head to him so their mouths could fuse once again.

His tongue plundered her mouth and his hands covered her breasts. And she could feel him, all along her body, feel the power of him, the heat. Feel the proof of how much he wanted her, silky and hard, pressing into her back.

And then he was turning her and guiding her down onto the sheets and right then, at that moment on that night, she was the happiest woman in Texas. There was only the feel of his big body settling against hers, only his kiss, only his skilled touch, on her breasts, her belly and lower.

He took away her panties and those wonderful fingers of his found the womanly core of her and she moaned into his mouth. He kissed her some more as he caressed her, bringing her higher, making her clutch his hard shoulders and press herself closer.

Closer…

And then she couldn't wait. Not one second longer. She eased her hand between them and she wrapped her fingers around him and she guided him into place.

When he came into her, she let out a soft cry at the sheer beauty of it, at the feel of him filling her. So perfectly. So right.

He kissed her throat, and then scraped the willing flesh there with his teeth. And then he licked her. And then he blew on her wet skin and she moaned and pulled him closer again, lifting her legs to wrap around his waist, pushing herself harder against him, demanding everything of him, wanting it all.

When he held her like this, when he worked his special magic on her skin, she had no doubts at all. She would follow him anywhere, and she would be happy.

Just the two of them and Trevor. And maybe, if they were lucky, more children. Three or four. Nine or ten…

She'd forgotten how many she wanted, how many they had finally agreed on. And what did it matter how many? She would love them all, every one.

And by then, she'd forgotten everything—everything but this, but the man who held her, the man who filled her. The pleasure was building, spinning fast, and then gathering tight.

Only to open outward, a sudden blooming, so hot and

perfect. She cried out again, loud enough that he had to cover her mouth with his hand.

She laughed against his fingers, a wild sound. And then he was laughing with her. And still the pleasure bloomed and grew. And all at once, they were silent, serious, concentrated, eyes wide open, falling into each other.

Falling and spinning, set gloriously free: the two of them, locked together. She was lost in his eyes. And more than happy to be so.

She whispered his name.

With a low groan, he gave hers back to her.


She must have slept for a time.

When she woke, he was braced up on an elbow, looking down at her, his eyes black velvet, his mouth an invitation to sin.

She reached up, curved her fingers around the back of his head, pulled him closer. They shared a quick, gentle kiss. "It's so good, to wake up and find you here. I want to do that for the rest of my life."

"And my darling, you shall. Now go back to sleep."

"Soon. Tell me about your parents. Are they angry, that you married me?"

"No. They're pleased. Very pleased."

She wasn't buying that. "They don't even know me. You met me and married me in like, ten minutes or less. How can they be pleased with that? I mean, I could understand if you said they were…accepting. But *pleased?*"

"They know me. They know that I'm happy, that I've found the woman I want to be with for a lifetime. They're relieved and they're grateful."

"Well, okay." She traced the shape of his ear. It was such a good-looking ear. "I get that. I mean, they were probably getting pretty concerned, right, that you wouldn't marry in time?"

"They were, yes." He caught her hand, kissed the tips of her fingers.

"But if you'd married the Princess of Alagonia, wouldn't that have made them a lot happier?"

"No. Evidently not. They told me they didn't think Lili and I would have been a good match."

"You'd think they might have said that earlier."

"My response exactly."

"Someone should change that ridiculous law."

"My mother's great-grandfather, who ruled Montedoro for fifty years, *did* change it. He abolished the law. And then my mother's father put the law in place once again."

"But why?"

"My mother's *grand*father didn't marry until late in life. He had eight children, but only one was legitimate, my mother's father, *my* grandfather. Then my grandfather had just one child, a daughter, legitimate, my mother. The family was dying out. My grandfather took action. He put the law back in place."

She laughed. "And then your mother obeyed it. She married young, brought in fresh blood and took her reproductive duties to heart."

"Yes, she did. And look at us now."

"Heirs and spares all over the place."

"That's right. So you see, the law has its uses."

She frowned, considering. "There must be any number of ways around it. You could marry someone in time to keep your inheritance, and then divorce her as soon as your thirty-third birthday has passed."

He nuzzled her neck. "Already planning how you'll get rid of me, eh?"

She laughed, and caught his face and kissed him, hard,

on the mouth. "Never. But you know what I'm saying, right?"

"We are Catholic. The heir to the throne always marries in the church. Divorce is not an option in the church. There is annulment, but there are specific grounds for that, none of them pretty. And you have to understand. In my family, we are raised to respect the Prince's Marriage Law. We believe it is a good law, good for Montedoro—especially after we saw what happened when my great-great-grandfather abolished it. And we grow up committed to the spirit of that law, to finding a proper marriage partner by the required date. My parents were good parents, parents who spent time with their children, what you would call in America 'hands-on' parents. My mother considers each of her nine children to be every bit as important as her throne."

"Well, all right," she said. "I guess I can't argue with success. But I do have a couple more questions."

"Ask."

"Do *we* have to marry in the church in order for you to keep your inheritance?"

"No. The heir must marry in the church. The rest of us are only required to be legally wed before the age of thirty-three. But, should I become the heir—which is most unlikely at this point—you and I would have to take steps for a church-sanctioned marriage. That would not be complicated, as neither of us has been married before."

"Do you want us to be married in the church?"

He kissed the tip of her nose. "I do, yes."

"Good answer." She slid her hands up his chest and wrapped them around his neck. "I want that, too."

"Then we shall take the necessary steps to make it happen as soon as we're settled in Montedoro."

"Agreed. I think we should seal it with a kiss."

"Beyond a doubt, we should."

So they kissed. A long, slow one. The kiss led to more kisses and then to the usual stimulating conclusion.

Rule told her again to go sleep.

She said, "Soon."

And then they talked for another hour about everything from the success of his plan to sell Montedoran oranges to a number of exclusive outlets in the U.S., to why his brother Alex and Princess Lili had never gotten along. Alex, Rule said, had always thought Lili was silly and shallow; Lili considered Alex to be overly brooding and grim, with a definite tendency toward overbearing self-importance.

Sydney learned that his brother Max's son was named Nicholas and Max's little girl was Constance. And Rule told her that in his great-grandfather's day, the economy of Montedoro was almost solely dependent on gambling revenues. His grandfather and his mother had made a point to expand the principality's economic interests beyond its traditional gambling base.

"Now," he said, "gambling accounts for only four percent of our nation's annual revenues."

She reminded him that he knew all about Ryan and Peter. But other than Liliana, she knew nothing of the women who had mattered in his life.

"You already know that I admire my mother," he said with a gleam in his eye.

"Your mother and your sisters don't count. I'm talking love affairs, Rule. You know that I am."

So he told her about the Greek heiress he'd loved when he was fourteen. "She had an absolutely adorable space between her two front teeth and she spoke with a slight lisp and she intended to run away to America and become a musical theater star."

"Did she?"

"Unfortunately, she was tone deaf. I heard her sing once. Once was enough."

"Destroyed your undying love for her, did it?"

"I was young and easily distracted. Especially when it came to love." He spoke of the girl he'd met in a Paris café when he was eighteen. And of an Irish girl he'd met in London. "Black hair, blue eyes. And a temper. A hot one. At first, I found her temper exciting. But in time it grew tiresome."

"Luckily there were any number of actresses and models just waiting for their chance with you."

"You make me sound like a Casanova."

"Weren't you?"

"No. I was not. Yes, I've spent time with a number of women, but seduction for its own sake has never interested me. I was…looking for someone. The *right* someone." He lowered his head until their noses touched. "You."

Her heart did that melty thing. "Oh, Rule…"

He kissed her forehead, her cheeks, and finally her lips—sweet, brushing kisses. "Will you please go to sleep now?" He tucked the covers closer around her. "Close your eyes…"

And she did.

The next day was Saturday. Sydney left Rule having breakfast with Trevor and Lani and spent the morning at the office, where things were pretty quiet and she got a lot done.

She returned home at lunchtime and spent the rest of the day with Rule and her son and her best friend. She and Rule went out to dinner that night and then, at home, made slow, wonderful love. They fell asleep with their arms wrapped around each other. Her last thought before she drifted off was that she had it all now. Her life was exactly as she'd once dreamed it might be.

Sunday she stayed home, too. She and Rule took Trevor to the park in the morning. She watched Rule pushing Trev on the swings and thought how already they seemed like father and son. Trev adored him. It was "Roo" this and "Roo" that. The feeling was clearly mutual. Rule seemed to dote on Trev. He never tired of listening to Trev babble on about the things that mattered to a curious two-year-old.

And an older lady, a woman there with her grandson, leaned close to Sydney when they sat on the bench together. "Your boy looks just like his daddy."

Sydney smiled at the woman. "He does, doesn't he?"

Later, at lunch, Trev was back into his knock-knock jokes. He and Rule played a never-ending game of them until Sydney put her hands over her ears and begged them to stop.

Trev laughed. "Mama says, 'No more knock-knock!'"

Rule piped up with, "Mama says, 'Touch your nose.'" He touched his nose and then Trev, delighted, touched his. And Rule said, "Mama says, 'Rub your tummy.'" They both rubbed their tummies.

Trev caught on about then and they were off on the "Mama" version of Simon Says. Sydney laughed along with them.

The woman at the park had been right. And Lani had noticed the resemblance, too. They were so much alike, really. They even had mannerisms in common—the way they each tipped their head, a little to the left, when thoughtful. Even the way they smiled was similar—slow and dazzling.

Sydney supposed it wasn't all that surprising, how much Trev resembled his new stepdad. The sperm donor she'd chosen had a lot of characteristics in common with Rule—hair and eye color, height and build. And the similarities weren't only physical. The donor had an advanced degree in business and enjoyed travel and sports. And the description of him compiled by the staff at the cryobank? All about how charming and handsome and bright and dynamic he was. How well-spoken and articulate, a born leader *and* a good listener. His profile also said that family was important to him and he believed in marriage, that he felt it could and should last a lifetime.

She'd selected that particular donor mostly because he sounded like the kind of man she'd given up on finding. After all, a woman hopes her child might inherit traits that she admires.

A little shiver skittered up her spine as she watched her son and Rule together and compared her husband with the man who had supplied half of her child's DNA. Life could be so strange and amazing. Really, she'd chosen her own personal fantasy man as her sperm donor, not even realizing that he was destined to materialize in the flesh and promptly sweep her off her feet into their very own happy-ever-after—let alone that he would so quickly become a doting father to her son.

That Sunday was sunny and clear, with a high in the mid-eighties, a little warm for mid-April. It was a great day for splashing around in the pool—which they did as soon as Trevor woke up from his nap. Later, Lani made dinner, a fabulous Greek-style shrimp scampi.

Monday it was off to work again. Rule showed up at a little after eleven. Sydney introduced him around the office and two of the partners were only too happy to join them for lunch at the Mansion.

It was a working lunch, and a very productive one. By the end of it, Rule had set up three dinner dates where he would introduce her colleagues to more potential clients. After lunch, he returned to the house and she went back to work.

Their days fell into a certain rhythm. The office owned her during the long weekdays, but she spent her nights with her new husband and managed to get most of the weekend free to be with Trevor, too. Rule spent a lot of time with her son and the growing bond between the man and the boy was something special to see. Rule would play with him for hours during the day and read him his bedtime stories most nights.

Sydney worked and worked some more. Rule often appeared to take her to lunch—and he moved forward on the goal he'd set for himself of giving her partners enough new business that they wouldn't consider themselves cheated when she moved on.

There were more tabloid stories. Sydney didn't read them, but evidently a few of her coworkers did. She found more than one discarded scandal rag on the lunch table in the break room. Somehow, they'd gotten her high school and college graduation pictures, and there were pictures of Rule, bare-chested on a sailboat with a blonde, and also wearing a tux at some gala event, a gorgeous redhead on his arm. Sydney hardly glanced at them. Rule said that when they got to Montedoro, a press conference would be arranged. They would answer questions for a roomful of reporters and let them take a lot of pictures. That should satisfy them if they hadn't already moved on to the next big story by then.

Twice during the weeks it took her to finish up at the firm, Rule had to travel. He had business in New York and spent four days in Manhattan. And he also returned briefly to Montedoro to meet with a certain luxury car manufacturer who was considering giving one of his new designs, a sleek high-end sports car, the name "Montedoro."

Sydney missed him when he was gone. Her bed seemed so empty without him there to keep her warm in the middle of the night. Trev missed him, too. "I sad, Mama. I want Roo," he would say. And she would remind him that Rule would return soon.

On the last Friday in April, Sydney came home late as usual. Rule was back from Montedoro. He and Lani had waited to have dinner with her. They'd even invited the ever-present but usually silent Joseph to join them. Lani had outdone herself with a crown roast of lamb. Rule opened a lovely bottle of Syrah. And Lani announced that she'd decided to take them up on their offer and come with them to Montedoro.

Sydney jumped from her chair and ran around the table and hugged her friend good and hard. "Whew. I didn't want to pressure you, but I really was hoping you would come with us."

Lani laughed. "Are you kidding? Miss the chance to live on the Mediterranean in the Prince's Palace? I couldn't pass it up."

Even Joseph was smiling. "Good news," he said and raised the glass of wine he'd hardly touched.

Lani said, "Life experience is everything for a novelist. Plus, well, what would I do without you?"

"Exactly." Sydney hugged her again. "And how could we possibly get along without *you?*"

Deep in the night, Sydney woke suddenly from a sound sleep. It was after three and she had no idea what had wakened her.

And then she heard Trev crying. "Mama…Mama…"

Beside her, Rule woke, too. He sat up. "I'll go…"

She kissed his beard-scratchy cheek and pushed him back down to the pillow. "No. I'll do it." She threw on a robe and went to see what was wrong.

Trev was fussy and feverish, his dark hair wet with sweat. He kept putting his hands to his cheeks and crying, "Hurt, Mama. Hurt…"

Lani came in, her hair every which way, a sleep mark on her cheek, belting her robe. "Can I do something?"

"It's all right. I think he's teething. Go back to bed. I've got him."

"Come get me if you need me."

"Will do."

Yawning, Lani returned to her room.

Sydney took Trev's temperature. It was marginally elevated. She gave him some children's acetaminophen and took him downstairs to get one of the teething rings she kept in the freezer. She was back in his room, sitting in the rocker with him as he fussed and chewed on the teething ring when Rule appeared in the doorway to the upstairs hall, bare-chested in a pair of blue pajama bottoms.

"He's not a happy camper," she said. "I think it's his teeth. I gave him a painkiller. It should take effect soon."

Trev pushed away from Sydney. "Roo! Hurt. I have hurt…" He held out his chubby little arms.

Rule came for him, scooping him up out of Sydney's lap without a word or a second's hesitation. Trev wrapped his arms around his stepfather's neck and held on, sticking the ring back in his mouth and burrowing his dark head against Rule's chest. Rule began walking him, back and forth across the bedroom floor.

Sydney, still in the rocker, stared up at the man and the little boy, at their two dark heads so close together, and tried to get a grip on exactly what she was feeling.

Jealousy?

Maybe a little. Rule had become nothing short of pro-prietary about Trev—and Trev about him. In recent weeks, with Rule around day in and day out, Trev had grown to count on him, to expect him to be there, to demand his attention. Since Rule was only too happy to spend lots of time with Trev, and did, it was natural that a powerful bond had swiftly developed between them.

And wasn't that bond a *good* thing? As a father figure, Rule had so far proved himself to be pretty much the ideal. So what was bothering her?

Did she want Rule to defer to her when it came to Trev, was that it? When he'd grabbed her son from her arms without so much as a do-you-mind, had that somehow threatened her, made her feel that her status as Trev's parent was in jeopardy? Lani and Trev had a close rela-tionship, but Lani always remembered that Sydney was the mom, that her claim on him came first.

Rule, though…

He didn't defer to her anymore, if he ever had. He seemed to consider himself as much Trev's dad as Sydney was his mom.

And what was wrong with that?

Wasn't that what she'd been hoping for all along?

Ugh. Maybe it was guilt—scratch the "maybe." *Prob-ably* it was guilt. *Her* guilt, because she knew she'd never been around enough. She worked killer hours and a lot of days she didn't see her son awake except early in the morning, when she kissed him goodbye on her way out the door.

No wonder he chose Rule over her when he needed comforting. Rule was more a consistent presence in his life than she was.

But that was going to change. Very soon. And it would change *because* of Rule, because of what he offered her and Trev, because of the kind of husband and father he was. Not only deeply committed to his family, but also an excellent provider.

As soon as she was finished at the firm, *she* would be available to Trev more consistently—constantly, in fact, at least at first. And even when she found interesting work in Montedoro, it was going to be work with reasonable hours for a change. She would truly have it all. Time to be a mom, time to be a wife, time to do good work that mattered.

It was all going to be fine and she needed to get over her guilt and her jealousy. Trev had a dad now, that was all that was happening here. Sometimes a child wanted his dad over his mom. And there was nothing at all wrong with that.

She leaned her head back in the rocker and closed her eyes.

The next moment—or so it seemed to her—Rule was whispering in her ear. "Come back to bed, sleepyhead."

She forced her heavy eyes to open, asked, "Trev?"

He put a finger to his lips, tipped his head toward the toddler bed across the room, where Trev was curled up under the blankets, his arm around his favorite stuffed dinosaur.

She gave Rule her hand and he pulled her out of the chair. He drew her close and she leaned against him as they returned to the master bedroom.

In bed, he gathered her close to him. "You work too hard." He stroked her hair.

"Not for long. Another week or so, the way I figure it, and I'm so outta there."

"I can't wait to take you home with me—you and Trevor both."

She traced his dark brows, one and then the other, by

feel more than sight. They had turned off the lamp. "I have a secret to tell you."

"I love secrets." He bent closer, kissed her temple. "Especially *your* secrets."

"Don't laugh."

"I promise, I won't." He stroked her hair.

"You and Trev look a lot alike."

He kissed her lips, a brushing kiss, his breath so warm across her cheek. "We do, a little, don't we—and is that your secret?"

"No. I'm getting to it, though. And it starts with the resemblance between you and Trev, which is pretty striking, really. Beyond the dark hair and eyes, you both tip your heads at the same angle when you're thinking. And when you smile…you make me think of him. In fact, that first day we met, remember how I've said I kept thinking how you looked familiar? Remember, I even asked you if we'd met before?"

"Yes. I remember."

"I've been thinking about that a lot lately, kind of marveling over it. And then I realized it's not surprising in the least."

"Why not?"

"Simple. The sperm donor I chose was a lot like you—and yes, that would be my big secret." She traced the so-manly strong line of his jaw. "I chose him because he was just like you—I mean, the you I didn't even know then. He had your same height and build, dark eyes and dark hair. I chose him because he seemed like the man I always hoped to meet someday. The man I had by then decided I would *never* meet."

He withdrew from her then, turning over onto his back beside her.

She wondered at that. "Rule? Are you okay? Did I say something that upset you?"

"Of course you didn't." He sounded…distant. And a little strange. "I'm perfectly all right."

"You don't *seem* all right."

He found her hand under the covers, twined his fingers with hers. "I'm fine."

"Good." She smiled into the darkness. "You sure you were never a sperm donor?"

"You're joking."

"Well, yeah. I guess I am. But sometimes, it's almost eerie, the resemblance between you and Trev."

He didn't say anything.

She went on, "I always kind of hoped to meet him. But he was a confidential donor. I left permission that he could contact me if he ever changed his mind. He didn't. Not so far, anyway—and that reminds me. I need to change my contact information with Secure Choice—that's the clinic I used, Secure Choice Cryobank." She waited for his response, thinking of his possessiveness concerning Trev—and also a little worried about the dreamy way she'd spoken of a man she'd never met.

Was he jealous? Would he try to talk her out of keeping her information current, want her to make it more difficult for the donor to get in touch should he ever decide he wanted to?

But then Rule only reached for her again. He eased his arm under her nape and drew her into him, bringing her to rest against his warm, hard chest. "Go to sleep."

She closed her eyes and let the steady, even sound of his heartbeat lull her.

Of course he'd never been a sperm donor. She knew what a donor went through. She'd researched the whole process when she decided on artificial insemination. It wasn't just a matter of doing the happy hand in a cup.

A man went through all kinds of testing before he could become a donor. Only a small percentage of applicants were accepted. A man had to donate weekly, at least, and he couldn't have sex for two days before each donation. He also couldn't go more than five days *without* ejaculating, because not often enough was as bad for sperm production as too often. Most sperm donors signed contracts for six months to a year of donations—six months to a year of having sex in a cup on a strict schedule. The money wasn't even all that much, averaging under a hundred dollars per viable donation.

To have been her donor, Rule would have had to sign on for all of the above with the fertility clinic she had used, or an affiliate. What were the odds of that?

He was a hardworking man who traveled the world doing business for his country. Not only would being a donor be unprofitable, time-consuming and a logistical nightmare for Rule, it just…wasn't like him. He felt so strongly about family and fatherhood. He wasn't a man who could help to give a child life and not want to be there while that child was growing up.

Still, she didn't get the way he'd pulled away from her when she talked about how much alike he and Trevor were, when she'd confessed that he, Rule, was pretty much her dream man come to life. He'd turned onto his back before she said anything about how she'd given permission to be contacted, so his original withdrawal really couldn't be chalked up to apprehension that the donor might show up someday.

She didn't like the way he'd said, *You're joking,* when she'd asked him if he'd ever been a donor. He could so easily have given her a simple, direct denial.

It wasn't that she actually suspected he might be Trevor's biological father. She only wondered why he'd seemed so defensive and why he'd pulled away from her when she'd only been trying to tell him that he was everything she'd ever wanted in a man.

## Chapter Eleven

But by the next morning, in the bright light of day, as Sydney hurried to get ready to head to the office, her vague suspicions about Rule…

Well, they seemed downright ridiculous.

He hadn't really pulled away from her last night, had he? He'd only rolled over to his back. And when she'd asked if anything was wrong, he'd told her there was nothing.

And his seeming evasiveness when she teased him about being a sperm donor? It just didn't strike her as all that odd now that she'd had a little time to think it over. He was very attached to Trevor. He didn't want to dwell on the stranger who had fathered her child. She could understand that.

She decided that she would put the whole issue from her mind. She had so much work to do and not all that much time to do it in. The last thing she needed was to waste her energy stewing about stuff she'd made up in her head.

Plus, if she wanted to dwell on something, why not choose something real? Something important. Something potentially quite wonderful.

As of that morning, her period was one week late. It was beginning to look as though she and her new husband were already getting their start on that larger family they both hoped for.

But she shouldn't get ahead of herself. She *had* been under a lot of stress lately—meeting and marrying Rule in the space of forty-eight hours, and then having to send him away to make his apologies to the "other woman" in his life. And then there was the way she was working like crazy to finish up at the firm, planning a move halfway around the world.

Yes. Her life was especially stressful right now. And stress could really mess up a woman's cycle.

She decided she would wait a few weeks before she said anything to Rule. No reason to get his expectations up unnecessarily—or her own, for that matter. She would let that question rest for a while, not allow herself to get too excited about it until more time had passed.

Trev was much better that morning. He seemed to be over the bout of teething pain. His temperature was normal and he was eating his breakfast cereal, chattering away, when she left for work.

He gave her a big kiss. "Come back soon, Mama!"

"Don't you worry, I will."

And that evening, she managed to get away from the officer earlier than usual. She was even in time to give Trev his bath before bed. Once he was in bed, Rule said he wanted to take her out to dinner.

They went to the Mansion. Sydney loved the food and

service there and Rule liked it, too. The staff knew him and protected his privacy.

He made a toast. "To us. To our family. To our whole lives together."

She clinked her wineglass with his, aglow with happiness, knowing that she had to be the most fortunate woman in all of Texas. After a couple of sips, she set her glass down and didn't pick it up again. Might as well be cautious. Just in case she really was pregnant.

Not that she thought she was. Uh-uh. She wasn't going there. Not yet.

Four days later, on the first Friday in May, Sydney said goodbye to Teale, Gayle and Prosser.

She left her desk clean and neat and her clients effectively shifted to other attorneys in the firm. She also departed on good terms with her former partners, all thanks to her strict dedication to doing things right—and her new husband's willingness to share his connections.

The next week was all about packing for the move. Lani, one of the most organized human beings on the planet, had already gotten a good head start on that. But there was more to do. Sydney got to work on the rest of the job with her usual enthusiasm. They were leaving the house furnished and in the hands of an excellent Realtor.

Their passports were current. Even Trevor's. Sydney had gotten his for him months before, when she'd been thinking of taking a vacation in Ireland.

On the second Friday in May, they boarded the private jet for Montedoro. Lani's brother, Carlos, and her parents, Iris and Jorge, came to the airport to see them off. There were also reporters. They snapped lots of pictures and asked an endless number of way-too-personal questions.

Rule told them he had no comment at this time and Joseph herded them up the ramp and into the plane.

The flight was a long one and there was a seven-hour time difference between Dallas and their destination. They took off from Love Field at two in the afternoon and arrived at the airport in Nice at eight the next morning. A limo was waiting to whisk them to Montedoro and the Prince's Palace. So were more paparazzi. Again, they hurried to get into the car and away from the questions and cameras.

The first sight of the palace stole Sydney's breath. White as a dove's wing against the clear blue sky, it was a sprawling edifice of crenellated towers and paladin windows and balconies and arches. It stood on a rocky promontory overlooking the sapphire-colored sea.

The driver took them around to a private entrance. By a little after nine, they were filing into Rule's apartment.

After the grandeur of the arched, marble-floored hallways decorated in gorgeous mosaics, Sydney was relieved that Rule's private space was more low-key. The furniture was simple, plush and inviting, the walls were of stucco or something similar, with tall, curving ceilings and dark wood floors covered with beautiful old rugs woven in intricate patterns, most of them deep reds and vivid blues. Balconies in the large sitting room and in the master suite opened onto stunning views of the main courtyard and the crowns of the palms and mimosas, the olive and oak trees that covered the hillside below. Farther out, the Mediterranean, dotted here and there with pretty sailboats and giant cruise ships, shone in the afternoon sun.

The palace staff set right to work unpacking and putting everything away. In no time, that job was done and the soft-spoken, efficient maids had vanished. Lani retreated to her room at one end of the apartment, probably to work on her novel or jot down her first impressions of Montedoro in her journal. Trev sat on a glorious red rug in the sitting room playing with his plastic blocks, and Rule was off somewhere conferring with his private secretary, Caroline.

For a while, Sydney leaned on the carved stone balcony railing, the doors to the sitting room wide open behind her, and stared out at the boats floating on the impossibly blue sea. There was a soft breeze, like the lightest brush of silk against her skin. She felt tempted to pinch herself. It almost seemed like a dream that they were actually here, in Montedoro, at last.

And it got even better. Her period was now almost three weeks late. She had no morning sickness, but she'd had none with Trev, either. What she did have were breasts.

They weren't huge or anything, but they were definitely fuller, and more sensitive than usual. That was the same as with Trev, too.

Another baby. She put her hand against her flat stomach, the way mothers had been doing since the beginning of time. *Another baby.* When she'd had Trevor, she'd told herself to be grateful for one. And she had been. So very grateful.

But now, well, she was pretty much positive she would be having her second. Incredible. Talk about impossible dreams coming true.

She'd bought a home test the week before. And today, as she leaned on the stone railing and admired the sea, she was thinking it was about time to take the test.

And about time to tell Rule that their family was growing.

"Mama! Come. Play…"

She turned to smile at her son, who had stacked several brightly colored blocks into a rickety tower and waved two more at her, one in each chubby hand. "All right, sweetheart. Let's play." She went and sat on the rug with him.

"Here, Mama." He handed her a drool-covered block. Lately, as his back teeth came in, anything he got his little hands on ended up with drool on it.

"Thank you." She wiped the drool off on her jeans and hooked the block at the base of his tower. As long as she was helping, she might as well improve the stability a tad.

A few moments later, Rule appeared. Trev cried his name in sheer delight, "Roo!" And he came right over and scooped him high into his big arms. "Roo, we play blocks!"

"I can see that. Quite a fine tower you have there."

"Mama helps."

"Oh, yes, she does." Rule gave her a smile. Her heart did a couple of somersaults. "My parents are impatient to meet you."

"I'm eager to meet *them*." She gazed up at him from her cross-legged seat on the red rug and wondered if there was a woman alive as fortunate as she. At the same time, she was just a little nervous to be meeting his mom and dad, aka Their Highnesses, for the first time. "But maybe I need a few tips on palace protocol first...."

He shook his head as he kissed the fingers that Trev was trying to stick into his mouth. "We're invited to their private apartment at six. We'll visit, you'll get to know them a little. Then we'll have an early meal. There will be no ceremony, no protocol to observe. Just the family. Just us. Together."

"Perfect," she said.

"I knew you would think so." He asked Trev, "How about you, young man? Ready to meet your new grandpa and grandma?"

Trev beamed. "Yes!"

* * *

The sovereign's apartments were larger than Rule's, but even the private foyer had a welcoming quality about it. She got the sense that real people lived there. The floor was marble, inlaid with ebony and jade, and the chandelier was a fabulous creation of ironwork and crystal. But the hall table had a bowl filled with shells on it and a family photo taken outside, beneath the wide-spreading branches of a gnarled oak tree. Sydney barely had time to pick out a much-younger Rule from the nine children arrayed at the feet of the two handsome dark-haired parents, before the thin, severe-looking woman who had opened the door to them was leading them on, down a hallway lined with oil portraits of princely relatives, the men wearing uniforms loaded down with ribbons and medals and the women resplendent in fancy ball gowns and glittering tiaras.

Rule had hold of Sydney's hand. He carried Trev high against his chest on his other arm. As they approached the end of the hall, he squeezed her fingers. She sent him a smile and squeezed back, all too aware of the fluttery, anxious sensation in her stomach.

The hallway ended at a sitting room. The tall woman nodded and left them. The same dark-haired man and woman as in the picture in the foyer rose from a matched pair of gold-trimmed velvet chairs to greet them.

"At last," said the woman, who was tall, full-figured and quite beautiful. She seemed ageless to Sydney. She could have been anywhere from forty to sixty. She had the eyes of an Egyptian goddess and a wide, radiantly smiling mouth. "Come. Come to me." She held out slender arms.

Sydney might have stood there, gaping in admiration at Rule's mom forever. Luckily, he still had her hand. He started forward and she went with him.

Then, all at once, they were there.

Rule said, "Mother. Father. This is Sydney, my wife."

And then Rule's mom was reaching for her, gathering her into those slender arms. "Sydney," she said, with such warmth and fondness. "I'm so pleased you're here with us."

"Uh. Hello." *Smooth, Sydney. Very smooth.* Really, she should have insisted that Rule at least tell her what to call this amazing creature. Your Highness? Your Sovereign Highness? Your Total Magnificence? What?

And then Rule's mom took her by the shoulders. She gave her a conspirator's grin. "You shall call me Adrienne, of course—except during certain state functions, before which, I promise you will be thoroughly briefed."

"Adrienne," Sydney breathed in relief. "Rule speaks of you often, and with deep affection."

Those Egyptian eyes gleamed. "I am so pleased he has found what he was seeking—and just in time, too."

And then Rule was saying, "And this is Trevor."

Rule's mom turned to bestow that glowing smile on Trev. "Yes. Trevor, I…" HSH Adrienne's sentence died unfinished. She blinked and shot a speaking glance at Prince Evan. It only lasted a split second, and then she recovered and continued, "Lovely to meet you." Trevor, suddenly shy, buried his head against Rule's neck. Adrienne laughed. She had an alto laugh, a little husky, and compelling. "How are you, Trevor?"

"I fine," Trevor muttered, his head still pressed tight to Rule.

Rule rubbed his back. "Say, 'Hello, Grandmother. So nice to meet you.'"

It was a lot of words for a suddenly shy little boy. But he said them, "'Lo, Gamma. Nice to meet you," with his face still smashed into Rule's neck.

"And it's a delight to meet you, as well." Adrienne loosed that husky musical laugh again.

And then Trevor's dad was taking Sydney's hand. "A Texas girl," he said in a voice as smooth and rich and deep as his son's. "Always a good choice."

Sydney thanked him and thought that he was almost as good-looking as his wife. No wonder Rule was drop-dead gorgeous. How could he be otherwise with a mom and dad like these two?

They all sat down. The severe-looking woman reappeared and offered cocktails. They sipped their drinks and Evan wanted to know about her parents. So she told them that she had lost them very young and been raised by her grandmother. They were sympathetic and admiring, of her Grandma Ellen and of the successes Sydney had achieved in her life. They knew she was an attorney and asked about her work. She explained a little about her experiences at Teale, Gayle and Prosser.

The talk shifted to Rule and the progress on his various projects. It was a bit formal, Sydney thought. But in a nice, getting-to-know-you sort of way.

She was so proud of Trev. He sat quietly on Rule's lap for a while, watching the adults, big dark eyes tracking from one face to another. Both Adrienne and Evan seemed taken with him. They kept sending him warm looks and smiles.

Slowly, Trev was drawn in. After twenty minutes or so, during a slight lull in the conversation, he held out his arms to Adrienne. "Gamma. Hug, please."

Adrienne reached for him and Rule passed him over. She wore a gorgeous designer jacket and a silk dress underneath. Sydney worried a little that Trev would drool on Her Highness's lovely outfit.

But Adrienne didn't seem concerned. She hugged him and kissed his cheek and he allowed it, all shyness fled.

Lani appeared about half an hour into the visit, ushered in by the thin woman. After a brief introduction, she took Trevor with her back to their rooms.

The rest of them went in to dinner, where they were joined by two of Rule's brothers—Maximilian, the heir apparent, who'd come up from his villa to meet Rule's bride, and Alexander, the one who'd been a prisoner in Afghanistan.

Sydney liked Maximilian from the first. He was almost as handsome as Rule and he seemed to her to be a kind man, and very charismatic. He had sad eyes, though. She remembered what Rule had told her, about Max losing his wife in a water-skiing accident, and wondered if he was still grieving the loss.

It was difficult to like Alex. He was darkly handsome like the rest of the family, but more powerfully built and very quiet. He seemed…angry. Or perhaps sunk in some deep depression. Sydney supposed his attitude wasn't all that surprising. She imagined that being kept prisoner by terrorists would give anyone a bad attitude. But she could easily see why he and Princess Lili didn't get along. Sydney doubted that Alex got along with anyone.

Rule's other brother, Alex's twin, Damien, was something of a jet-setter. He was off on a friend's yacht. Two of his sisters, the youngest and second-youngest, Rory and Genevra, were away at school. Alice and Rhiannon were at an event in Luxembourg. And the oldest sister, Arabella, had gone to Paris. When they were home from school, Rory and Genevra still lived at the palace. The three older sisters had their own villas.

Dinner was several courses. The food was delicious. There was wine. Excellent French wine. As she'd done since she first suspected she might be pregnant, Sydney took care to drink very little of it.

Later, back in their own apartment, she and Rule celebrated her move to Montedoro by making love—twice. Once, while standing up against the tall, beautifully carved bedroom doors. Very well hung, those doors, she'd teased, as he was moving so deliciously inside her. Those doors didn't rattle once no matter how enthusiastic they became.

Eventually, they got into bed, where they made love the second time. It was after that second time, when she lay tucked close against him, that she told him, "Your mother says there's a large library here at the palace. A lot of books on Montedoran history. She also says the palace librarian can answer just about any question I might have about your country."

He stroked her arm in an idle, thoroughly distracting way. "Going to become a Montedoran scholar, are you?"

"I need to catch up, to understand how things work here, so I can begin to consider the kind of work I want to do, to discover where and how I can be most useful to my new country."

"So ambitious." He said it admiringly as he caressed her breast.

"You know I lose IQ points when you do that…"

He covered her breast with his warm hand. "I love your breasts."

"Good. You'll be seeing a lot of them as the years go by."

He caught her nipple between his fingers and squeezed. She sighed. He said, in a gentle, careful voice, "I believe they are fuller than they used to be."

It was the perfect opportunity to tell him that there was

a reason her breasts were bigger: she was having his baby. But instead, she elbowed him in the ribs. "Oh. You like them because they're *bigger*."

He nuzzled her hair. "*Are* they bigger?"

She got up on one elbow, where she could see his eyes. "Yes." She knew then. She could see it in his face, in the breathless way he looked at her. *He* knew already. She gave him a teasing smile. "My breasts are bigger. It's a miracle."

He asked, almost shyly, "Sydney…is it possible that you…?"

She smiled even wider. "That I *what,* Rule?"

"Don't tease me. Please." His eyes had gone dark as the middle of the night. It was a soft, yearning sort of darkness. He really, really wanted to know.

And her heart just…expanded. It felt suddenly twice as big as a moment before, as if it were pushing at her ribs, trying to make more room inside her chest. "I think so," she whispered. "I think we're going to have a baby."

He held her gaze, steadily, surely. "You *think?*"

"All the signs are there. The same ones I had with Trev. And my period is almost three weeks late. I haven't taken the home test I bought yet, though."

He touched her chin, brushed his thumb across her lips. "When will you take it?"

She smiled against his touch. "How about tomorrow morning?"

"Sydney…"

"What?"

"That's all. Just Sydney. Sydney, Sydney, Sydney…" He took her shoulders and pulled her close so he could kiss her. A long kiss, so tender. So thorough. So right.

She settled back onto his chest again, her chin on her arms. "So. You're happy?"

He stroked her hair. "I am. I can't tell you how happy."

"You're a good father. Trev is crazy about you."

He smoothed her hair, guided it behind her ear. "Trevor is everything I ever wanted in a son. And you are everything I ever dreamed of in a wife."

She remembered his mother's reaction at her first sight of Trev and smiled to herself. "Did you see how surprised your mother was when she met Trev? I'm guessing she noticed the uncanny resemblance between you two."

His hand stilled on her hair. "What makes you think that?"

Had something changed in his eyes?

She asked herself the question—and then decided it was nothing. He was stroking her hair again, regarding her so tenderly. She said, "I thought she looked pretty stunned when she saw him—you didn't notice the look on her face?"

"Hmm. Yes, I suppose…"

She asked, "Did you see it, or didn't you?" At his shrug, she frowned. "It was only there for a second and then gone. I guess I might have imagined it…."

He framed her face between his hands. "Come here. Kiss me."

She pretended to consider. "Well, now. That's a pretty tempting offer."

"Come here. Let me show you *how* tempting…."

She lifted up over him and then, with a happy sigh, settled her mouth on his. He was right. The kiss tempted her to kiss him some more.

Kisses led to more caresses and they made love again. Slowly. Beautifully.

She gazed up at his unforgettable face above her and thought how it just kept getting better between them. How there was nothing, ever, that could tear them apart.

* * *

An hour later, Rule lay in the dark staring up at the ceiling, listening to his wife's even, relaxed breathing beside him.

*His pregnant wife...*

He was sure of it. And so was she. The test in the morning was only a formality. She was having his baby.

His *second* baby.

And yes. He'd seen that look on his mother's face, too.

His mother had known that Trevor was his. One look at the boy and she'd had no doubt.

Very soon now, Her Sovereign Highness would be summoning him for a private talk. She was going to want to discuss the startling resemblance between him and his supposed stepson.

She would also be going after his father, working on the poor man. She would be insisting that her Prince Consort tell her the truth if he knew *anything* about what was really going on with Rule and his new wife and the child who was the mirror image of Rule at that age. One way or another, Adrienne would get to the bottom of it.

And as soon as she knew the truth, she was going to be after Rule to come clean with his wife. His mother was as much about integrity and truth in life and marriage as his wife was.

Rule felt the day of reckoning approaching. He had everything now: the woman he'd almost given up on finding; a healthy, happy, perfect son—and a second child on the way.

The only real question was how much he was going to lose when Sydney finally learned the truth.

Sydney's hands were shaking.

She turned her back to the test wand she'd left on the

corner of the serpentine marble counter and held both hands out in front of her. Yep. Her fingers trembled like leaves in the wind.

"Silly," she whispered. "So silly…" With a low moan, she lifted her hands and covered her face with them.

Really, there was no reason she should be such a bundle of nerves over this. She was either pregnant or not—and she just knew that she *was.* In a moment, the timer would go off and she would have proof.

No reason to be freaked out over it. No reason at all.

Rule tapped on the bathroom door. "Sydney? Are you all right in there?" As if in response to his question, the timer she'd set on the marble enclosure around the ginormous sunken tub started beeping. "Sydney! Are you all right?"

She went over and flipped the switch on the timer. It fell blessedly silent.

Rule didn't. "Sydney, my God!" He pounded on the door.

She whirled, stalked to the door, twisted the lock and flung it wide. He stood there looking fabulous, wearing nothing but a worried expression. Through clenched teeth she informed him, "I am *fine.* Get it? Fine."

He held out his arms.

With a cry, she threw herself into them, wrapped her arms around his lean bare waist and held on tight. She buried her face against his beautiful hard chest. "It's time," she said into that wonderful trail of hair that started between his perfect pectoral muscles and went on down, all the way to heaven. "I can't look."

"Sydney…" He said her name in that special way that only he could, so tenderly, so reassuringly. He stroked her back and then he took her chin and tipped it up. His dark eyes were waiting. "We both know what the test will say." He brushed a kiss across her lips.

Her mouth trembled. Sheesh. She was a trembling fool. She bit her lower lip to make it stop and then she said, "I *know* we both know. But what if we're wrong?"

He drew in a slow breath and dared to suggest, "Only one way to find out."

She shoved her face into his chest again, feeling like Trevor, the day before, clinging to his precious *Roo* upon meeting his new grandparents. "*You* look. I can't do it."

He chuckled. Oh, wasn't that just like a man? To chuckle at a time like this. He chuckled, and then he kissed the top of her head and then he gently took hold of her arms. "You will have to release me if you want me to be the one to look."

Reluctantly, with another soft cry, she let go of him and stepped out of his way. "Do it. Now."

He indicated the wand on the edge of the marble sink counter and slanted her a questioning glance.

She nodded.

He went to it, picked it up, frowned at it.

What? Suddenly, he couldn't read? She said, "The little window, it either says 'pregnant' or 'not pregnant.'"

He made a big show of squinting at the wand. "Well, now, let's see here…"

"I am going to grab that thing and hit you on the head with it. Just see if I don't."

He waved his free hand in a shushing kind of gesture. "All right, all right. It says… Well, what do you know? It says…"

"Rule. Stop it. I mean it. You stop it right now."

And then he dropped the wand in the sink, turned and grabbed her, lifting her high, spinning her around. She squealed and then she laughed. And then he was letting her down, slowly, the short silk nightie she wore catching, riding up, leaving her bare from the waist down. Her feet touched the floor toes-first.

Finally, he leaned close and whispered in her ear, "Pregnant."

*Pregnant.* The magic word.

She threw her arms around him. "Oh, I can't believe it. It's true. It's really true. We're having a baby. We really, really are. How amazing is that?"

"Extremely amazing," he agreed.

And then he scooped her high in his arms and carried her back to the bed where they celebrated the positive test result in their favorite way.

Later, Sydney asked Rule if he would mind keeping the news about the baby to themselves for a while. She was only a few weeks along, after all. No one else needed to know for another month or so, did they? She wanted a little time to have it be just between the two of them.

He kissed her. "However you want it."

"You're so easy."

"For you, anything," he told her. And he meant it.

He was feeling so good—about their life together, about the new baby, about everything—that he almost succeeded in forgetting his dread of the eventual moment of truth concerning Trevor.

And as that day went by and the one after that and his mother failed to invite him to a private audience, his dread diminished even further. For whatever reason, it appeared that his mother was not going to call him to task on the subject of his look-alike "stepson." Perhaps she'd decided that the similarity was merely a coincidence. Or perhaps she simply didn't wish to interfere.

Or possibly, she had come to the conclusion that when

Rule was ready to talk about it with her, he would. Whatever her rationale on the subject, she was staying out of it.

Rule was grateful. And relieved.

That first Tuesday, they got through the press conference where they formally announced their marriage to the press, though by then, their marriage was old news in the fast-moving world of the scandal sheets. Wednesday, they visited with the archbishop of Montedoro to request a wedding in the church. The archbishop was only too happy to help speed up the process. They took their expedited marriage classes on Thursday and Friday and then, quickly and quietly, on the Saturday after Rule moved his new family to Montedoro, he and Sydney were married in the church.

Rule had three days of meetings in Paris that next week. Sydney, Lani and Trevor stayed in Montedoro, where Sydney and his mother spent some time alone, getting to know each other a little. In bed the night of his return from France, Sydney said that his mother had asked her about Trevor's father.

Rule kept his voice light and easy. "And what did you tell her?"

"The truth, of course. That I wanted a family and I didn't have a man and so I went to a sperm bank. She took it well, I think. She smiled and said what a determined woman I am."

"And you are." He kissed her. She kissed him back. Nature took its course from there.

The next day, Liliana returned to Montedoro for a brief visit at HSH Adrienne's invitation. Sydney got to meet her. The two hit it off—the delicate Alagonian princess and Rule's tall, brilliant and determined American bride. Rule wasn't really all that surprised that they got along. They were both good women with tender hearts.

at last realized that his child and his true love "mattered more than royal blood." He'd returned to claim the woman he'd "always loved" and the child he'd "left behind."

There was even a long explanation of how Sydney had "put it out" that her child was the result of artificial insemination. But *The International Sun* wasn't fooled and neither should its readership be.

"A picture is worth a thousand words." And the pictures showed clearly that the child in question was Prince Rule's. At least the prince had "done the right thing" in the end and married the mother of his child. Since "all was well that ended well," *The Sun* wished the prince and his newfound family a lifetime of happiness.

It was ugly, stupid, insulting and riddled with clichés. Not to mention mostly fiction. However, within the general ridiculousness lurked the all-important twin kernels of truth: that Trevor was in fact Rule's child. And that Sydney really had used a sperm bank.

And that was why deciding what to do in response to this absurd flight of pseudo-literary fantasy was of the utmost importance. Really, anything he did—from making no statement, to issuing an outraged denial, to suing the paper for slander—could make things worse. And no matter what he did next, some ambitious and resourceful reporter might decide to dig deeper. It was possible that someone, somehow, could unearth the fact that he'd been a donor at Secure Choice. If that happened, and he still hadn't told Sydney his secret…

No. He couldn't allow even the possibility that it might go that far.

He was going to have to tell her. Now. Today. And when he did, she was going to be angry with him. More than angry. She might never forgive him. But if she found out in the tabloids, the likelihood was exponentially greater that he would lose her forever.

Rule shoved the tabloid aside, braced his elbows on the desk pad and put his head in his hands. He should have told her by now, should have told her weeks ago. Should have told her at the first....

*Should have told her...*

How many times had he reminded himself of that? A hundred? Five hundred?

And any one of those times, he *could* have told her.

Yes, it would have been bad.

But not as bad as it was going to be now.

He'd made his choice—the wrong choice—a hundred, five hundred, a thousand times. He'd wagered their happiness on that choice. He should have known better than that. Wagers were not a good idea—not when it came to the things that mattered most.

Half an hour later, Rule and his father met in Evan's private office. Also in the meeting were Donahue Villiers, a family advocate, or legal advisor, and Leticia Sprague, Palace Press Secretary. Leticia had been a trusted member of the palace staff for over twenty years.

They discussed what their next move should be and decided that Donahue would be in contact with the paper's legal department to discuss the lawsuit the family intended to file. He would also demand that the paper print a full retraction which, he would assure them, would go a long way toward mollifying Prince Rule once a settlement for damages was under discussion. Leticia suggested that Rule release a statement wherein he refuted the story and made his outrage at such ridiculous allegations crystal clear.

Rule's father said, "Before we proceed with any of this,

there must be a *family* conference. Her Sovereign Highness must be brought up to speed and given the opportunity to make her wishes in the matter known. So, of course, must Sydney."

And that was it. The meeting ended. Leticia and Donahue left Rule and his father alone.

Rule and Evan exchanged a long, bleak glance.

And then Evan said, "It's not the end of the world, son."

Rule started to speak.

Evan put up a hand. "You will get through this—with your family intact. And you *could* look on the bright side."

Rule made a scoffing sound. "So unfortunate that there isn't one."

"Of course there is. The article is absurd. *The International Sun* is going to end up looking very bad."

"It's a tabloid. It's not as though they care if they look bad."

His father regarded him solemnly for a moment. "What you did, becoming a donor, you did in a good cause. With an honest heart."

"I was an idiot. It was an act of rebellion against everything I am, everything we stand for as Bravo-Calabrettis."

Patiently, his father continued, "You would never have found the wife you wanted if not for your 'act of rebellion.' There would be no Trevor. And that you finally arranged to meet Sydney, that you pursued her and convinced her to make a family with you, that you became a real father to your son…I find that not only admirable, but truly honorable."

Rule wanted to grab the crystal paperweight from the corner of his father's desk and smash it against the far wall. "You don't understand. Sydney still doesn't know. I still haven't told her."

"Then you *will* tell her. Right away."

"I could lose her over this."

"I don't think you will. She loves you. She will stick by you."

Rule said nothing to that. What was there to say? Evan had been for honesty with Sydney from the first. His father wouldn't rub it in. That wasn't Evan's way. But the knowledge that his father had been right all along made this unpleasant discussion doubly difficult.

Evan said, "I think it's time that you told your mother the truth."

Rule gave him a scowl. "Wonderful."

His father said gently, "You can't put it off any longer. One look at that child and your mother was certain he had to be yours. She asked me what *I* knew. I told her that you had taken me into your confidence and gotten my agreement that I would keep your secret. I said that if she demanded it, I would tell her everything, I would break my word to you."

Rule affected an American accent. "Gee, thanks, Dad."

His father's chuckle had little humor in it. "Once she saw Trevor, I couldn't have kept her in the dark if she needed to know. She rules my heart as she rules this land. Maybe that's beyond your understanding."

Rule thought of Sydney. "No. I understand. I do."

"As it turned out, I didn't have to break my word to you. Your mother said that I should keep your secret for you, that she preferred to respect your wishes in the matter."

"So she only knows that Trevor is mine."

"As I said, I never told her the truth outright. She has drawn her own conclusions and kept them to herself. It's time that you were honest with her."

"I have to tell Sydney first."

"Of course you do."

* * *

Sydney wasn't in their apartment when Rule entered a few minutes later, the offending tabloid rolled in his hand. Lani told him that she'd gone to the palace library and would return by eleven.

It was ten forty-five.

Trevor tugged on his trouser leg. "Roo. Come. Play…"

His heart like a large ball of lead in his chest, he got down on the floor with his son, set the rolled paper to the side and helped him build a fanciful machine with a set of connectable plastic wheels and gears.

Trevor glanced up, a plastic propeller in his hand. "See, Roo. 'Peller." He stuck the propeller on a bright-colored stick and blew on it. Then he chortled in delight as it spun. Rule tried to laugh with him, but didn't succeed. Trevor bent to fiddle with the wheels and cogs some more, leaving Rule to stare down longingly at his dark head. Rule wanted to grab him and hold him close and never, ever let him go, as if by clutching his son tight, he might somehow escape the impending moment of truth.

But there was no escape. He was done with this lie.

It wasn't long before he heard brisk footsteps approaching from the foyer. And then Sydney was there, laughing, asking Lani how many pages she'd written.

"Three paragraphs," Lani grumbled, pushing her glasses higher on her nose. "It's just not coming together."

"It will," Sydney reassured her friend. "It always does."

"Yeah, well. I hope you're right."

"Persistence is the key."

Lani grumbled something else. Rule didn't make out the words over the rushing of his own blood in his ears as Sydney's footsteps came closer.

She stood above them. "What kind of fantastical machine is this?"

For a moment, Rule stared at her pretty open-toed shoes, her trim ankles. Then, forcing his mouth to form a smile, he lifted his head to meet her eyes. "You'll have to ask your son."

Trev glanced up. "Hi, Mama. I make a machine, a machine with a 'peller."

"I see that and I…" Her glance had shifted. Rule followed her gaze. The paper beside him had opened halfway, revealing the outrageous headline and half of the pictures. "What in the…?"

He grabbed the paper and swiftly rolled it up again. "We need a few moments in private, I think."

Both of her eyebrows lifted. And then she nodded. "Well, I guess we do."

Trev sat looking from Rule to Sydney and back again, puzzled by whatever was going on between the grown-ups. "Mama? Roo?"

Rule laid a hand against his son's cheek. "Trevor," he said, with all the calm and gentleness he could muster. "Mama and I have to talk now."

Trev blinked. "Talk?" He frowned. And then he announced, "Okay. I build machine!"

Lani put her laptop aside. "C'mon, Trev." She jumped up from the sofa and came to stand over them. "How 'bout a snack?" She reached down and lifted him into her arms.

Trevor perked up. "I want graham crackers and milk. In the *big* kitchen." He loved going down to the palace kitchens where the chefs and prep staff doted on him.

"Graham crackers and milk in the big kitchen it shall be."

"Thank you." Rule forced a smile for Lani as he rose from the floor.

With a quick nod, Lani carried Trevor to the door. He heard it close behind her.

He and Sydney were alone in the apartment.

She said, "Well?"

He handed her the tabloid.

She opened it and let out a throaty sound of disbelief. "Please. They have got to be kidding."

"Sydney, I—"

She put up a hand. "Give me a minute. Let me read this garbage."

So they stood there, on either side of Trevor's pile of bright plastic wheels and cogs, as she read the damned thing through. She was a quick study. It didn't take her long.

Finally, in disgust, she tossed the paper to the floor again. "That is the most outrageous bunch of crap I've ever read. Do you believe it? The nerve of those people. We're suing, right?"

"I believe that is the plan."

"You *believe?* It's a pack of lies. Not a single shred of truth in the whole disgusting thing."

"Well, and that's the problem, actually. There *is* some truth in it. More than a shred."

"What are you talking about?" She regarded him sideways. "Rule, what's wrong?"

He gulped—like a guilty child caught stealing chocolates. "There's something I really must tell you."

"What?" She was starting to look frightened. "Rule. *What?*"

"You should...sit down, I think." He tried to take her arm.

She eased free of his grip. "Okay. You're scaring me. Whatever it is, you need to just go ahead and say it."

"I will, of course. It's important and I should have told you long ago, right at the first."

"Rule." Now she was the one reaching for him. She took

hold of both of his arms and she looked him squarely in the eye. "Tell me. Whatever it is, tell me right now."

Was there any way to do this gently? He couldn't think of one. So he went ahead and just said it outright. "I was a donor for Secure Choice Cryobank. It was my profile you chose. Trevor is my son."

have said it, might have come clean about it, why now?" And then she blinked. He watched comprehension dawn in her eyes. "That stupid article. The pictures. You and Trevor, so much alike. It even mentions that I 'claim' to have used a sperm donor. You're afraid someone might do more digging, and reach the truth. You couldn't *afford* to keep me in the dark any longer."

What could he give her but shamefaced confirmation? "Yes. That's right."

"Oh, Rule. I thought it was bad, when you had to rush back here to Montedoro to explain yourself to Lili the morning after our wedding. I was…disappointed in you then. But I told myself that you had never lied to me. That you were a truly honest man, that you didn't have a lying bone in your body…" Though her eyes were dry, a sob escaped her. She covered her mouth again for a moment, hard, with her palm that time, as though she could stuff that sob back inside. When she had control of herself, she lowered her hand and said, "What a fool I was. How could I have *been* such a fool? All the signs were there. I saw them, *knew* them. And still you convinced me not to believe the evidence of my own eyes."

"I wanted to tell you," he heard himself say, and then cursed the words for their weakness.

Her sweet, wide mouth curved in a sneer. "Then why *didn't* you tell me?"

He said it right out. "At the first? Because I knew I wouldn't have a chance with you if I did."

"You couldn't know that."

"Of course I knew. After your wonderful grandmother who taught you that honesty was everything. After those bastards, Ryan and Peter…"

She waved her hand that time, dismissing his excuses.

"If not at the beginning, why not that night I asked you directly if you'd ever been a donor?"

"We've been so happy. I didn't want to lose that, our happiness. I didn't want to lose *you.*"

"Were you *ever* going to tell me?" Her voice was furious and hopeful, both at the same time.

He longed to reassure her. To give her more lies. But he couldn't. Some…line had been crossed. All that was left to him now was the brutal truth. "I don't think so. I kept telling myself I would, but there was always an excuse, to wait a little longer, to put it off. I kept choosing the excuses over telling you what you had a right to know."

"So, then." The hope was gone. Only her cool fury remained. "You were never going to tell me."

He refused to look away. "No. I wasn't willing to risk losing you."

"And how's that worked out for you, Rule?" Her sarcasm cut a ragged hole in his heart.

He answered without inflection. "As of now, I would have to say not very well."

She sat very still. She…watched him. For the longest, most terrible stretch of time. And then she said, "I don't get it. It makes no sense to me, that you would become a donor. Why did you? It's…not like you. Not like you at all."

"Does it matter now?"

"It matters to me. I am trying very hard to understand."

"Sydney, I—"

"Tell me." It was a command.

He obeyed. "My reasons were… They seemed real to me, seemed valid, at the time." How could he make her see when he still didn't completely understand it himself? He gave it his best shot. "I wanted…something. I wanted my life to be more than the sum of its parts. I wanted what my parents have together. What Max and Sophia had. It seemed I went through the motions of living but it wasn't a rich life. Not a full life. I enjoyed my work, but when I came home I wanted someone to come home to." He shook his head. "It makes no sense, does it?"

She was implacable. "Go on."

He tried again. "There were women. They were… strangers to me. I enjoyed having sex with them, but I didn't want them beyond the brief moments of pleasure they gave me in bed. I looked into their eyes and I didn't feel I would ever truly know them. Or they, me. I was alone. I had business, in Dallas. I spent over a year there."

"When?"

"Starting a little more than four years ago. I would go down to San Antonio on occasion, to visit with my family there. But it was empty, my life. I had only casual friends at that time. Looking back, I can't remember a single connection I made that mattered to me other than in terms of my business. Except for one man. He turned up at a party I went to. We'd been at Princeton together. We…touched base. Talked about old times. He'd been a donor. He'd come from an American public school, was at Princeton on full scholarship. He became a donor partly for the money—which, he told me, laughing, wasn't really much at all. But also because he said it did his heart good. It felt right, he said. To help a couple who had everything but the child they wanted most. That struck a chord with me. It seemed that being a donor would be…something good, that I could do, something I could give—but you're right. It wasn't like me. I'm a Bravo-Calabretti all the way to the core. I just refused to see that until it was too late and my profile was available to clients. Until two women had chosen me as their donor."

Those lightless eyes widened. "*Two* women?"

"The other didn't become pregnant. By the time she ordered again, I'd had my profile taken down."

"Just two of us? But…I can't believe more women wouldn't have chosen you."

Under other circumstances, he might have laughed. "My profile was only available for a short period of time. I withdrew my samples when I realized what an idiot I'd been to become a donor in the first place. Secure Choice was not the least happy with me. Our agreement was for ten pregnancies resulting in births or nine months of availability. I made arrangements to reimburse them for the money they would have made *if* I'd fulfilled my commitment with them. In the end, I simply couldn't…let it go. And that's the basic job of a donor. To *donate* and let it go."

She continued for him. "But that was never going to work for you, was it? You realized that you *had* to know—if there were children, if they were all right…" She understood him so well.

He said softly, "Yes. And that was my plan, after I found out that you had become pregnant. That was all I ever intended to do, make certain that you and the child were provided for. I swear it to you. As long as you and Trevor were all right, I was never going to contact you or interfere in your life in any way. I had assured myself that you were a fine mother *and* an excellent provider. I knew Trevor was healthy. I knew you would do all in your considerable power to make certain he had a good start in life."

"Yes. I could give him everything—except a father."

It was her first misreading of his motives. He corrected her. "I didn't think of it that way. I swear that I didn't."

She crossed her long, slim legs, folded her hands tightly

in her lap and accused, "Oh, please. You are all about being a father. We both know that."

Her words hit him like blows.

They were much too true.

And they proved all over again what a hopeless idiot he'd been to become a donor in the first place, how little he'd understood his own mind and heart.

"All right," he said. "I'm guilty. Guilty in a hundred ways. It *is* important to me. That my child have a father."

"So you set out to see that he did."

He felt, somehow, like a bug on a pin under the cool regard of those watchful eyes of hers. And in the back of his mind a cruel voice would not stop whispering, *You have lost her. She will leave you. She will leave you now.* Somehow, no matter what happened, he had to make her see the most basic motivation for his actions concerning her. "No. I swear to you, Sydney. It wasn't…that way. It was *you*."

"Oh, please."

He repeated, insisted, "*You*. It was you. Yes, Trevor mattered. He mattered more than I can say. But *you* were the starting point. I pursued *you,* not my son. I lied, yes, by omission. I never told you why I happened to be in that parking lot outside of Macy's that first day we met. That it was because of you that I was there, in the first place. Because you fascinated me. So bright and capable. So successful. And apparently, so determined to have a family, with or without a man at your side. I told myself I only wanted to see you in the flesh, just one time. That once I'd done that, I could let you go, let Trevor go. Return here to Montedoro, make my proposal to Lili…"

"You were lying to *yourself*."

"Yes. The sight of you that first time, getting out of your car in the parking garage…the sight of you only made me realize I had to get closer, to see you face-to-face, to look in your eyes. To hear your voice, your laugh. I followed you into the store. And as soon as you granted me that adorable, disbelieving sideways glance while you pretended to read a price tag on a frying pan, I knew that there had to be more. Every word you spoke, every moment in your presence, it only got worse. Stronger. I swear to you, I didn't set out to seduce and marry you."

She made another of those low, scoffing sounds.

And he was the one putting up a hand. "Yes," he confessed, "it's what I did in the end. But it started with *you*. It was always about you. And by that first evening we spent together, when we had dinner at the Mansion, I knew I wanted you for my wife."

Her eyes were emerald-bright now. With tears.

The tears gave him new hope.

Hope she dashed by turning away and stealing a slow breath. When she faced him again, the tear-sheen was gone.

She said in the cold, logical voice of an accuser, "You had so many options. *Better* options than the ones you chose."

He didn't deny it. "I know. In hindsight, that's all so painfully clear."

"You could have asked to see me as soon as you managed to find out you'd been my donor. I *would* have seen you. I was as fascinated by the idea of you—of the man I had chosen as my donor—as you claim you were by me."

"As I *am* by you," he corrected. "And I had no reason to believe you would have been happy to see me. It seemed to me that the last thing a single mother really wants is a visit from a stranger who might try to lay a claim on her child."

"I had given permission for you to contact me. That should have been enough for you to have taken a chance."

"Yes. I see that, now that I know you. But I didn't know you then. I didn't know how you would react. And it seemed wrong for me to…interfere in your life."

"If you had sought me out at the beginning, you would have had more than two years until the marriage law went into effect. We would have had the time to get through all this garbage. *You* would have had time for the truth."

"Sydney, I know that. I see that now. But it's not what I did. Yes, I should have been braver. I should have been… truer. I should have taken a chance, arranged to meet with you early on. But I hesitated. I hesitated much too long. I see that. And by the time I acted, I was down to the wire."

"Wire or not," she said, refusing to give him an inch, as he'd known that she would, "you owed it to me to tell me the truth before you asked me to marry you. You owed that to me then, at the very least."

"I know that. We've already been through that. But by then there was all you had told me about how you valued honesty."

"So you should have been honest."

"And what about Ryan and Peter? What about your distrust of men? You would have assumed right away that I was only after Trevor."

She looked at him unwavering. "Telling me the truth was the right thing to do."

"Yes. And then I would have lost you. You were not about to give a third man the benefit of the doubt. It was too big a risk. We were getting along so beautifully. I couldn't stand to lose you when I'd only just found you. Are you going to deny that I *would* have lost you?"

"No. You're right. At that time, I…didn't know you well enough. I would have broken it off for a while, slowed things down between us. I would have needed more time to learn to trust you."

"You would have needed longer than I could afford."

She made a low sound. "Because of the Prince's Marriage Law."

"Yes."

"You're telling me you were trapped." She spoke with disdain.

"No. I'm telling you that I knew what I wanted, at last. After all the years of being so sure I would never find it, find *you*. I wanted you. I wanted our child. And I wanted my inheritance, too. I made choices to give myself— and us—the best chance that we could both get what we wanted."

"And you kept making choices. Kept making the *same* choice. To lie to me. Over and over and over again. Since our marriage, I can't even count the times when you could have made a different choice."

"I know it. And we're back to the beginning again. Back to where I remind you that we have been so happy, and that telling you the truth would have destroyed our happiness, back to where I say I did what I did because I couldn't bear to lose you."

She stood up. And then, looking down at him, she said, "In making the choice to lie to me, you stole *my* choices. You treated me like a child, someone not fully responsible, someone unable to deal with the facts and make reasonable decisions based on all the available information. For generations, men did that to women, treated them as incompetent, as unable to face reality and make rational choices. Treated them as possessions rather than thinking human beings. I will not be treated as your possession, Rule, no matter how prized. Do you understand?"

He did understand. And at that point, there was nothing left for him but to admit the wrong he'd done her—done them both—and pay the price for it. "Yes. I understand."

"It matters. That you believe in me. That you trust me. That you treat me as your equal."

"And I see that," he said. "I do."

"But given the same set of circumstances, you would lie to me all over again—don't you tell me that you wouldn't."

He wanted to deny it. But somehow, he couldn't. And his denial wouldn't matter anyway. He couldn't undo what he'd done. What mattered now was that, no matter what the circumstances, he wouldn't lie to her again. "I simply didn't want to lose you. That's all. I lied because I was certain the truth would cost me what we have together. And now, you can be assured I see that I made the wrong choice. I swear I'll never lie to you again." Her face was set against him. He shook his head. "But then, I look at you and I see that it doesn't matter what I promise you. I see in your eyes that I'm going to lose you anyway."

Her cold expression changed. She looked…puzzled. And also disbelieving. And then she actually rolled her eyes. "Of course you're not going to lose me, Rule."

He gaped at her, convinced he couldn't have heard her right. "What did you just say?"

"I said you're not going to lose me. I would never leave you. I'm your wife and I love you more than my life. But I am not the least happy with you. And I'm not going to hide how I feel about this, or pretend to get past it when I'm *not* past it. You may end up wishing that I *would* go."

"My God," he said, hope rekindled, catching fire. "I would never wish for you to go. You have to know that."

"We'll see."

He rose. His arms ached to reach for her. But her expression signaled all too clearly the reception he would get if he tried. "I want our marriage," he said, and longed to give her words back to her. *I love you more than my life.* But it seemed wrong to speak of his love now, wrong and cheap. So instead, he said, "I want only you, always. That isn't going to change, no matter what you do, no matter how angry you are at me."

"We'll see," she said again. And for a moment, he saw the sadness in her eyes. Men had disappointed her before. And now he was just like the others.

Except he wasn't. He refused to be.

Whatever it took, he would be more, better, than he had been until now. Whatever the cost, he would win back her trust again and reclaim his right to stand at her side.

She was watching him, assessing him. "How much do your parents know?"

"My father knows everything. I confided in him. But my mother knows nothing—beyond being certain that Trevor is my son as well as yours."

"You told her?"

"No. She guessed that he was mine the moment she saw him. She asked my father what he knew. He offered to betray my confidence and tell her everything. She didn't think that would be right, so she declined his offer to break his word to me."

"I do like your mother."

"Yes," he said dryly. "Like you, she is thoroughly admirable—and you remind me I need to speak with her."

She indicated the tabloid she'd tossed to the floor and asked him wearily, "About all this?"

He nodded. "By now, she'll have had her morning look at the newspapers, including *The Sun.* I have to go to her and explain."

Sydney said, "We'll go together."

It was more than he'd hoped for. Much more. "Are you sure?"

"I'll just leave a note for Lani."

They met with his mother in the apartments she shared with his father. It was just the four of them—Adrienne, Evan, Rule and Sydney.

Rule told the whole story all over again. His mother's face remained unreadable throughout.

When he was done at last, she turned to Sydney. "I am so sorry that my son misled you."

Sydney replied with a slow nod. "Yes. I am, too."

Rule stared straight ahead. He felt like the bad child in school, sent to the corner to sit on a stool facing the wall and contemplate the terrible extent of his transgressions.

His mother said, "All right. Where are we now in terms of dealing with *The International Sun* and their absurd pack of lies?"

His father outlined the brief earlier meeting with Leticia and Donahue, concluding with, "To start, at least, Donahue will demand a retraction."

His mother looked at Rule, at Sydney, and then at Rule again. "Would a retraction satisfy you two?"

*Satisfy me?* Rule thought. Hardly. What would satisfy him was to have his wife once again look at him with affection and desire, to have her forgiveness. "That would be fine," he said, not caring in the least anymore about the damned tabloid story.

"It's *not* fine with me," Sydney said.

He glanced at her, took in the tightness of her mouth, the spots of hectic color high on her cheeks. She was as furious at the tabloid as she was at him. It hurt him, to look at her. It made him yearn for the feel of her skin under his hand, for the pleasure of simply holding her. Despair dragged at him. She'd said she wouldn't leave him.

But how long would it be before she allowed him to hold her again?

Sydney went on, "The retraction, yes. Absolutely. They should *start* with a retraction. And then we should sue their asses off."

"Their asses," his mother repeated, exchanging a glance with his father. "I do admire your enthusiasm, Sydney."

"It's an outrage." Sydney pressed her lips more tightly together. She blew out a hard breath through her nose.

His mother said, "I agree. And we will have a retraction."

"It's not enough," Sydney insisted. "That article is a gross misrepresentation of Rule's integrity, of his character. Rule would never simply walk away and desert a woman who was pregnant with his child. Never."

Rule realized he was gaping at her again. He couldn't help it. She astonished him. As infuriated as she was at him, she still defended him. He reminded her gently, "Sydney. It's just a silly tabloid story. It doesn't matter."

Her eyes were green fire. "Of course it matters. It's a lie. And they deserve to have their noses rubbed in it. I think we should hold a press conference and tell the world what liars they are. I think we need to tell the world the truth."

*Tell the world the truth.* She couldn't be serious.

He said, with slow care, "You want me to tell the world that I was your sperm donor? That it took me more than two years to get up the nerve to approach you? That when I did, I didn't tell you I was your child's father, but instead seduced you and got you to marry me under false pretenses?"

"Yes," she said hotly. "That's what I want from you, Rule. I want you to tell the truth."

For the first time on that awful day, he felt his own anger rising. It was all coming much too clear. "You want to see me humiliated. And it's not enough for you that *The Sun* should make me look like a fool. You want to see me make a fool of *myself.*"

She sucked in a sharp breath and put her hand to her throat. "No. No, that's not it. That's not what I meant."

He told her icily, "Of course it's what you meant."

"Oh, Rule," she said softly after several seconds had passed. "You don't get it. You don't get it at all."

He said nothing. He had nothing to say.

Finally, his mother spoke softly. "Whatever action the two of you decide to take, you have our complete support. I can see this is something the two of you must work out between yourselves."

## Chapter Fourteen

But Rule and Sydney didn't work it out. They returned to their apartment—together, but not speaking.

That night, Rule slept in the small bedroom off the master suite. He lay alone in bed in the darkness and realized he wasn't angry anymore.

He missed his anger.

It was a lot easier to be furious than it was to be ashamed.

Now his anger had left him, he could see that for Sydney it was as it had always been; it was about honesty. She saw that insane press conference of hers as a way to clear the air once and for all, to lay the truth bare for everyone to see. She saw it as a way to beat *The International Sun* at its own game. She was an American, an egalitarian to the core.

She didn't have generations of proud, aristocratic Calabretti ancestors behind her, staring down their formidable noses, appalled at the very idea that one of their own would even consider getting up in a public forum and explaining his shameful personal shortcomings to the world at large.

Such things were not done.

A Calabretti had more pride than that.

*He* had more pride than that. Too much pride. He could see that now.

He was not about to tell the world the unvarnished truth about his private life. Even if he'd behaved in an exemplary fashion, that would have been extraordinarily difficult for him.

But his behavior had not been exemplary. Far from it.

He'd been an imbecile. On any number of levels. And it just wasn't in him, to stand up and confess his own idiocy to the world.

The next day was as bad as the one before it. He and Sydney were polite with each other. Excruciatingly so. But they hardly spoke.

In his office, the phone rang off the hook. Every newspaper, every magazine, every radio and TV station wanted a few brief words with Prince Rule. He declined to speak with any of them.

And he stayed another night in the extra room. And then another after that.

The weekend went by. He spent time with his son. He and Sydney continued to speak to each other only when necessary.

Monday evening they had a meeting with Jacques Fournier, the architect they'd chosen, about the renovations at the villa. Sydney sent Rule an email about that on Monday afternoon.

An email. She was one room away, but she talked to him via email.

Do you want me to contact Fournier and tell him we won't be available tonight?

He zipped her off a one-word reply. Yes.

She didn't email back to update him on her conversation with Fournier. Just as well. He didn't really care if the architect was annoyed with them for backing out on him.

What he cared about was making things right with his wife. Unfortunately, he had no idea how to do that.

Or if he *did* have an idea, he had altogether too much pride to go through with it.

That evening, she surprised him.

She came and hovered in the doorway to his little room. Hope flared in him yet again, that this might mean she was ready to forgive him. But her face gave him nothing. She seemed a little nervous, maybe. But not like a woman on the verge of offering to mend a serious breach.

"I called Fournier," she said.

He set the book he'd been trying to read aside. "Thank you," he said stiffly.

"Fournier said it was fine, to call and reschedule when we were…ready." Her sweet mouth trembled.

He wanted to kiss the trembling away. But he stayed in the room's single chair, by the window. "All right."

"I'm sure he must know about that awful article…"

He shrugged. "He might."

"Not that it matters what the architect knows." She looked tired, he thought. There were dark smudges beneath her eyes. Was she having as much trouble sleeping as he was? "I… Oh, Rule…" She looked at him sadly. And pleadingly, too.

His heart beat faster. Hope, that thing that refused to die, rose up more strongly, tightening his throat, bringing him to his feet. "Sydney…"

And then she was flying at him and he was opening his

arms. She landed against his chest with a soft cry and he gathered her into him.

He held on tight.

And she was holding him, too, burying her face against his chest, sighing, whispering, "Rule. Oh, Rule…"

He lowered his lips to her fragrant hair, breathed in the longed-for scent of her. "Sydney. I'm so sorry. I can't tell you…"

"I know." She tipped her head back, met his waiting gaze.

Crying. She was crying, tears leaking from the corners of her eyes, leaving shining trails along her flushed cheeks.

"Don't cry." He caught her face between his hands, kissed the tear trails, tasted their salty wetness. "Don't cry…"

"I want…to make it right with us. But I don't know how to make it right."

He dared to kiss her lips—a quick kiss, and chaste. It felt wrong to do more. "You can't make it right. *I* have to do that."

She searched his face. "Please believe me. I didn't suggest that press conference to shame you. I swear that I didn't."

"I know. I see that now. Don't worry on that account. I understand."

"I'm…too proud, Rule. I know that I am. Too proud and too difficult. Too demanding."

He almost laughed. "Too prickly."

"Yes, that, too. A kinder, gentler woman would be over this by now."

He kissed the tip of her nose. "I have no interest in a kinder, gentler woman. And you are not *too* anything. You are just right. I wouldn't want you to change. I wouldn't want you to be anyone other than exactly who you are, any way other than *as* you are."

"Oh, Rule…"

He took her shoulders and he set her gently away from him. "Can you forgive me?"

She shut her eyes, drew herself taller. And when she looked at him again, she wasn't smiling. "I'm working on it."

Strangely, he understood exactly what she was telling him. "But you aren't succeeding. You can't forgive me."

She pressed her lips together, shook her head—and started to speak.

He touched his thumb to her mouth. "Never mind. You don't have to answer. Let it be for now."

"I miss you so. It hurts so much."

Gruffly, he confessed, "For me, as well."

She took his hand, placed it on her still-flat belly where their unborn baby slept. The feel of that, the *promise* of that, came very close to breaking his heart. "We have to… do something," she said in a torn little whisper. "We have to…get past this. For the baby's sake, for Trev. For the sake of our family. *I* have to get past this, put aside my hurt pride that you lied, that you didn't treat me as an equal. We have to move on. But then, just when I'm sure I'm ready to let it go, I think of all the times you might have told me, might have *trusted* me…."

"Shh," he said, and lifted his hand to touch her lips again with the pads of his fingers. "It's not your fault. I am to blame and I know that I am. Somehow, I have to make you believe that I do trust you in all ways, that no matter how hard the truth is, I will never lie to you again."

She let out a ragged breath. "I *want* to believe you. So much."

He lifted her chin and brushed one last kiss against her

tender lips. "Give it time," he said again. "It will be all right." Would it? *Yes.* Somehow, he would make it so.

She stepped back and turned. And then she walked away from him.

It was the hardest thing he'd ever done, to watch her go. To *let* her go. Not to call her back. Not to grab her close again and kiss her senseless. Not to promise them both that everything was all right now.

When it wasn't all right.

When something precious was shattered between them and he knew that, as the one who had done the shattering, it was up to him to mend a thousand ragged pieces into one strong, shining whole.


The answer came to him in the middle of the night.

Or rather, in the middle of the night, he accepted fully how far he was actually willing to go to make things right.

He saw at last that he was going to have to do the one thing he'd said he would never do, the thing he'd rejected out of hand because it was going to be difficult for him. More than difficult. Almost impossible.

But whatever it took, if it gave him a chance of healing the breach between him and Sydney, he was ready to do it. To move forward with it.

And to do so willingly.

*Pride,* she had told him. *"I'm...too proud, Rule."*

They were alike in that. Both of them prideful, unwilling to bend.

But he would bend, finally. He would do the hardest thing. And he would do it gladly.

If it meant he would have her trust once more. If it meant she would see and believe that he knew the extent of the damage he'd done and would never do such a thing again.

He turned over on his side and closed his eyes and was sound asleep in seconds.

When he woke, it was a little after seven. He rose, showered, shaved and dressed.

Then he went to his office where he got out the stack of messages he'd tossed in the second drawer of his desk—the stack he'd known somewhere in the back of his mind he shouldn't throw away.

Not yet. Not until he was willing to make his choice from among them.

He chose quickly. It wasn't difficult: Andrea Waters. She was a household name, with her own prime-time news and talk show in America, on NBC. She was highly respected as a television journalist. And women loved her warmth and personal charm.

He glanced at his watch.

It would be two in the morning in New York City. He would have to wait several hours until he could call her producer back himself.

He made the first call to New York at two that afternoon. By seven that evening, everything was arranged.

Now, to tell his wife. He rose from his desk to go and find her.

And there was a tap at his office door.

At seven in the evening? Caroline wasn't out there to screen visitors. He'd told her she could go more than an hour before.

He called, "It's open. Come in."

The door opened—and Sydney slipped through.

He stood there behind his desk and drank in the sight of her. His lady in red—a red skirt and silk blouse, wearing those pearls her grandmother had given her, her hair smooth on her shoulders, just as it had been that first day, when he saw her in the parking garage and couldn't stop himself from following her inside. She looked tired, though. There were still shadows under her eyes.

"I've been waiting to talk to you," she said. "I...couldn't wait any longer. I came to find you."

"It's been a busy day. I'm finished here now, though." He tried on a smile. "I was just coming to find *you*...."

Hesitantly, she returned his smile. "I hardly slept at all last night."

"I know how that goes." His voice sounded strange to his own ears—a little rusty, rougher than usual. "I haven't been getting a lot of sleep, either."

"I told you yesterday that I wasn't there yet, I...hadn't really forgiven you."

"And I said I understood. I meant what I said."

"Oh, but Rule..." Her smile widened. And all at once, her whole face had a glow about it. She hardly even seemed tired anymore. She had her hands folded in front of her. He thought she looked so young right then. A girl, an innocent. Looking at her now he would never have guessed that she'd given birth to his son, that she carried his second child under her heart. "Something happened," she said. "Something wonderful."

*Something wonderful.* His heart beat a swift tattoo beneath his ribs. "Tell me."

"I don't know. I...I was lying there, alone in our bed. It was almost one in the morning. I was thinking of how I missed you, beside me, in the dark. Thinking that I knew, I understood, why you had kept the truth from me. Objectively I could see how it must have been for you. Waiting too long to contact me, knowing you were up against the deadline of the marriage law. Telling yourself you were only waiting for the right moment to say the words. And then hearing about Ryan, about Peter. Fearing that if you told me the truth, I would suspect that you only wanted Trevor. And then, when you *didn't* tell me, I could see how it only got harder for you, how every day the truth became more and more impossible for you to reveal."

He shook his head. "None of which is any excuse."

She put her hands to her cheeks, as if to cool the hectic color in them. "I just want you to know that I *did* understand…I *do* understand, intellectually." She let her left hand drop to her side. Her right, she laid above her breast. "But my heart…my heart wanted you to trust in me. My heart wanted you to be bigger than your very realistic fears. My heart wanted you to give me the truth no matter the cost."

"And I should have trusted you," he said. "I was wrong. Very wrong. And I want you to stop torturing yourself because you can't forgive me."

She laughed then. A happy laugh, young and so free. And her eyes had that tear-shine, the same as the day before. She sniffed, swiped the tears away. "But that's just it. I was lying there, thinking about everything, how wrong things had gotten between us, how I wanted to work it out but my heart wouldn't let me. And all of a sudden, just like that…I saw *you.* I saw you, Rule. I…felt you, as though you were there, in our dark bedroom with me. And I saw that you love me and I love you and that's what matters, that's what makes it all worthwhile. And I didn't even need to think about forgiveness anymore. It just… happened. I let my anger and my hurt and my resentment go. I realized I do believe in you. I believe in your goodness and your basic honesty. I believe that you love me as I love you. I want…our family back. I want *us* back." She was crying again, the tears dribbling down her cheeks, over her chin.

"Sydney…" He was out from behind his desk and at her side in four long strides. "Sydney…"

She fell against him, sobbing. "Rule, oh, Rule…"

He wrapped his arms around her and held on tight. "Shh. Shh. It's all right. It's going to be all right…"

Finally, pressing herself close, she tipped her chin back and he met her shining, tear-wet eyes. "Rule. I love you, Rule."

"And I love you, Sydney. With all of my heart. You *are* my heart. I looked for you for far too long. I'm so glad I finally found you. I'm so glad what we have together is stronger than my lies." He lowered his head.

And he kissed her. A real kiss. A deep kiss. A kiss of love and tears and laughter. A kiss to reaffirm their life together. Again. At last…

That kiss went on forever. And still it wasn't long enough.

But finally, he lifted his head. He took her face between his hands and brushed away the tear tracks. "I think you're right. I think we're going to make it, after all."

"I know we will. I always knew—or at least, I kept promising myself that somehow, eventually, it would all work out."

"I was coming to find you when you knocked on the door."

She held his gaze, searching. "What? What is it?"

"You wanted me to call a press conference…."

"Yes. I see now that was probably a bad idea."

"At first, I though it was a bad idea, too. Mostly because of my pride."

"It's okay, Rule. Truly."

"But I reconsidered."

"You're kidding."

"No. I did reconsider—and I still decided against it."

"It's fine. I understand."

"Instead, I'm going to give Andrea Waters an exclusive interview."

She gasped. And then she made a sputtering sound.

He laughed then. "My darling, I believe you are speechless. I don't remember that ever happening before."

She groaned. "Oh, you…" And she gave him a teasing punch on the arm.

"Ouch!" He grinned.

"Really, Rule. You're not serious."

"Oh, yes I am. I'm going to tell the truth about you and me and our son. I'm going to tell it on *Andrea Waters Tonight*."

"Um. *Everything?*"

"Well, I think it would be acceptable to *manage* the message, at least to a degree."

She reached up, laid her hand on the side of his face. That simple touch meant so much to him. It was everything. To have her in his arms again, to feel her cool palm against his cheek, to know they were together, and that they always would be. "It isn't necessary," she said in a whisper. "It was too much for me to ask of you."

"No. It wasn't."

She touched his lips with her thumb. "Shh. Hear me out." She waited for his nod before she spoke again. "Yes, when it comes to us, to you and me, I demand total honesty. But I certainly don't expect you to share all your secrets with the rest of the world."

He took her hand, opened it, kissed the soft heart of her palm the way he'd always loved to do. "I think it should be possible to do this with dignity. With integrity."

"You can cancel. I'll be completely accepting of that."

He only shook his head and kissed her palm again.

She said, "Okay. If you're determined to do this…"

"Yes?"

"I want to be there, beside you, when Andrea Waters starts asking the questions."

He turned her hand over, kissed the backs of her fingers, one by one. "I was hoping you would say that."

"Are we going to New York?"

"No. She will come here, to Montedoro. There will be a tour of the palace as part of the broadcast. And then we'll sit down, the three of us, and chat."

"Chat." Sydney shivered.

"Are you cold, my darling?"

"With your arms around me?" Her green gaze didn't waver. "Never. But I *am* a little scared."

"Don't be. It's going to go beautifully. I'm sure of it."

"Kiss me, Rule."

And he did, for a very long time.

## Epilogue

Her Royal Highness Liliana, Princess of Alagonia, Duchess of Laille, Countess of Salamondo, sat alone in her bedroom in her father's palace.

She wore a very old, very large green The Little Mermaid T-shirt, bought on a trip to America years before—and nothing else. Perched cross-legged on her bed, she held a delicate black plate decorated with yellow poppies and piled high with almond cookies. Lili intended to eat every one of those cookies. It was her second plate of them. She'd finished the first plateful a few minutes before.

Also, close at hand, she had a big box of tissues. Already, she'd used several of those. The discards littered the bed around her.

She was watching the television in the armoire across the room. It was *Andrea Waters Tonight,* an American program. Andrea Waters was interviewing Rule and Sydney.

Lili thought the interview was absolutely wonderful. Such a romantic story. She'd had no idea. Rule, a sperm donor? She never would have imagined that, not in a hundred thousand years. And Sydney's little boy, Trevor—he was Rule's all along.

Of course, Lili should have guessed. The resemblance was nothing short of striking.

And didn't Sydney look adorable? She was such a handsome woman. And she sat so close to Rule, holding his hand. And the glances those two shared…

*That.* Yes. Exactly. Lili wanted that, what Rule and Sydney had. She wanted real love, strong love, true love, forever, with the right man.

Unfortunately, that she would ever find the right man was looking less and less likely. Especially after what had happened with Alex.

Really, how *could* she?

With Alex, of all people?

And now, just look at the mess she was in.

Lili ate another almond cookie, whipped out another tissue and blotted up tears. Unceremoniously, she blew her nose.

And then she sighed.

Rule and Sydney. They looked so happy. They *were* so happy. And Lili was happy *for* them.

Yes, it was true. She'd been something of a fool over Rule for all those years. He was so handsome and such a good man and he'd always treated her with warmth and affection. She'd let her vivid imagination carry her away. She'd dreamed of being Rule's bride.

She'd thought that she loved him. And she *did* love him. But now, at last, she understood that the love she felt for Rule wasn't the kind of love a woman feels for the man to whom she binds her life.

Again, Lili wondered if she would ever find that man.

It was beyond doubtful. Maybe even impossible, given her current condition.

Besides the cookies and the tissues, Lili also had her phone. It was on the bed beside her. She reached out and grabbed it and dialed the number she'd been putting off calling for too long now.

She waited, hardly daring to breathe, as the phone rang. And rang. Finally, an answering machine picked up.

Alex's recorded voice said, "I'm not available. Leave a message."

She waited for the beep and then she said, "Alexander. You are the most exasperating man." She wanted to blurt out the truth right then and there. But it wasn't a good idea. Not on the phone. "Read the letter I sent you," she said. "And then you'd better call me, Alex. We really do need to speak privately." She waited some more. Maybe he was there, listening. Maybe for once he'd behave like a reasonable person and pick up the phone.

But he didn't. She heard the click that meant the machine had disconnected her.

Very gently, she hung up.

And after that, she just sat there, not even crying anymore, not even wanting another almond cookie, feeling terrible about everything. Wondering what was going to happen when her father found out.

\* \* \* \* \*

*Watch for Lili and Alex's story,*
*THE PRINCE SHE HAD TO MARRY,*
*coming in November 2012,*
*only from Harlequin Special Edition.*

# THE ANNIVERSARY PARTY

Dear Reader,

I am a big believer in celebrating milestones, and for Special Edition, this is a big one! Thirty years… it hardly seems possible, and yet April 1982 was indeed, yep, thirty years ago! When I walked into the Harlequin offices (only *twenty* years ago, but still), the first books I worked on were Special Edition. I loved the line instantly—for its breadth and its depth, and for its fabulous array of authors, some of whom I've been privileged to work with for twenty years, and some of whom are newer, but no less treasured, friends.

When it came time to plan our thirtieth anniversary celebration, we wanted to give our readers something from the heart—not to mention something from our very beloved April 2012 lineup. So many thanks to RaeAnne Thayne, Christine Rimmer, Susan Crosby, Christyne Butler, Gina Wilkins and Cindy Kirk for their contributions to *The Anniversary Party*. The Morgans, Diana and Frank, are celebrating their thirtieth anniversary along with us. Like us, they've had a great thirty years, and they're looking forward to many more. Like us, though there may be some obstacles along the way, they're getting their happily ever after.

Which is what we wish you, Dear Reader. Thanks for coming along for the first thirty years of Special Edition—we hope you'll be with us for many more!

We hope you enjoy *The Anniversary Party*.

Here's to the next thirty!

All the best,

Gail Chasan
Senior Editor, Special Edition

## Chapter One
### by RaeAnne Thayne

With the basket of crusty bread sticks she had baked that afternoon in one arm and a mixed salad—*insalata mista,* as the Italians would say—in the other, Melissa Morgan walked into her sister's house and her jaw dropped.

"Oh, my word, Ab! This looks incredible! When did you start decorating? A month ago?"

Predictably, Abby looked a little wild-eyed. Her sister was one of those type A personalities who always sought perfection, whether that was excelling in her college studies, where she'd emerged with a summa cum laude, or decorating for their parents' surprise thirtieth anniversary celebration.

Abby didn't answer for a moment. She was busy arranging a plant in the basket of a rusty bicycle resting against one wall so the greenery spilled over the top, almost to the front tire. Melissa had no idea how she'd managed it but somehow Abby had hung wooden lattice from her ceiling to form a faux pergola over her dining table. Grapevines, fairy lights and more greenery had been woven through the lattice and, at various intervals, candles hung in colored jars like something out of a Tuscan vineyard.

Adorning the walls were framed posters of Venice and the beautiful and calming Lake Como.

"It feels like a month," Abby finally answered, "but actually, I only started last week. Greg helped me hang the lattice. I couldn't have done it without him."

The affection in her sister's voice caused a funny little twinge inside Melissa. Abby and her husband had one of those perfect relationships. They clearly adored each other, no matter what.

She wished she could say the same thing about Josh. After a year of dating, shouldn't she have a little more confidence in their relationship? If someone had asked her a month ago if she thought her boyfriend loved her, she would have been able to answer with complete assurance in the affirmative, but for the past few weeks something had changed. He'd been acting so oddly—dodging phone calls, canceling plans, avoiding her questions.

He seemed to be slipping away more every day. As melodramatic as it sounded, she didn't know how she would survive if he decided to break things off.

*Breathe,* she reminded herself. She didn't want to ruin the anniversary dinner by worrying about Josh. For now, she really needed to focus on her wonderful parents and how very much they deserved this celebration she and Abby had been planning for a long time.

"You and Greg have really outdone yourself. I love all the little details. The old wine bottles, the flowers. Just beautiful. I know Mom and Dad will be thrilled with your hard work." She paused. "I can only see one little problem."

Abby looked vaguely panicked. "What? What's missing?"

Melissa shook her head ruefully. "Nothing. That's the problem. I was supposed to be helping you. That's why I'm here early, right? Have you left anything for me to do?"

"Are you kidding? I've still got a million things to do. The chicken cacciatore is just about ready to go into the oven. Why don't you help me set the table?"

"Sure," she said, following her sister into the kitchen.

"You talked to Louise, right?" Abby asked.

"Yes. She had everything ready when I stopped at her office on my way over here. I've got a huge gift basket in the car. You should see it. She really went all out. Biscotti, gourmet cappuccino mix, even a bottle of prosecco."

"What about the tickets and the itinerary?" Abby had that panicked look again.

"Relax, Abs. It's all there. She's been amazing. I think she just might be as scarily organized as you are."

Abby made a face. "Did you have a chance to go over the details?"

"She printed everything out and included a copy for us, as well as Mom and Dad. In addition to the plane tickets and the hotel information and the other goodies, she sent over pamphlets, maps, even an Italian-English dictionary and a couple of guidebooks."

"Perfect! They're going to be so surprised."

"Surprised and happy, I hope," Melissa answered, loading her arms with the deep red chargers and honey-gold plates her sister indicated, which perfectly matched the theme for the evening.

"How could they be anything else? They finally have the chance to enjoy the perfect honeymoon they missed out on the first time." Abby smiled, looking more than a little starry-eyed. Despite being married for several years, her sister was a true romantic.

"This has to be better than the original," she said. "The bar was set pretty low thirty years ago, judging by all the stories they've told us over the years. Missed trains, lousy hotels, disappearing luggage."

"Don't forget the pickpocket that stole their cash and passports."

Melissa had to smile. Though their parents' stories always made their honeymoon thirty years ago sound dismal, Frank and Diane always laughed when they shared them, as if they had viewed the whole thing as a huge adventure.

She wanted that. She wanted to share that kind of joy and laughter and tears with Josh. The adventure that was life.

Her smile faded, replaced by that ache of sadness that always seemed so close these days. *Oh, Josh.* She reached into the silverware drawer, avoiding her sister's gaze.

"Okay. What's wrong?" Abby asked anyway.

She forced a smile. "Nothing. I'm just a little tired, that's all."

"Late night with Josh?" her sister teased.

Before she could stop them, tears welled up and spilled over. She blinked them back but not before her sharp-eyed sister caught them.

"What did I say?" Abby asked with a stunned look.

"Nothing. I just…I didn't have a late night with Josh. Not last night, not last week, not for the last two weeks. He's avoiding my calls and canceled our last two dates. Even when we're together, it's like he's not there. I know he's busy at work but…I think he's planning to break up with me."

Abby's jaw sagged and Melissa saw shock and some-thing else, something furtive, shift across Abby's expres-sion.

"That can't be true. It just…can't be."

She wanted to believe that, too. "I'm sorry. I shouldn't have said anything. Forget it. You've worked so hard to make this night perfect and I don't want to ruin it."

Abby shook her head. "You need to put that wacky idea out of your head right now. Josh is crazy about you. It's clear to anybody who has ever seen the two of you to-gether for five seconds. He couldn't possibly be thinking of breaking things off."

"I'm sure you're right," she lied. Too much evidence pointed otherwise. Worst of all was the casual kiss good-night the past few times she'd seen him, instead of one of their deep, emotional, soul-sharing kisses that made her toes curl.

"I'm serious, Missy. Trust me on this. I'm absolutely positive he's not planning to break up with you. Not Josh. He loves you. In fact…"

She stopped, biting her lip, and furiously turned back to the chicken.

"In fact what?"

Abby's features were evasive. "In fact, would he be out right now with Greg buying the wine and champagne for tonight if he didn't want to have anything to do with the Morgan family?"

Out of the corner of her gaze, Melissa saw that amaz-ingly decorated dining room again, the magical setting her sister had worked so hard to create for their parents who loved each other dearly. She refused to ruin this night for Abby and the rest of her family. For now, she would focus on the celebration and forget the tiny cracks in her heart.

She pasted on a smile and grabbed the napkins, with

their rings formed out of entwined grapevine hearts. "You're right. I'm being silly. I'm sure everything will be just fine. Anyway, tonight is for Mom and Dad. That's the important thing."

Abby gave her a searching look and Melissa couldn't help thinking that even with the worry lines on her forehead, Abby seemed to glow tonight.

"It is about them, isn't it?" Abby murmured. Though Melissa's arms were full, her sister reached around the plates and cutlery to give her a hug. "Trust me, baby sister. Everything will be just fine."

Melissa dearly wanted to believe her and as she returned to the dining room, she did her very best to ignore the ache of fear that something infinitely dear was slipping away.

"Hello? Are you still in there?"

His friend Greg's words jerked Josh out of his daze and he glanced up. "Yeah. Sorry. Did you say something?"

"Only about three times. I've been asking your opinion about the champagne and all I'm getting in return is a blank stare. You're a million miles away, man, which is not really helping out much here."

This just might be the most important day of his life. Who could blame a guy if he couldn't seem to string two thoughts together?

"Sorry. I've got a lot of things on my mind."

"And champagne is obviously not one of those things."

He made a face. "It rarely is. I'm afraid I'm more of a Sam Adams kind of guy."

"I hear you. Why do you think I asked you to come along and help me pick out the wine and champagne for tonight?"

He had wondered that himself. "Because my car has a bigger trunk?"

Greg laughed, which eased Josh's nerves a little. He had to admit, he had liked the guy since he met him a year ago when he first started dating Melissa. Josh was married to Melissa's sister, Abby, and if things worked out the way he hoped, they would be brothers-in-law in the not-so-distant future.

"It's only the six of us for dinner," Greg reminded him. "I'm not exactly buying cases here. So what do you think?"

He turned back to the racks of bottles. "No idea. Which one is more expensive?"

Greg picked one up with a fancy label that certainly looked pricey.

"Excellent choice." The snooty clerk who had mostly been ignoring them since they walked in finally deigned to approach them.

"You think so?" Greg asked. "We're celebrating a big occasion."

"You won't be disappointed, I assure you. What else can I help you find?"

Sometime later—and with considerably lightened wallets—the two of them carried two magnums of champagne and two bottles of wine out to Josh's car.

"I, uh, need to make one last quick stop," he said after pulling into traffic. "Do you mind waiting?"

"No problem. The party doesn't start for another two hours. We've got plenty of time."

When Josh pulled up in front of an assuming storefront a few moments later, Greg looked at the sign above the door then back at him with eyebrows raised. "Wow. Seriously? Tonight? I thought Abby was jumping the gun when she said she suspected you were close to proposing.

She's always right, that beautiful wife of mine. Don't tell her I said that."

Josh shifted, uncomfortably aware his fingers were shaking a little as he undid his seatbelt. "I bought the ring two weeks ago. When the jeweler told me it would be ready today, I figured that was a sign."

"You're a brave man to pick a ring out without her."

Panic clutched at his gut again, but he took a deep breath and pushed it away. He wanted to make his proposal perfect. Part of that, to his mind, was the element of surprise.

"I found a bridal magazine at Melissa's apartment kind of hidden under a stack of books and she had the page folded down on this ring. I snapped a quick picture with my phone and took that in to the jeweler."

"Nice." Greg's admiring look settled his stomach a little.

"I figure, if she doesn't like it, we can always reset the stone, right?"

"So when are you going to pop the question?"

"I haven't figured that out yet. I thought maybe when I take her home after the party tonight, we might drive up to that overlook above town."

"That could work."

"What about you? How did you propose to Abby?"

"Nothing very original, I'm afraid. I took her to dinner at La Maison Marie. She loves that place. Personally, I think you're only paying for overpriced sauce, but what can you do? Anyway, after dinner, she kept acting like she was expecting something. I *did* take her along to shop for rings a few weeks earlier but hadn't said anything to her since. She seemed kind of disappointed when the dessert came and no big proposal. So we were walking around on the grounds after dinner and we walked past this waterfall and pond she liked. I pretended I tripped over something and did a stupid little magician sleight of hand and pulled out the ring box."

"Did you do the whole drop-to-your-knee thing?"

"Yeah. It seemed important to Abby. Women remember that kind of thing."

"I hope I don't forget that part."

"Don't sweat it. When the moment comes, whatever you do will be right for the two of you, I promise."

"I hope so."

The depth of his love for Melissa still took him by surprise. He loved her with everything inside him and wanted to give her all the hearts and flowers and romance she could ever want.

"It will be," Greg said. "Anyway, look at how lousy Frank and Diane's marriage started out. Their honeymoon sounded like a nightmare but thirty years later they can still laugh about it."

That was what he wanted with Melissa. Thirty years—and more—of laughter and joy and love.

He just had to get through the proposal first.

## Chapter Two
### by Christine Rimmer

"Frank. The light is yellow. Frank!" Diana Morgan stomped the passenger-side floor of the Buick. Hard. If only she had the brakes on her side.

Frank Morgan pulled to a smooth stop as the light went red. "There," he said, in that calm, deep, untroubled voice she'd always loved. "We're stopped. No need to wear a hole in the floor."

Diana glanced over at her husband of thirty years. She loved him so much. There were a whole lot of things to worry about in life, but Frank's love was the one thing Diana never doubted. He belonged to her, absolutely, as she belonged to him, and he'd given her two beautiful, perfect daughters. Abby and Melissa were all grown up now.

The years went by way too fast.

Diana sent her husband another glance. Thirty years together. Amazing. She still loved just looking at him.

He was the handsomest man she'd ever met, even at fifty-seven. Nature had been kind to him. He had all his hair and it was only lightly speckled with gray. She smoothed her own shoulder-length bob. No gray there, either. Her hair was still the same auburn shade it had been when she married him. Only in her case, nature didn't have a thing to do with it.

A man only grew more distinguished over the years. A woman had to work at it.

The light turned green. Frank hit the gas.

*Too hard,* Diana thought. But she didn't say a word. She only straightened her teal-blue silk blouse, re-crossed her legs and tried not to make impatient, worried noises. Frank was a wonderful man. But he drove too fast.

Abby and her husband, Greg, were having them over for dinner tonight. They were on their way there now—to Abby's house. Diana was looking forward to the evening. But she was also dreading it. Something was going on with Abby. A mother knows these things.

And something was bothering Melissa, too. Diana's younger daughter was still single. She'd been going out with Josh Wright for a year now. It was a serious relationship.

But was there something wrong between Josh and Melissa? Diana had a sense about these things, a sort of radar for emotional disturbances, especially when it came to her daughters. Right now, tonight, Diana had a suspicion that something wasn't right—both between Melissa and Josh *and* between Abby and Greg.

"Remember Venice?" Frank gave her a fond glance.

She smiled at him—and then stiffened. "Frank. Eyes on the road."

"All right, all right." He patiently faced front again. "Remember that wonderful old hotel on the Grand Canal?"

She made a humphing sound. "It was like the rest of our honeymoon. Nothing went right."

"I loved every moment of it," he said softly.

She reminded him, "You know what happened at that hotel in Venice, how they managed to lose our luggage somewhere between the front desk and our room. How hard can it be, to get the suitcases to the right room? And it smelled a bit moldy in the bathroom, didn't you think?"

"All I remember is you, Diana. Naked in the morning light." He said it softly. Intimately.

She shivered a little, drew in a shaky breath and confessed, "Oh, yes. That. I remember that, too." It was one of the best things about a good marriage. The shared memories. Frank had seen her naked in Venice when they were both young. Together, they had heard Abby's first laugh, watched Melissa as she learned to walk, staggering and falling, but then gamely picking herself right back up and trying again. Together, they had made it through all those years that drew them closer, through the rough times as well as the happy ones....

*A good marriage.*

Until very recently, she'd been so sure that Abby and Greg were happy. But were they? Really? And what about Melissa and Josh?

Oh, Lord. Being a mother was the hardest job in the world. They grew up. But they stayed in your heart. And when they were suffering, you ached right along with them.

"All right," Frank said suddenly in an exasperated tone. "You'd better just tell me, Diana. You'd better just say it, whatever it is."

Diana sighed. Deeply. "Oh, Frank…"

"Come on," he coaxed, pulling to another stop at yet another stoplight—at the very last possible second. She didn't even stomp the floor that time, she was that upset. "Tell me," he insisted.

Tears pooled in her eyes and clogged her throat. She sniffed them back. "I wasn't going to do it. I wasn't going to interfere. I wasn't even going to say a word…"

He flipped open the armrest and whipped out a tissue. "Dry your eyes."

"Oh, Frank…" She took the tissue and dabbed at her lower lid. If she wasn't careful, her makeup would be a total mess.

"Now," Frank said, reaching across to pat her knee. "Tell me about it. Whatever it is, you know you'll feel better once we've talked it over."

The light changed. "Go," she said on a sob.

He drove on. "I'm waiting."

She sniffed again. "I think something's wrong between Abby and Greg. And not only that, there's something going on with Melissa, too. I think Melissa's got…a secret, you know? A secret that is worrying her terribly."

"Why do you think something's going on between Abby and Greg?"

"I sensed it. You know how sensitive I am— Oh, God. Do you think Abby and Greg are breaking up? Do you think he might be seeing someone else?"

"Whoa. Diana. Slow down."

"Well, I am *worried.* I am *so* worried. And Melissa. She is suffering. I can hear it in her voice when I talk to her."

"But you haven't told me *why* you think there might be something wrong—with Melissa, or between Abby and Greg. Did Abby say something to you?"

"Of course not. She wants to protect me."

"What about Melissa?"

"What do you *mean,* what about Melissa?"

"Well, did you *ask* her if something is bothering her?"

Another sob caught in Diana's throat. She swallowed it. "I couldn't. I didn't want to butt in."

Frank eased the car to the shoulder and stopped. "Diana," he said. That was all. Just her name.

It was more than enough. "Don't you look at me like that, Frank Morgan."

"Diana, I hate to say this—"

"Then don't. Just don't. And why are we stopped? We'll be late. Even with family, you know I always like to be on time."

"Diana…"

She waved her soggy tissue at him. "Drive, Frank. Just drive."

He leaned closer across the console. "Sweetheart…"

She sagged in her seat. "Oh, fine. What?"

"You know what you're doing, don't you?" He said it gently. But still. She knew exactly what he was getting at and she didn't like it one bit.

She sighed and dropped the wadded tissue in the little wastepaper bag she always carried in the car. "Well, I know you're bound to tell me, now don't I?"

He took her hand, kissed the back of it.

"Don't try to butter me up," she muttered.

"You're jumping to conclusions again," he said tenderly.

"Am not."

"Yes, you are. You've got nothin'. Zip. Admit it. No solid reason why you think Melissa has a secret or why you think Abby and Greg are suddenly on the rocks."

"I don't need a solid reason. I can *feel* it." She laid her hand over her heart. "Here."

"You know it's very possible that what's really going on is a surprise anniversary party for us, don't you?"

Diana smoothed her hair. "What? You mean tonight?"

"That's right. Tonight."

"Oh, I suppose. It could be." She pictured their dear faces. She loved them so much. "They are the sweetest girls, aren't they?"

"The best. I'm the luckiest dad in the world—not to mention the happiest husband."

Diana leaned toward him and kissed him. "You *are* a very special man." She sank back against her seat—and remembered how worried she was. "But Frank, if this *is* a party, it's still not *it.*"

"It?" He looked bewildered. Men could be so thick-headed sometimes.

Patiently, she reminded him, "The awful, secret things that are going on with our daughters."

He bent in close, kissed her cheek and then brushed his lips across her own. "We are going to dinner at our daughter's house," he whispered. "We are going to have a wonderful time. You are not going to snoop around trying to find out if something's wrong with Abby. You're not going to worry about Melissa."

"I hate you, Frank."

"No, you don't. You love me *almost* as much as I love you."

She wrinkled her nose at him. "More. I love you more."

He kissed her again. "Promise you won't snoop and you'll stop jumping to conclusions?"

"And if I don't, what? We'll sit here on the side of the road all night?"

"Promise."

"Fine. All right. I promise."

He touched her cheek, a lovely, cherishing touch. "Can we go to Abby's now?"

"I'm not the one who stopped the car."

He only looked at her reproachfully.

She couldn't hold out against him. She never could. "Oh, all right. I've promised, already, okay? Now, let's go."

With a wry smile, he retreated back behind the wheel and eased the car forward into the flow of traffic again.

Abby opened the door. "Surprise!" Abby, Greg, Melissa and Josh all shouted at once. They all started clapping.

Greg announced, "Happy Anniversary!" The rest of them chimed in with "Congratulations!" and "Thirty years!" and "Wahoo!"

Frank was laughing. "Well, what do you know?"

Diana said nothing. One look in her older daughter's big brown eyes and she knew for certain that she wasn't just imagining things. Something was going on in Abby's life. Something important.

They all filed into the dining room, where the walls were decorated with posters of the Grand Canal and the Tuscan countryside, of the Coliseum and the small, beautiful town of Bellagio on Lake Como. The table was set with Abby's best china and tall candles gave a golden glow.

Greg said, "We thought, you know, an Italian theme—in honor of your honeymoon."

"It's lovely," said Diana, going through the motions, hugging first Greg and then Josh.

"Thank you," said Frank as he clapped his son-in-law on the back and shook hands with Josh.

Melissa came close. "Mom." She put on a smile. But her eyes were as shadowed as Abby's. "Happy thirtieth anniversary."

Diana grabbed her and hugged her. No doubt about it. Melissa looked miserable, too.

Yes, Diana had promised Frank that she would mind her own business.

But, well, sometimes a woman just couldn't keep that

kind of promise. Sometimes a woman had to find a way to get to the bottom of a bad situation for the sake of the ones she loved most of all.

By the end of the evening, no matter what, Diana would find out the secrets her daughters were keeping from her.

Frank leaned close. "Don't even think about it."

She gave him her sweetest smile. "Happy anniversary, darling."

## Chapter Three
### by Susan Crosby

Abby Morgan DeSena and her husband, Greg, had hosted quite a few dinner parties during their three years of marriage, but none as special as this one—a celebration of Abby's parents' thirtieth wedding anniversary. Abby and her younger sister, Melissa, had spent weeks planning the Italian-themed party as a sweet reminder for their parents of their honeymoon, and now that the main meal was over, Abby could say, well, so far, so good.

For someone who planned everything down to the last detail, that was high praise. They were on schedule. First, antipasti and wine in the living room, then chicken cacciatore, crusty bread sticks and green salad in the dining room.

But for all that the timetable had been met and the food praised and devoured, an air of tension hovered over the six people at the table, especially between Melissa and her boyfriend, Josh, who were both acting out of character.

"We had chicken cacciatore our first night in Bellagio, remember, Diana?" Abby's father said to her mother as everyone sat back, sated. "And lemon sorbet in prosecco."

"The waiter knocked my glass into my lap," Diana reminded him.

"Your napkin caught most of it, and he fixed you another one. He even took it off the tab. On our newlywed budget, it made a difference." He brought his wife's hand to his lips, his eyes twinkling. "And it was delicious, wasn't it? Tart and sweet and bubbly."

Diana blushed, making Abby wonder if the memory involved more than food. It was inspiring seeing her parents so openly in love after thirty years.

Under the table, Abby felt her hand being squeezed and looked at her own beloved husband. Greg winked, as if reading her mind.

"Well, we don't have sorbet and prosecco," Abby said, standing and stacking dinner plates. "But we certainly have dessert. Please sit down, Mom. You're our guest. Melissa and I will take care of everything."

It didn't take long to clear the table.

"Mom and Dad loved the dinner, didn't they?" Melissa asked as they entered Abby's contemporary kitchen.

"They seemed to," Abby answered, although unsure whether she believed her own words. Had her parents noticed the same tension Abby had? Her mother's gaze had flitted from Melissa to Josh to Abby to Greg all evening, as if searching for clues. It'd made Abby more nervous with every passing minute, and on a night she'd been looking forward to, a night of sweet surprises.

"How about you? Did you enjoy the meal?" Abby asked

Melissa, setting dishes in the sink, then started the coffee-maker brewing. "You hardly touched your food."

She shrugged. "I guess I snacked on too many bread sticks before dinner."

Abby took out a raspberry tiramisu from the refrigerator while studying her sister, noting how stiffly Melissa held herself, how shaky her hands were as she rinsed the dinner plates. She seemed fragile. It wasn't a word Abby usually applied to her sister. The conversation they'd had earlier in the evening obviously hadn't set Melissa's mind at ease, but Abby didn't know what else to say to her tightly wrung sister. Only time—and Josh—could relieve Melissa's anxiety.

Abby set the fancy dessert on the counter next to six etched-crystal parfait glasses.

Melissa approached, drying her hands, then picked up one of the glasses. "Grandma gave these to you, didn't she?"

"Mmm-hmm. Three years ago as a wedding present. I know it's a cliché, but it seems like yesterday." Abby smiled at her sister, remembering the wedding, revisiting her wonderful marriage. She couldn't ask for a better husband, friend and partner than Greg. "Grandma plans to give you the other six glasses at your wedding. When we both have big family dinners, we can share them. It'll be our tradition."

Melissa's face paled. Her eyes welled. Horrified, Abby dropped the spoon and reached for her.

"I—I'll grab the gift basket from your office," Melissa said, taking a couple steps back then rushing out.

Frustrated, Abby pressed her face into her hands. If she were the screaming type, she would've screamed. If she were a throw-the-pots-around type, she would've done that, too, as noisily as possible. It would've felt *good.*

"I thought Melissa was in here with you," said a male voice from behind her.

Abby spun around and glared at Josh Wright, the source of Melissa's problems—and subsequently Abby's—as he peeked into the kitchen. He could be the solution, too, if only he'd act instead of sitting on his hands.

"She's getting the anniversary gift from my office," Abby said through gritted teeth, digging deep for the composure she'd inherited from her father.

Josh came all the way into the room. He looked as strained as Melissa. "Need some help?" he asked, shoving his hands into his pockets instead of going in search of Melissa.

"Coward." Abby began dishing up six portions of tiramisu.

"Guilty," Josh said, coming up beside her. "Give me a job. I can't sit still."

"You can pour the decaf into that carafe next to the coffeemaker."

Full of nervous energy, his hands shaking as much as Melissa's had earlier, he got right to the task, fumbling at every step, slopping coffee onto the counter.

"Relax, would you, Josh?" Abby said, exasperated. "You're making everyone jumpy, but especially Melissa. My sister is her mother's daughter, you know. They both have a flair for the dramatic, but this time Melissa is honestly thrown by your behavior. She's on the edge, and it's not of her own making."

"But it'll all come out okay in the end?"

The way he turned the sentence into a question had Abby staring at him. He and her kid sister were a study in contrasts, Melissa with her black hair and green eyes, Josh all blond and blue-eyed. They'd been dating for a year, were head over heels in love with each other, seeming to validate the theory that opposites attract. It was rare that they weren't touching or staring into each other's eyes, communicating silently.

Tonight was different, however, and Abby knew why. She just didn't know if they would all survive the suspense.

"Whether or not it all turns out okay in the end depends on how long you take to pop the question," Abby said, dropping her voice to a whisper.

"You know I'm planning the perfect proposal," he whispered back. "Your husband gave me advice, but if you'd like to add yours, I'm listening."

She couldn't tell him that Melissa thought he was about to break up with her—that was hers to say. But Abby could offer some perspective.

"Here's my advice, Josh, and it has nothing to do with how to set a romantic scene that she'll remember the rest of her life. My advice is simple—do it sooner rather than later." She spoke in a normal tone again, figuring even if someone came into the room, they wouldn't suspect what she and Josh were talking about. "When Greg and I were in college, I misunderstood something he said. Instead of asking him to clarify it, I stewed. And stewed some more. I blew it all out of proportion."

She dug deep into memories she'd long ago put aside. "Here's what happens to a couple at times like that. He asks what's wrong, and she says it's nothing. He asks again. She *insists* it's nothing. A gulf widens that can't be crossed because there's no longer a bridge between them, one you used to travel easily. It doesn't even matter how much love you share. Once trust is gone, once the ability to talk to each other openly and freely goes away, the relationship begins to unravel. Someimes it takes weeks, sometimes months, even years, but t happens and there's no fixing it."

"But you fixed it."

They almost hadn't, Abby remembered. They came so close to breaking up. "At times like that, it can go either way. Even strong partners struggle sometimes in a marriage."

"How do you get through those times?"

"You put on a smile for everyone, then you try to work t out alone together so that no one else gets involved."

"Don't you talk to your mom? She's had a long, successful marriage. She'd give good advice, wouldn't she?"

Abby smiled as she pictured her sweet, sometimes overwrought mother. "Mom's the last one I'd ask for advice," she said.

"I'm going to see what's taking so long," Diana said to her husband, laying her napkin on the table.

"Diana." Implied in his tone of voice were the words he didn't speak aloud—*Don't borrow trouble.*

"I'm sure they'll be right out," Greg said, standing, suddenly looking frantic. Her cool, calm son-in-law never panicked.

It upped her determination to see what was wrong. Because something definitely was.

"I'm going." Diana headed toward the kitchen. She could hear Abby speaking quietly.

"I adore my mother, but she makes mountains out of molehills. Greg and I are a team. We keep our problems to ourselves. And you know she would take my side, as any parent would, and that isn't fair to Greg. She might hold on to her partiality long after I've forgotten the argument. So you see, Josh, sometimes the best way to handle personal problems is to keep other people in the dark. Got it?"

"Clear as a bell."

Diana slapped a hand over her mouth and slid a few feet along the wall outside the kitchen before she let out an audible gasp. Her first born *was* keeping her in the dark about something, just as Diana had suspected. And Frank had pooh-poohed the whole thing.

Men just didn't get it. It wasn't called women's intuition for nothing—and she wasn't just a woman but a mother. Mothers saw every emotion on their children's faces, knew every body movement.

She'd *known* something was wrong with Abby. Now it'd been verified, not by rumor but by the person in question, no less. Abby and Greg were on the verge of separating. Her daughter had hidden their problems, not seeking advice from the one who loved her most in the world. Diana could've helped, too, she was sure of it.

*Keep other people in the dark.* The words stung. She wasn't "other people." She was Abby's mother.

And what about Melissa? What was her problem—because she definitely had one, something big, too. Had she confided in Abby?

Diana moved out of range, not wanting to hear more distressing words, not on the anniversary of the most wonderful day of her life. But she had to tell Frank what she'd learned, had to share the awful news with her own partner so that she could make it through the rest of the evening.

At least she could count on Frank to understand.

She hoped.

## Chapter Four
### by Christyne Butler

*D*on't think, don't feel.

*Just keep breathing and you'll get through this night unscathed.*

*Unscathed, but with a broken heart.*

Melissa squared her shoulders, brushed the wetness from her cheeks and heaved a shuddering breath that shook her all the way to her toes.

*There. Don't you feel calmer?*

No, she didn't, but that wasn't anyone's fault but her own.

She'd fallen in love with Josh on their very first date and after tonight, she'd probably never see him again.

The past two weeks had been crazy at her job. Trying to make it through what had been ten hours without her usual caffeine fix, having decided that two cups of coffee and three diet sodas a day weren't the best thing for her, had taken its toll. She'd been moody and pissy and okay, she was big to admit it, a bit dramatic.

Hey, she was her mother's daughter.

But none of that explained why the man of her dreams was going to break her heart.

Another deep breath did little to help, but it would have to do. Between helping her sister plan tonight's party and Josh's strange behavior, Melissa knew she was holding herself together with the thinnest of threads.

The scent of fresh coffee drifted through the house and Melissa groaned. Oh, how she ached for a hot cup, swimming in cream and lots of sugar.

Pushing the thought from her head, she picked up the gift basket that held everything her parents would need for a perfect second honeymoon in Italy. There was a small alcove right next to the dining room, a perfect place to stash it until just the right moment.

Turning, she headed for the door of her sister's office when the matching antique photo frames on a nearby bookshelf caught her eye.

The one on the right, taken just a few short years ago, was of Abby and Greg standing at the altar just after being presented to their friends and family as Mr. and Mrs. Gregory DeSena. Despite the elaborate setting, and the huge bridal party standing other either side of them, Melissa right there next to her sister, Abby and Greg only had eyes for each other. In fact, the photographer had captured the picture just as Greg had gently wiped a tear from her sister's cheek.

The other photograph, a bit more formal in monochrome colors of black and white, showed her mother and father on their wedding day. Her mother looked so young, so beautiful, so thin. Daddy was as handsome as ever in his tuxedo, his arm around his bride, his hand easily spanning her waist. The bridal bouquet was larger and over-the-top, typical for the early '80s, but her mother's dress…

Melissa squeezed tighter to the basket, the cellophane crinkling loudly in the silent room.

Abby had planned her wedding with the precision of an army general, right down to her chiffon, A-line silhouette gown with just enough crystal bling along the shoulder straps to give a special sparkle. Their mother looked the opposite, but just as beautiful wearing her own mother's gown, a vintage 1960 beauty of satin, lace and tulle with a circular skirt that cried out for layers of crinoline, a square-neck bodice and sleeves that hugged her arms.

A dress that Melissa had always seen herself wearing one day.

The day she married Josh.

Of course, she'd change into something short and sexy and perfect for dancing the night away after the ceremony, but—

"Oh, what does it matter!" Melissa said aloud. "It's not going to happen! It's never going to happen! Josh doesn't want to date you anymore, much less even think about getting down on one knee."

She exited the room and hurried down the long hall, tucking the basket just out of sight. They would have dessert, present the gift and then she would find a way to get Josh to take her home as soon as possible.

For the last time.

This was all Greg's fault.

As heartbreaking as it was, because she and Frank had always loved Greg, Diana knew deep in her heart that the man they'd welcomed in their home, into their hearts, was on the verge of walking out on their daughter.

How could Greg do this to Abby?

They were perfect together, complemented each other so well because they were so alike. Levelheaded, organized to a fault, methodical even.

Diana paused and grabbed hold of the stairway landing.

Could that be it?

Could Abby and Greg be too much alike? Had her son-in-law found someone else? Someone cute and bubbly who hung on his every word like it was gold?

Abby had mentioned a coworker of Greg's they'd run into one night while out to dinner. She'd said he'd been reluctant to introduce them, which seemed strange as the woman had literally gushed at how much she enjoyed working with Abby's husband when she'd stopped by their table.

The need to get to Frank, to squeeze his hand and have him comfort her, rolled over Diana. She needed him to tell her that everything would be all right, that she'd been right all along, and promise her they'd fight tooth and nail for their daughter so she didn't lose this beautiful home.

"Mom?"

Diana looked up and found Melissa standing there.

"Are you okay?" Melissa asked. "You look a little pale."

"I'm fine."

"You've got a death grip on the railing."

Diana immediately released her hold. "I just got a bit light-headed for a moment."

Concern filled her daughter's beautiful eyes. She motioned to the steps that led to the second floor. "Here, let's sit."

"But your sister is—"

"Perfectly capable of pulling dessert together all on her own," Melissa took her arm and the two of them sat. "Disgustingly capable, as we both know."

Diana sat, basically because she had no choice, taking the time to really look at her daughter. She'd been crying. Her baby suffered the same fate as she did when tears came—puffy eyes. And while Melissa had been acting strange during dinner, this was the first true evidence Diana had that something was terribly wrong.

"Darling, you seem a bit...off this evening." Diana kept her tone light after a few minutes of silence passed. "How is everything with you? You didn't eat very much tonight."

Melissa stared at her clenched hands. "Everything is just fine, mother. It's been a long week and I'm very tired."

"Yes, you said you've been working long hours. That's probably cut into your free time with Josh."

"Y-yes, it has, but I don't think that's going to be a problem much longer."

"What does that mean?"

Melissa rose, one hand pressed against her stomach. "It's nothing. You were right. We should get back into the dining room. You know how Abby gets when things go off schedule."

Yes, she did know. Oh, the divorce was going to upset Abby's tidy world, but that didn't mean that Diana wouldn't be there for her other daughter, as well. She still had no idea what was bothering her youngest, but she would find out before this evening was through.

And she would make things right.

For both her girls.

She'd easily found the time to attend Abby's debates, girl scout meetings and band concerts and never missed a dance recital, theatre production or football game while Melissa was on the cheerleading squad. Her daughters might be grown, but they still needed their mother.

Now more than ever.

Diana stood, as well. "Yes, let's go back and join everyone."

They walked into the room and Diana's gaze locked with Frank's. Her husband watched her every step as she moved around the table to retake her seat next to him. Thirty years of marriage honed his deduction skills to a razor-sharp point, and she knew that he knew she'd found out something.

"Okay, let's get this celebration going." Greg spoke from where he stood at the buffet filling tall fluted glasses with sparkling liquid, having already popped open the bottle. "Josh, why don't you hand out the champagne to everyone?"

Frank leaned in close. "What's wrong?"

Diana batted her eyes, determined not to cry as his gentle and caring tone was sure to bring on the waterworks. "Not now, darling."

"So you were worried for nothing?"

"Of course not. I was right all along—" She cut off her words when Abby came in with a tray of desserts in her hands. "Dear, can I help with those?"

"No, you stay seated, Mom. It'll only take me a moment to hand these out."

True to her words, the etched-crystal parfait dishes were soon at everyone's place setting and, immediately after, Josh placed a glass in front of Frank and Diana.

Diana watched as he then went back to get two more for Greg and Abby and one last trip for the final two glasses.

"Here you go, sweetheart." He moved in behind Melissa and reached past her shoulder to place a glass in front of her.

"No, thank you." Her baby girl's voice was strained.

"You don't want any champagne?" Josh was clearly

confused. "You love the stuff. We practically finished off a magnum ourselves last New Year's Eve."

Melissa shook her head, her dark locks flying over her shoulder. "I'm sure. I'll just h-have—" She paused, pressing her fingertips to her mouth for a quick moment. "I'd prefer a cup of coffee. Decaf, please."

Oh, everything made sense now!

The tears, the exhaustion, the hand held protectively over her still flat belly, the refusal of alcohol. Her motherly intrusion might have been late in picking up on Melissa's distress, but the realization over what her baby was facing hit Diana like a thunderbolt coming from the sky.

Her heart didn't know whether to break for the certain pain Abby was facing over the end of her marriage or rejoice with the news that she was finally going to be a grandmother!

Her baby was having a baby!

## Chapter Five
### by Gina Wilkins

During the year he and Melissa Morgan had been to-gether, Josh Wright thought he'd come to know her family fairly well, but there were still times when he felt like an outsider who couldn't quite catch on to the family rhythms. Tonight was one of those occasions.

The undercurrents of tension at the elegantly set dinner table were obvious enough, even to him.

Melissa had been acting oddly all evening. Abby and Greg kept exchanging significant looks, as though mes-sages passed between them that no one else could hear. Even Melissa and Abby's mom, Diana, typically the life of any dinner party, was unnaturally subdued and introspec-tive tonight. Only the family patriarch, Frank, seemed as steady and unruffled as ever, characteristically enjoying the time with his family without getting drawn in to their occasional, usually Diana-generated melodramas.

Josh didn't have a clue what was going on with any of them. Shouldn't he understand them better by now, considering he wanted so badly to be truly one of them soon?

He dipped his spoon into the dessert dish in front of him, scooping up a bite of fresh raspberries, an orange-liqueur flavored mascarpone cheese mixture and ladyfingers spread with what tasted like raspberry jam. "Abby, this dessert is amazing."

She smiled across the table at him. "Thank you. Mom and Dad had tiramisu the first night of their honeymoon, so I tried to recreate that nice memory."

"Ours wasn't flavored with orange and raspberry," Diana seemed compelled to point out. "We had a more traditional espresso-based tiramisu."

Abby's smile turned just a bit wry. "I found this recipe online and thought it sounded good. I wasn't trying to exactly reproduce what you had before, Mom."

"I think this one is even better," Frank interjected hastily, after swallowing a big bite of his dessert. "Who'd have thought thirty years later we'd be eating tiramisu made by our own little girl, eh, Diana?"

Everyone smiled—except Melissa, who was playing with her dessert without her usual enthusiasm for sweets. It bothered Josh that Melissa seemed to become more withdrawn and somber as the evening progressed. Though she had made a noticeable effort to participate in the dining table conversation, her eyes were darkened to almost jade and the few smiles she'd managed looked forced. As well as he knew her, as much as he loved her, he sensed when she was stressed or unhappy. For some reason, she seemed both tonight, and that was twisting him into knots.

Maybe Abby had been right when she'd warned him that his nervous anticipation was affecting Melissa, though he thought he'd done a better job of hiding it from her. Apparently, she knew him a bit too well, also.

Encouraged by the response to his compliment of the dessert, he thought he would try again to keep the conversation light and cheerful. Maybe Melissa would relax if everyone else did.

Mindful of the reason for this gathering—and because he was rather obsessed with love and marriage, anyway—he said, "Thirty years. That's a remarkable accomplishment these days. Not many couples are able to keep the fire alive for that long."

He couldn't imagine his passion for Melissa ever burning out, not in thirty years—or fifty, for that matter.

He felt her shift in her seat next to him and her spoon clicked against her dessert dish. He glanced sideways at her, but she was looking down at her dish, her glossy black hair falling forward to hide her face from him.

Frank, at least, seemed pleased with Josh's observation.

"That's it, exactly." Frank pointed his spoon in Josh's direction, almost dripping raspberry jam on the tablecloth. "Keeping the fire alive. Takes work, but it's worth it, right, hon?"

"Absolutely." Diana looked hard at Abby and Greg as she spoke. "All marriages go through challenging times, but with love and patience and mutual effort, the rewards will come."

Abby and Greg shared a startled look, but Frank spoke again before either of them could respond to what seemed like a sermon aimed directly at them. "I still remember the day I met her, just like it was yesterday."

That sounded like a story worth pursuing. Though everyone else had probably heard it many times, Josh encouraged Frank to continue. "I'd like to hear about it. How did you meet?"

Frank's smile was nostalgic, his eyes distant with the memories. "I was the best man in a college friend's wedding. Diana was the maid of honor. I had a flat tire on the way to the wedding rehearsal, so I was late arriving."

Diana shook her head. Though she still looked worried about something, she was paying attention to her husband's tale. "The bride was fit to be tied that it looked as though the best man wasn't going to show up for the rehearsal. She was a nervous wreck, even though her groom kept assuring her Frank could be counted on to be there."

Frank chuckled. "Anyway, the minute I arrived, all rumpled and dusty from changing the tire, I was rushed straight to a little room off the church sanctuary where the groom's party was gathered getting ready to enter on cue. I didn't have a chance to socialize or meet the other wedding party members before the rehearsal began. Five minutes after I dashed in, I was standing at the front of the church next to my friend Jim. And then the music began and the bridesmaids started their march in. Diana was the third bridesmaid to enter."

"Gretchen was first, Bridget next."

Ignoring the details Diana inserted, Frank continued, "She was wearing a green dress, the same color as her eyes. The minute she walked into the church, I felt my heart flop like a landed fish."

Diana laughed ruefully. "Well, that doesn't sound very romantic."

Frank patted her hand, still lost in his memories. "She stopped halfway down the aisle and informed the organist that she was playing much too slowly and that everyone in the audience would fall asleep before the whole wedding party reached the front of the church."

"Well, she was."

Frank chuckled and winked at Josh. "That was when I knew this was someone I had to meet."

Charmed by the story, Josh remembered the first moment he'd laid eyes on Melissa. He understood that "floppy fish" analogy all too well, though he'd compared his own heart to a runaway train. He could still recall how hard it had raced when Melissa had tossed back her dark hair and laughed up at him for the first time, her green eyes sparkling with humor and warmth. He'd actually wondered for a moment if she could hear it pounding against his chest.

"So it was love at first sight?"

Frank nodded decisively. "That it was."

"And when did you know she was 'the one' for you? That you wanted to marry her?"

"Probably right then. But certainly the next evening during the ceremony, after I'd spent a few hours getting to know Diana. When I found myself mentally saying 'I do' when the preacher asked 'Do you take this woman?' I knew I was hooked."

Josh sighed. This, he thought, was why he wanted to wait for the absolute perfect moment to propose to Melissa. Someday he hoped to tell a story that would make everyone who heard it say "Awww," the way he felt like doing now. "You're a lucky man, Frank. Not every guy is fortunate enough to find a woman he wants to spend the rest of his life with."

Three lucky men sat at this table tonight, he thought happily. Like Frank and Greg, he had found his perfect match.

Melissa dropped her spoon with a clatter and sprang to her feet. "I, uh— Excuse me," she muttered, her voice choked. "I'm not feeling well."

Before Josh or anyone else could ask her what was

wrong, she dashed from the room. Concerned, he half rose from his seat, intending to follow her.

"What on earth is wrong with Melissa?" Frank asked in bewilderment.

Words burst from Diana as if she'd held them in as long as she was physically able. "Melissa is pregnant."

His knees turning to gelatin, Josh fell back into his chair with a thump.

After patting her face with a towel, Melissa looked in the bathroom mirror to make sure she'd removed all signs of her bout of tears. She was quite sure Abby would say she was overreacting and being overly dramatic—just like their Mom, Abby would say with a shake of her auburn head—but Melissa couldn't help it. Every time she thought about her life without Josh in it tears welled up behind her eyes and it was all she could do to keep them from gushing out.

Abby had tried to convince her she was only imagining that Josh was trying to find a way to break up with her. As much as she wanted to believe her sister, Melissa was convinced her qualms were well-founded. She knew every expression that crossed Josh's handsome face. Every flicker of emotion that passed through his clear blue eyes. He had grown increasingly nervous and awkward around her during the past few days, when they had always been so close, so connected, so easy together before. Passion was only a part of their relationship—though certainly a major part. But the mental connection between them was even more special—or at least it had been.

She didn't know what had gone wrong. Everything had seemed so perfect until Josh's behavior had suddenly changed. But maybe the questions he had asked her dad tonight had been a clue. Maybe he had concluded that he didn't really want to spend the rest of his life with her. That only a few men were lucky enough to find "the one."

She had so hoped she was Josh's "one."

Feeling tears threaten again, she drew a deep breath and lifted her chin, ordering herself to reclaim her pride. She would survive losing Josh, she assured herself. Maybe.

Forcing herself to leave Abby's guest bathroom, she headed for the dining room, expecting to hear conversation and the clinking of silverware and china. Instead what appeared to be stunned silence gripped the five people sitting at the table. Her gaze went instinctively to Josh, finding him staring back at her. His dark blond hair tumbled almost into his eyes, making him look oddly disheveled and perturbed. She realized suddenly that everyone else was gawking at her, too. Did she see sympathy on her father's face?

Before she could stop herself, she leaped to a stomach-wrenching conclusion. Had Josh told her family that he was breaking up with her? Is that why they were all looking at her like…well, like that?

"What?" she asked apprehensively.

"Why didn't you tell me?" Josh demanded.

It occurred to her that he sounded incongruously hurt, considering he was the one on the verge of breaking her heart. "Tell you what?"

"That you're pregnant."

"I'm—?" Her voice shot up into a squeak of surprise, unable to complete the sentence.

"Don't worry, darling, we'll all be here for you," Diana assured her, wiping her eyes with the corner of a napkin. "Just as we'll be here for you, Abby, after you and Greg split up. Although I sincerely hope you'll try to work everything out before you go your separate ways."

"Wait. What?" Greg's chair scraped against the floor

as he spun to stare at his wife. "What is she talking about, Abby?"

Melissa felt as if she'd left a calm, orderly dinner party and returned only minutes later to sheer pandemonium.

"What on earth makes you think I'm pregnant?" she asked Josh, unable to concentrate on her sister's sputtering at the moment.

He looked from her to her mom and back again, growing visibly more confused by the minute. "Your mother told us."

Her mother sighed and nodded. "I've overheard a few snippets of conversation today. Enough to put two and two together about what's going on with both my poor girls. You're giving up caffeine and you're feeling queasy and we've all noticed that you've been upset all evening."

"Mom, I don't know what you heard—" Abby began, but Melissa talked over her sister.

"You're completely off base, Mom," she said firmly, avoiding Josh's eyes until she was sure she could look at him without succumbing to those looming tears again. "I'm giving up caffeine because I think I've been drinking too much of it for my health. I'm not pregnant."

Regret swept through her with the words. Maybe she was being overly dramatic again, but the thought of never having a child with Josh almost sent her bolting for the bathroom with another bout of hot tears.

She risked a quick glance at him, but she couldn't quite read his expression. He sat silently in his chair, his expression completely inscrutable now. She assumed he was deeply relieved to find out she wasn't pregnant, but the relief wasn't evident on his face. Maybe he was thinking about what a close call he'd just escaped.

Her mom searched her face. "You're not?"

Melissa shook her head. "No. I'm not."

"Then why have you been so upset this evening?"

Rattled by this entire confrontation, she blurted, "I'm upset because Josh is breaking up with me."

Josh made a choked sound before pushing a hand through his hair in exasperation. "Why do you think I'm breaking up with you?"

"I just, um, put two and two together," she muttered, all too aware that she sounded as much like her mother as Abby always accused her.

"Well, then you need to work on your math skills," Josh shot back with a frustrated shake of his head. "I don't want to break up with you, Melissa. I want to ask you to marry me!"

## Chapter Six
### by Cindy Kirk

Bedlam followed Josh Wright's announcement that he planned to propose to Melissa Morgan. Everyone at the table started talking in loud excited voices, their hands gesturing wildly.

Family patriarch Frank Morgan had experience with chaotic situations. After all, he and his wife Diana had raised two girls. When things got out of hand, control had to be established. Because his silver referee whistle was in a drawer back home, Frank improvised.

Seconds later, a shrill noise split the air.

His family immediately stopped talking and all turned in his direction.

"Frank?" Shock blanketed Greg DeSena's face. Though he'd been married to Frank's oldest daughter, Abby, for three years, this was a side to his father-in-law he'd obviously never seen.

Frank's youngest daughter, Melissa, slipped into her chair without being asked. She cast furtive glances at her boyfriend, Josh. It had been Josh's unexpected proclamation that he intended to propose to her that had thrown everyone into such a tizzy.

Even though Frank hadn't whistled a family meeting to order in years, his wife and daughters remembered what the blast of air meant.

"Darling." Diana spoke in a low tone, but loud enough for everyone at the table to hear clearly. "This is our anniversary dinner. Can't a family meeting wait until another time?"

Her green eyes looked liked liquid jade in the candlelight. Even after thirty years, one look from her, one touch, was all it took to make Frank fall in love all over again.

If they were at their home—instead of at Greg and Abby's house—he'd grab her hand and they'd trip up the stairs, kissing and shedding clothes with every step. But he was the head of this warm, wonderful, sometimes crazy family and with the position came responsibility.

"I'm sorry, sweetheart. This can't wait." Frank shifted his gaze from his beautiful wife and settled it on the man who'd blurted out his intentions only moments before. "Josh."

His future son-in-law snapped to attention. "Sir."

Though Frank hadn't been a marine in a very long time, Josh's response showed he'd retained his commanding presence. "Sounds like there's something you want to ask my daughter."

"Frank, no. Not now," Diana protested. "Not like this."

"Mr. Morgan is right." Josh pushed back his chair and stood. "There *is* something I want to ask Melissa. From the misunderstanding tonight, it appears I've already waited too long."

Frank nodded approvingly and sat back in his chair. He liked a decisive man. Josh would be a good addition to the family.

"If you want to wait—" Diana began.

Before she could finish, Frank leaned over and did what he'd wanted to do all night. He kissed her.

"Let the man say his piece," he murmured against her lips.

Diana shuddered. Her breathing hitched but predictably she opened her mouth. So he kissed her again. This time deeper, longer, until her eyes lost their focus, until she relaxed against his shoulder with a happy sigh.

Josh held out his hand to Melissa. His heart pounded so hard against his ribs, he felt almost faint. But he was going to do it. Now. Finally.

With a tremulous smile, Melissa placed her slender fingers in his. The lines that had furrowed her pretty brow the past couple of weeks disappeared. His heart clenched as he realized he'd been to blame for her distress. Well, he wouldn't delay a second longer. He promptly dropped to one knee.

"Melissa," Josh began then stopped when his voice broke. He glanced around the table. All eyes were on him, but no one dared to speak. Abby and Greg offered encouraging smiles. His future in-laws nodded approvingly.

His girlfriend's eyes never left his face. The love he saw shining in the emerald depths gave him courage to continue.

"When I first saw you at the office Christmas party, I was struck by your beauty. It wasn't until we began dating that I realized you are as beautiful inside as out."

Melissa blinked back tears. Josh hoped they were tears of happiness.

"This past year I've fallen deeper and deeper in love with you. I can't imagine my life without you in it. I want your face to be the last I see at night and the first I see every morning. I want to have children with you. I want to grow old with you. I promise I'll do everything in my power to make you happy."

He was rambling. Speaking from the heart to be sure, but rambling. For a second Josh wished he had the speech he'd tinkered with over the past couple of months with him now, the one with the pretty words and poetic phrases. But it was across the room in his jacket pocket and too late to be of help now.

Josh slipped a small box from his pocket and snapped open the lid. The diamond he'd seen circled in her bride's magazine was nestled inside. The large stone caught the light and sparkled with an impressive brilliance. "I love you more than I thought it was possible to love someone."

He'd told himself he wasn't going to say another word but surely a declaration of such magnitude couldn't be considered rambling.

Her lips curved upward and she expelled a happy sigh. "I love you, too."

Josh resisted the urge to jump to his feet and do a little home-plate dance. He reminded himself there would be plenty of time for celebration once the ring was on her finger.

With great care, Josh lifted the diamond from the black velvet. He was primed to slip it on when she pulled her hand back ever-so-slightly.

"Isn't there something you want to ask me?" Melissa whispered.

At first Josh couldn't figure out what she was referring to until he realized with sudden horror that he hadn't actually popped the question. Heat rose up his neck. Thankfully he was still on one knee. "Melissa, will you make me the happiest man in the world and marry me?"

The words came out in one breath and were a bit garbled, but she didn't appear to notice.

"Yes. Oh, yes."

Relief flooded him. He slid the ring in place with trembling fingers. "If you don't like it we can—"

"It's perfect. Absolutely perfect." Tears slipped down her cheeks.

He stood and pulled her close, kissing her soundly. "I wanted this to be special—"

"It is special." Melissa turned toward her family and smiled through happy tears. "I can't imagine anything better than having my family here to celebrate with us."

"This calls for a toast." Flashing a smile that was almost as bright as his daughter's, Frank picked up the nearest bottle of champagne. He filled Diana's glass and then his own before passing the bottle around the table.

Greg filled his glass and those of Josh and Melissa's but Abby, his wife, covered her glass with her hand and shook her head.

Frank stood and raised his glass high. "To Josh and Melissa. May you be as happy together as Diana and I have been for the past thirty years."

Words of congratulations and the sound of clinking glasses filled the air.

Nestled in the crook of her future husband's arm, Melissa giggled. Normally her mom knew everything before everyone else. Not this time.

"You thought I was pregnant because I wanted decaf

coffee," she said to her mother, "but yet you don't find it odd that Abby hasn't had a sip of alcohol tonight?"

For a woman like Diana who prided herself on being in the "know," the comment was tantamount to waving a red flag in front of a bull. She whirled and fixed her gaze on her firstborn, who stood with her head resting against her husband's shoulder. "Honey, is there something you and Greg want to tell us?"

Abby's cheeks pinked. She straightened and exchanged a look with her husband. He gave a slight nod. She took one breath. And then another. "Greg and I, well, we're... we're pregnant."

"A baby!" Diana shrieked and moved so suddenly she'd have upset her glass of champagne, if Frank hadn't grabbed it. "I can't believe it. Our two girls, all grown up. One getting married. One having a baby. This is truly a happy day."

Everyone seemed to agree as tears of joy flowed as freely as the champagne, accompanied by much back-slapping.

"Have you thought of any names?" Diana asked Abby and Greg then turned to Melissa and Josh. "Any idea on a wedding date?"

Suggestions on both came fast and furious until Abby realized the party had gotten off track. She pulled her sister aside. "The anniversary gift," she said in a low tone to Melissa. "We need to give them their gift."

"I'll get it." In a matter of seconds, Melissa returned, cradling the large basket in her arms.

Josh moved to her side, as if he couldn't bear to be far from his new fiancée. Greg stood behind his wife, his arms around her still slender waist.

"Mom and Dad," Melissa began. "You've shown us what love looks like."

"What it feels like," Abby added.

With a flourish, Melissa presented her parents with a basket overflowing with biscotti, gourmet cappuccino mix, and other items reminiscent of their honeymoon in Italy…along with assorted travel documents. "Congratulations on thirty years of marriage."

"And best wishes for thirty more," Abby and Melissa said in unison, with Josh and Greg chiming in.

"Oh, Frank, isn't this the best evening ever?" Diana's voice bubbled with excitement. "All this good news and gifts, too."

She exclaimed over every item in the basket but grew silent when she got to the tickets, guidebooks and brochures. Diana glanced at her husband. He shrugged, looking equally puzzled.

"It's a trip," Abby explained.

Melissa smiled. "We've booked you on a four-star vacation to Italy, so you can recreate your honeymoon, only this time in comfort and style."

"Oh, my stars." Diana put a hand to her head. When she began to sway, her husband slipped a steadying arm around her shoulders.

"I think your mom has had a bit too much excitement for one day." Frank chuckled. "Or maybe a little too much of the vino."

"I've only had two glasses. Or was it three?" Instead of elbowing him in the side as he expected, she laughed and refocused on her children. "Regardless, thank you all for such wonderful, thoughtful presents."

Abby exchanged a relieved glance with Melissa. "We wanted to give you and Dad the perfect gift to celebrate your years of happiness together."

"You already have," Frank said, his voice thick with emotion.

He shifted his gaze from Abby and Greg to Melissa and Josh before letting it linger on his beautiful wife, Diana. A wedding in the spring. A grandbaby next summer. A wonderful woman to share his days and nights. Who could ask for more?

\* \* \* \* \*

# HEART & HOME

Heartwarming romances where love can
happen right when you least expect it.

## SPECIAL EDITION®

**COMING NEXT MONTH**
AVAILABLE APRIL 24, 2012

**#2185 FORTUNE'S UNEXPECTED GROOM**
*The Fortunes of Texas: Whirlwind Romance*
**Nancy Robards Thompson**

**#2186 A DOCTOR IN HIS HOUSE**
*McKinley Medics*
**Lilian Darcy**

**#2187 HOLDING OUT FOR DOCTOR PERFECT**
*Men of Mercy Medical*
**Teresa Southwick**

**#2188 COURTED BY THE TEXAS MILLIONAIRE**
*St. Valentine, Texas*
**Crystal Green**

**#2189 MATCHMAKING BY MOONLIGHT**
**Teresa Hill**

**#2190 THE SURPRISE OF HER LIFE**
**Helen R. Myers**

You can find more information on upcoming Harlequin® titles,
free excerpts and more at www.HarlequinInsideRomance.com.

HSECNM0412

# REQUEST YOUR FREE BOOKS!

## 2 FREE NOVELS PLUS 2 FREE GIFTS!

# SPECIAL EDITION

## Life, Love & Family

**YES!** Please send me 2 FREE Harlequin® Special Edition novels and my 2 FREE gifts (gifts are worth about $10). After receiving them, if I don't wish to receive any more books, I can return the shipping statement marked "cancel." If I don't cancel, I will receive 6 brand-new novels every month and be billed just $4.49 per book in the U.S. or $5.24 per book in Canada. That's a saving of at least 14% off the cover price! It's quite a bargain! Shipping and handling is just 50¢ per book in the U.S. and 75¢ per book in Canada.* I understand that accepting the 2 free books and gifts places me under no obligation to buy anything. I can always return a shipment and cancel at any time. Even if I never buy another book, the two free books and gifts are mine to keep forever.

235/335 HDN FEGF

Name _____ (PLEASE PRINT) _____

Address _____ Apt. # _____

City _____ State/Prov. _____ Zip/Postal Code _____

Signature (if under 18, a parent or guardian must sign)

### Mail to the **Reader Service:**
**IN U.S.A.:** P.O. Box 1867, Buffalo, NY 14240-1867
**IN CANADA:** P.O. Box 609, Fort Erie, Ontario L2A 5X3

Not valid for current subscribers to Harlequin Special Edition books.

**Want to try two free books from another line?**
**Call 1-800-873-8635 or visit www.ReaderService.com.**

* Terms and prices subject to change without notice. Prices do not include applicable taxes. Sales tax applicable in N.Y. Canadian residents will be charged applicable taxes. Offer not valid in Quebec. This offer is limited to one order per household. All orders subject to credit approval. Credit or debit balances in a customer's account(s) may be offset by any other outstanding balance owed by or to the customer. Please allow 4 to 6 weeks for delivery. Offer available while quantities last.

**Your Privacy**—The Reader Service is committed to protecting your privacy. Our Privacy Policy is available online at www.ReaderService.com or upon request from the Reader Service.

We make a portion of our mailing list available to reputable third parties that offer products we believe may interest you. If you prefer that we not exchange your name with third parties, or if you wish to clarify or modify your communication preferences, please visit us at www.ReaderService.com/consumerschoice or write to us at Reader Service Preference Service, P.O. Box 9062, Buffalo, NY 14269. Include your complete name and address.

HSE11B

# The heartwarming conclusion of

## from fan-favorite author
# TINA LEONARD

With five brothers married, Jonas Callahan is under no
pressure to tie the knot. But when Sabrina McKinley
admits her bouncing baby boy is his, Jonas does
everything he can to win over the woman he's loved
for years. First the last Callahan bachelor must uncover
an important family secret...before he can take
the lovely Sabrina down the aisle!

## A Callahan Wedding

**Available this May
wherever books are sold.**

*After a bad decision—or two—Annie Mendes*
*is determined to succeed as a P.I. But her first assignment*
*could be her last, because one thing is clear: she's not cut*
*out to be a nanny. And Louisiana detective Nate Dufrene*
*seems to know there's more to her than meets the eye!*

*Read on for an exciting excerpt of the upcoming book*
*WATERS RUN DEEP by Liz Talley…*


THE SOUND OF A CAR behind her had Annie scooting off the
road and checking over her shoulder.

Nate Dufrene.

Her heart took on a galloping rhythm that had nothing to
do with exercise.

He slowed beside her. "Wanna ride?"

"I'm almost there. Besides, I wouldn't want to get your
seat sweaty."

His gaze traveled down her body before meeting her
eyes. Awareness ignited in her blood. "I don't mind."

Her mind screamed, *get your butt back to the house and
leave Nate alone.* Her libido, however, told her to take the
candy he offered and climb into his car like a naughty little
girl. Damn, it was hard to ignore candy like him.

"If you don't mind." She pulled open the door and
climbed inside.

The slight scent of citrus cologne, which suited him,
filled the car. She inhaled, sucking in cool air and Nate.
Both were good.

"You run often?" he asked.

"Three or four times a week."

"Oh, yeah? Maybe we can go for a run together."

Her body tightened unwillingly as thoughts of other
things they could do together flitted through her mind. She

shrugged as though his presence wasn't affecting her. Which it *so* was. Lord, what was wrong with her? *He* wasn't her assignment.

"Sure." No way—not if she wanted to keep her job. As he parked, she reached for the door handle, but his hand on her arm stopped her. His touch was warm, even on her heated flesh.

"What did you say you were before becoming a nanny?"

Alarm choked out the weird sexual energy that had been humming in her for the past few minutes. Maybe meeting him on the road wasn't as coincidental as it first seemed. "A real-estate agent."

*Will Nate discover Annie's secret?*
*Find out in WATERS RUN DEEP by Liz Talley,*
*available May 2012 from Harlequin® Superromance®.*

*And be sure to look for the other two books*
*in Liz's THE BOYS OF BAYOU BRIDGE series,*
*available in July and September 2012.*

# Love Inspired

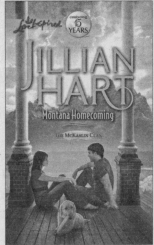

Hoping to shield the secret she carries, Brooke McKaslin returns to Montana on family business. She's not planning on staying long—until she begins working for reporter Liam Knightly. Liam is as leery of relationships as Brooke but as their romance develops, Brooke worries that her secret may ruin any chance at love.

# Montana Homecoming

### By fan-favorite author

# JILLIAN HART

## THE McKASLIN CLAN